For Love

They gazed at each other. She drew breath and her lips moved, but she did not say what she had been about to say. He did not even try to speak.

He had held her thus that night at Vauxhall, folded against himself, almost into himself. She had been heart of his heart, almost flesh of his flesh. . . . She would not have resisted. She would have opened for him, received him, trusted him . . . but honor had held him back.

And so the restless yearning, the incompleteness, unrecognized, firmly denied, had driven him like a scourge ever since.

Had he been so deceived on that evening? Had she known even then?

"Did you know on that night," he found himself whispering to her, "that the very next day you would betroth yourself to him?"

"No." She was whispering too. "No, I did not know."

It had not been an act, then, her tenderness and her ardor on that evening. It had been real. She really had loved him.

"Christina." There was nothing else to say. Just her name and all the pain of its utterance.

"I did not know," she said again, and tipped her head to rest her forehead beneath his chin again.

The Last Waltz

Mary Balogh

A SIGNET BOOK

SIGNET
Published by the Penguin Group
Penguin Putnam Inc., 375 Hudson Street,
New York, New York 10014, U.S.A.
Penguin Books Ltd, 27 Wrights Lane,
London W8 5TZ, England
Penguin Books Australia Ltd,
Ringwood, Victoria, Australia
Penguin Books Canada Ltd, 10 Alcorn Avenue,
Toronto, Ontario, Canada M4V 3B2
Penguin Books (N.Z.) Ltd, 182-190 Wairau Road,
Auckland 10, New Zealand

Penguin Books Ltd, Registered Offices:
Harmondsworth, Middlesex, England

First published by Signet, an imprint of Dutton NAL,
a member of Penguin Putnam Inc.

First Printing, November, 1998
10 9 8 7 6 5 4 3 2 1

Chapter 1

"What you need to do now, Wanstead," Mr. John Cannadine said, slouching inelegantly in a deep chair beside the crackling fire, "is take a wife."

Viscount Luttrell, who was leaning against the mantel, warming his legs against the fire, swirled the brandy in his glass and chuckled. "I have ever noted," he said, "that those with leg shackles want company. What you need to do, Wanstead, is acquire skill in dodging scheming chits and matchmaking mamas—for which I might offer my humble services. They are all about you like bees around a July flower bed."

"What you need to do, Wanstead," Mr. Ralph Milchip said—he was at the sideboard, pouring himself another glass of brandy, "is tell them all that you mean to go back to Montreal in the spring. And after you get there, back into the wilderness—by canoe. That will put the wind up them in a hurry."

Viscount Luttrell took a sip of his liquor. "Not so, old chap," he said. "Wanstead's connections with Canada and the wilderness and canoes and mosquitoes and fur-trapping are at least half his lure to the fair sex, had you not noticed? They sense a savage just beneath the veneer of his respectability and they find him irresistible. I would wager that there are chits lying awake in their beds at this very moment dreaming of being rowed upriver by our semiconscious friend here."

But the semiconscious friend was not completely descended into inebriation or sleep or whatever it was that held him stretched out in the chair opposite Mr. Cannadine's, his arms draped limply along its arms, his empty glass on the floor beside him, his eyes closed. The Earl of Wanstead chuckled.

"It would almost be worth marrying one of them and taking her over just to see her reaction when confronted with the reality of one of those canoes, not to mention one of those journeys," he said. He yawned. "Why do I need a wife, John? Convince me."

After walking back to his rented rooms in London with his friends following the third ball they had attended in two weeks, and after chatting and drinking with them for an hour or more, he was finding the warmth of the fire—as well, perhaps, as the inner warmth of the brandy he had drunk—quite lulling. His married friend's answer was quite predictable, of course. He began to check off points on his fingers.

"One," he said, "you have inherited the title and property and will need a hostess for the entertaining you will be expected to do. Two, for the same reasons you will need an heir, or preferably two or more. Three, you are—how old?" He looked up, frowning.

"One-and-thirty," his lordship said obligingly.

"You are one-and-thirty. Of an age when a man begins to think of his mortality and the need to perpetuate his line. Four, you were wealthy even before inheriting but now you are as rich as Croesus. An heir is clearly needed. Five, I have it on the best authority—Ralph and Harry here—that you have a strong aversion to brothels and green rooms and such, but you cannot tell me that you also have an aversion to women. Six—"

"Exactly how many points are there to be, old chap?" the viscount asked, strolling away from the heat of the fire and plopping himself down in a chair not far distant. "As many as you have fingers? Or will you start all over again once you run out?"

"You will be terrifying poor Wanstead, John," Mr. Milchip said, leaning back against the sideboard. "I know *my* knees are beginning to knock together."

"And *six*," John Cannadine said, undaunted, "there is a

certain satisfaction in having a mate, Wanstead, a woman who understands one and devotes all her energies to one's comfort."

"Mrs. Cannadine will understand this late night, then?" the viscount asked, winking across the room at Ralph Milchip. "And forgive it?"

"Assuredly she will," John Cannadine said without hesitation. "She is in a delicate way again, you know, and wished to retire early. She did *not* also wish to drag me away from my friends—and she knows perfectly well I am *with* my friends. She knows she can trust me."

"Bravo, John," the earl said, his eyes still closed. "The trouble is, one grows cynical with age. Ten years ago there was not a young lady with an ounce of worldly experience who would afford me a second glance. Their mamas—and papas—were like icebergs around me. This year, despite the fortune I have amassed, if I had returned from Canada as plain Gerard Percy, partner in a fur-trading company, do you think I would have received a single invitation to a *ton* party? Or been the recipient of one melting glance from a delicately reared female? Or of one gracious smile from her mama? But I am the Earl of Wanstead, owner of Thornwood Hall in Wiltshire, a large and prosperous estate. As such, I am suddenly eligible."

"*Very* eligible," Ralph Milchip echoed. "But who would have thought ten years and more ago, Gerard, that you would ever inherit? Wanstead had his heir and a second son, both robust enough by all accounts. But both dead within ten years of his own death." He shook his head.

"Which only proves my point about an heir or four," John Cannadine said. "You danced twice tonight with Lizzie Gaynor, Wanstead. She had Miffling—the *duke* of, I would have you know—dangling after her in the spring, but rumor had it that she did not like him. Perhaps it was his bald head or his paunch or his gout that she objected to or the fact that he is sixty if he is a day. Some girls are fussy about such things." He paused to chuckle again. "She clearly likes *you*."

"She is remarkably pretty," the earl said. "So is her younger sister."

"A baron's daughter," Mr. Cannadine said. "Excellent breeding and a sizable dowry, or so Laura tells me. You could hardly do better, Gerard."

"I wonder," the earl said, reaching over the side of his chair only to discover that his glass was empty. He returned it to its place on the floor—he really did not need more to drink. "I wonder if she would have liked me, John, if she had met me eighteen months ago as Mr. Percy, wealthy trader."

His friend tutted. "You are too sensitive by half," he said. "The point is she would not even have *met* you."

"There is nothing as cozy as a coal fire on a November evening," Viscount Luttrell said. He had set down his glass beside his chair and laced his fingers behind his head. "The trouble is, one hates the thought of having to step out into the street again. Ugh!" He shivered at the very thought. "Did you not tell me that the late earl had a sister, still living at Thornwood, Gerard?"

"Margaret?" he said. "Yes."

"And how old is she, pray?" the viscount asked. "I have never seen her in town."

The earl thought. "She was still a child when I left there twelve years ago at the age of nineteen," he said. "She must be twenty or so now."

"Well, there you are," the viscount said. "You can marry Lady Margaret, Gerard, and keep everything in the family."

"My own first cousin?" The earl frowned. "Sight unseen, Harry? She might well be an antidote. Though she was a pretty enough child, I must admit—all blond hair and big eyes. Followed me around like a little puppy."

"Perfect," the viscount said. "We have found Wanstead a bride, fellows. Now we can retire to our beds happy men. Except that we have to go out into the cold in order to find those beds."

"I believe," his lordship said, "I would prefer to wed Miss Campbell. *Not* that I have any immediate intentions of marrying anyone. But Jeannette is at least from my world. She was my friend long before I made my fortune and even longer before I inherited a title I never coveted. The only trouble is—oh, deuce take it, the trouble is she is a *friend*."

"And therefore is quite ineligible as a wife," Ralph Milchip said.

"Miss Campbell who is keeping house for her brother here?" the viscount asked. "Your associate's daughter from Canada, Gerard?"

Yes. When Robert Campbell had wanted to send his son to London to replace the agent there who was returning to Montreal, he had suggested that the older, more experienced Gerard Percy, a partner in the company, go with him for a year or so. And Jeannette had been eager to accompany her brother. The Campbells had not known at that time that Gerard Percy was also the Earl of Wanstead. He had heard the news himself only the week before when the first boat to come from England following the spring breakup of the ice in the St. Lawrence River had brought mail. By that time he had held the title for almost a year—his cousin Gilbert had died the summer before, and presumably Gilbert's younger brother had predeceased him. Gerard had not heard of Rodney's death, but then why should he? There had been no communication between him and Thornwood Hall since he left England.

"Jeannette would certainly be a wise choice," the earl said. "She knows the sort of life she would be going back to."

"You positively intend then, Wanstead, to return to Canada?" Ralph Milchip asked. "Despite the change in your status? I can remember how eager you were to go there years ago in the hope of making your fortune. But your situation was different then."

The earl shrugged and exerted himself sufficiently to sit forward in order to poke the fire into renewed life.

"What is there to stay for?" he asked. "Thornwood Hall is well run. I had the steward up for a few days and looked over all the books with him. I am not needed there. I came over just for a year, to set Andrew Campbell on his feet here, so to speak. He is already doing well enough without me."

But in truth, he thought, matters were not quite as simple

as he had expected when he had agreed to come to England. His title had seemed an empty thing, an embarrassment even, when he was still in Montreal. Here he had come to realize more clearly that he was now a part of the very fabric of the upper classes. He had even begun to feel, however reluctantly, that perhaps there were responsibilities he should assume—being an active landowner, for example; taking his seat in the Upper House, for example; begetting an heir, for example.

"What you should do, Wanstead," John Cannadine said— he had slipped even farther into his chair so that seated across from him, all one saw was a pair of stout legs and a tousled head, "is choose a bride. Get all the possibles together and make a sensible choice. You will not regret it."

Viscount Luttrell chuckled. "Parade 'em all in Hyde Park, Wanstead," he said. "Drill 'em like a company of recruits. And then pick the best one. The mind boggles."

"Or gather them all at Thornwood," the Earl of Wanstead said, listening to his own voice rather as if it proceeded from someone else's mouth. "See which one I like best. Or if I like any of them. Or if they like me, for that matter."

There was something dreadfully wrong with his suggestion, he thought even as he made it. He had agreed to come to England. He had had *no* intention of going to Thornwood. He hated the place.

"I say," Ralph Milchip said, "a house party. Is that what you mean, Gerard? Are we invited? I have always wanted to set eyes on the place, I must confess."

"A house party?" the viscount said more dubiously. "In the winter? Definitely not a good idea, old chap. Unless you were to make it a *Christmas* house party, of course."

"That is exactly what I mean," the earl said, yawning. What the deuce time was it? What was he suggesting now? A Christmas house party at Thornwood?

"Splendid!" John Cannadine said. "Laura's parents are in Italy for the winter, and mine are too far away for us to travel given the present delicate state of Laura's health— and the children are always obnoxiously restless during long journeys. Thornwood would be just the thing, Wanstead. Are you serious?"

"Do you hear me laughing?" the earl asked.

His friends all left together less than half an hour later. But a great deal of damage had been done in the interim. Irretrievable damage, the earl feared as he wended his way to bed. He was going down to Thornwood after all, it seemed. For Christmas. He was giving a house party there. Several guests had already been invited, either first- or secondhand. There were the Cannadines, children included, Luttrell, the Milchips—Ralph had declared that Sir Michael and Lady Milchip, his parents, would be delighted by an invitation, as would his younger brother and sister. And among the four of them—or more accurately, among three of them since the earl himself had contributed little—they had drawn up a list of guests to be invited that would fill Thornwood to the rafters.

There was no reason he should not go there, the earl thought. It was his property. It made sense to go down there and look it over and meet his neighbors at least once before he returned to Montreal. It would be the civilized thing to do. And going there would give him something to do over Christmas. He had been rather bored, truth to tell, since Andrew Campbell, only four-and-twenty years old and ambitious to rise in the ranks of the company, was anxious to show everyone that he did not need to have an older partner overseeing his work.

And perhaps he *should* give some consideration to marrying. Not that he felt any burning duty to beget heirs. He had not been brought up to expect Thornwood or the title to be his—his father had been a younger son, and his uncle had had two sons of his own, Gilbert two years older than he, and Rodney one year younger. But it was true that he felt a certain squeamishness about engaging the services of whores or even about setting up a mistress. And yet he had needs that sometimes gnawed at him by day and kept him awake by night.

Hosting a Christmas house party at Thornwood was perhaps after all a very good idea, despite the fact that it had come to him on the spur of the moment. Or had it, indeed, come to him at all? He had a suspicion that it might have been suggested to him. He frowned as his valet helped him off with his form-fitting coat and began to brush it lovingly before hanging it up. Had he been talked into doing something that he had no wish to do?

He remembered then with painful clarity why in fact it was not a good idea at all, why he had no wish to go back to Thornwood—ever.

He would have to inform his friends tomorrow morning, before they began to spread the word, that there was to be no house party after all.

He looked about him, shivering, after he had stripped off his waistcoat and shirt. He reached for the nightshirt that had been set out for him, and pulled it hastily over his head.

But why should there not be a house party? Was he afraid to go to Thornwood? Was that what had kept him from there even though he had been in England for almost three months? Was he really afraid? The idea, when it was brought consciously to mind, seemed absurd. But there was only one way to prove that he was not.

He would write to Thornwood first thing in the morning, he decided, to give notice of his intended visit. He would go down as soon as all the invitations had been sent out and answered, and he would prepare for his guests himself.

The three occupants of the drawing room sat close to the fire. It was built high and crackled cheerfully, but it had a large space to heat. The candles had already been lit although it was only early evening. But it was mid-December, a time of year when darkness fell almost before afternoon was out. The two ladies who sat on either side of the hearth stitched away at their embroidery, their heads bent to the task, one gray-haired and wearing a white lace cap, the other dark-haired and black-capped. The youngest of the three, who had drawn her chair as close to the blaze as she possibly could, was doing nothing more productive than drumming her fingers impatiently on the arms of her chair.

Dinner was late—an unheard-of occurrence at Thorn-

wood Hall, where punctuality had always been considered a
moral virtue. And there was no knowing when it would be
served since it awaited the arrival of my lord, and his letter
had not stated the exact hour at which my lady might expect
him. He had written only to announce that he would arrive
today.

Lady Margaret Percy crossed one leg over the other and
swung the dangling foot in time with her drumming fingers.

"It is cold in here," she complained.

"You have the draft from the door on your back, dear,"
Lady Hannah Milne, her aunt, told her. "Why do you not exchange places with me?"

"Do stay where you are, Aunt," the Countess of Wanstead
said, looking up briefly. "You should have worn a warmer
dress, Meg. And you should have brought down a shawl to
wrap about your shoulders. It is December, after all. It is
foolishness itself to dress for the evening in muslin at this
time of year."

She knew why her sister-in-law had donned such an inappropriate gown, of course. She wanted to look her petti-
est tonight for my lord's benefit. The countess could
understand that even if she herself had not been similarly
motivated. Quite the contrary, in fact. She still wore black
even though it was no longer necessary to do so. She might
by now have graduated to gray or lavender or even to other
colors. Gilbert had been dead for almost seventeen months
after all. But in the past week, since receiving his lordship's
letter, she had been glad she had not yet left off her mourning. She would certainly not do so for a while now. She
would not have it appear that she was trying to impress him.

"I am hungry," Margaret announced. "I do not know why
we cannot eat, Christina."

"You know exactly why." The countess smiled to soften
the abruptness of her words. "When his lordship has written
to announce his intention of arriving today, Meg, it would
be ill-mannered indeed to dine without him."

"But what if he has changed his mind?" her sister-in-law
asked reasonably enough. "What if he is putting up at an inn
somewhere for the night and does not come on here until to-

morrow? Perhaps at this very minute he is in the middle of his dinner. What if he did not even start out today? Are we to starve until he does come?"

"I do not believe his lordship would say he is coming and then not come, dear," her aunt told her. "It would be discourteous to Christina."

The countess bent her head to her work again. It was a seductive idea that he might not come until tomorrow after all, but on the whole she hoped he would come today so that this waiting, this suspense, might be at an end. "We will wait one more hour," she said. "If he has not come by then, we will eat."

"Another hour!" The words were a complaint in themselves, but Margaret did not argue further. Her fingers continued to drum on the chair arms.

If he did not come soon, Christina thought suddenly, she herself would surely explode into a thousand pieces. She had woken early in the morning after a night of fitful sleep, dreading his arrival, wondering how she would possibly face it since there was no avoiding it. And yet as the day progressed she had found herself wishing that he would come—*now*. If not sooner.

She wished he had stayed half a world away for the rest of his life.

"I wonder what he is like now," Margaret said with a sigh, her eyes on the coals. "I have only dim memories of him. He left Thornwood before Papa died when I was eight years old and never came back. It was good riddance, Gilbert used to say. He said Gerard was wild and reckless. What he meant was that he was a rake."

"Meg!" Christina said with sharp reprimand. And yet it was true, she thought, even if it was unladylike to say so. He had been wild.

"Oh, dear," Lady Hannah said, "I am not sure he was ever so very bad. Most young men are high-spirited. Not Gilbert, of course, or even Rodney—they were always patterns of propriety, may God rest their souls. But there are plenty of young men who feel obliged to sow their wild oats before settling down to perfectly decent lives when they marry. The time to which your brother referred, Meg, was many years ago. We may expect a different man altogether now. He is Wanstead now."

Christina's lips thinned as she concentrated on her embroidery.

"I do not care if he *is* still a rake," Margaret said. "I do not care if he is still wild. I do not even care if he is vulgar. I daresay he will be, will he not, after spending ten years in *business*? In Canada of all places. Mr. Evesham says it is a primitive and savage country, not fit even to be visited by a gentleman. Perhaps Cousin Gerard has become a savage himself. Perhaps he paints his face and his body and wears feathers in his hair and beats his breast." She chuckled merrily.

"Oh, my," her aunt commented.

"I hope," Margaret said, gazing into the fire, her drumming fingers stilled, "he will be interesting at least. Life has been so dreadfully dull since—since Papa's death. Not that anything has changed in the last year and a half since my cousin has been my guardian, but perhaps now that he is coming here . . ."

"Whatever he is and whatever he might do," Christina said firmly—all this speculation about how he might have changed, how he might have remained the same, was making her decidedly nervous again, "we will discover soon enough. Only one thing is certain. He is the earl now. Master of Thornwood." And of everyone living here, a voice said inside her head though she did not speak the words aloud. She breathed deeply and evenly to quell the pointless panic she felt.

"Whoever would have expected," Margaret said, "that Papa would die and Rodney and Gilbert too and that Gerard would inherit? Poor Papa. He had his heir and a spare and all for naught. And I was a mere daughter. Though for all that I think he used to like Gerard well enough despite what Gilbert said afterward. Gilbert, of course, would not allow us even to mention his name."

No. He had not, Christina remembered. He had made a particular point of it early in their marriage. Mr. Gerard

Percy, he had said, speaking with the sort of pompous formality she had soon learned was customary with him, was everything that was to be abhorred in a gentleman—if the circumstances of his birth allowed him even to claim that title for himself. He was ungrateful for the privileged upbringing his uncle had given him after the death of his own parents, raising him at Thornwood as his own son; he had become a wastrel, a gamer, a womanizer, a drinker, a fortune hunter. And finally he had repudiated his dubious claim to be called a gentleman by taking up business and commercial pursuits. Christina would kindly take note of the fact that his name was never again to be mentioned.

It was a command she had never felt inclined to disobey.

But through a bizarre twist of fate the prodigal cousin was now the Earl of Wanstead and had been for almost seventeen months. Gilbert's father had died before Christina's marriage. Her brother-in-law had drowned in Italy two years after her wedding. Gilbert had died of a sudden heart seizure after almost nine years of a marriage that had produced two healthy daughters and two stillborn sons.

And now the new—the almost new—Earl of Wanstead was coming home. To gloat? To stay? Merely to pay a courtesy visit before disappearing for another ten years or longer? His letter had provided no answers. They would have to wait and see—all his dependents. Christina found herself having to draw a steadying breath again.

"I hope there will be some changes here," Margaret said wistfully. "I hope—"

But she was not destined to tell them what else it was she hoped. Lady Hannah had held up a staying hand and they all assumed a listening attitude. Margaret leaned forward and gripped the arms of her chair, Christina sat with her needle suspended above her work, and Lady Hannah kept her hand upraised. The rumble of wheels and the clopping of horses' hooves on the cobbled terrace below were distinctly audible. And then there was the muffled sound of voices, one of them shouting out commands.

"No!" Christina said sharply as Margaret jumped to her

feet. "Please do not look out the window, Meg. Someone might glance up and see you. It would not be at all genteel."

Margaret pulled a face, but she slumped down into her chair again without argument. "We should at least go down," she said, "and meet him in the hall. Oh, do let's."

Christina had thought of it. But it would not be the right thing to do. It would be like meeting and greeting a guest to the house. He was not a guest. He was the master.

"We will remain here," she said, stiffening her spine, which was already straight as an arrow, and lowering her needle with a determinedly steady hand to her work. But she felt suddenly breathless, as if she had been running uphill or as if someone had sucked half the air from the room. She could hear the blood pounding like a drumbeat in her ears. He was the Earl of Wanstead, owner of Thornwood and everything and everyone within its gates. And he was no longer safely far away in Canada. He was here—entering Thornwood at this very moment. The feeling of total helplessness that had been assailing her ever since the arrival of his letter washed over her again.

What a dreadful fate it was sometimes to be a woman. To be dependent. To have to sit and wait. To be helpless to order one's own life no matter how carefully and sensibly one tried to plan.

"Quite right, dear," Lady Hannah said. "I daresay he will wish to change out of his traveling clothes and make himself more presentable before paying his respects to us."

Margaret sighed audibly and began the finger-drumming again.

She would simply not be able to bear it, Christina thought as she stitched doggedly on, if he chose to change his clothes before waiting on them in the drawing room. She would not be able to bear it if he delayed even one more minute downstairs. She might alarm her companions by starting to scream. She might—

The double doors opened.

Chapter 2

The Earl of Wanstead set out for Wiltshire on a gray and chilly December day that matched his mood. He was delayed early in the afternoon by the necessity of having a damaged wheel repaired, with the result that darkness had fallen by the time he arrived at Thornwood. His carriage drove along the deserted village street, once and still so familiar to him, turned to pass between the tall stone gateposts into the park—someone had opened the gates in advance—and proceeded up the long, winding driveway, its lamps beaming feebly ahead, and making looming, ominous shadows of the tall, dense trees of the forest to either side.

Gloom descended also on the Earl of Wanstead—or rather a darker gloom. And he realized that the ball of something heavy that had sat low in his stomach all day was not his midday meal—it had preceded that reasonably appetizing repast. It was dread. A dread of going back into that other, long-dead life—or what he had thought was long-dead.

But it was too late to change his mind now, he thought as the deeper rumbling of the wheels and sudden vibrations alerted him to the fact that his carriage was being drawn over the cobbled terrace before the house. The conveyance drew to a halt even as he thought it, and he looked out the window at the curving sweep of the horseshoe steps leading up to the main doors of the house.

The doors opened as he was stepping down from the carriage. Thornwood Hall, he thought as he climbed the steps rather reluctantly and entered the great domed hall, which he had foolishly hoped might be warm. His home—no, merely his house. There were two people waiting to greet him. He had half expected to find all the servants formally lined up for his inspection. And he had more than half expected the ladies to be waiting there. It was a relief to see only the butler and the housekeeper—he remembered both from his uncle's time.

"My lord," the butler said with pompous formality. "Welcome home. I trust you had a pleasant journey?"

"A tedious one," his lordship said, looking about him and shivering. But there was little point in asking why fires had not been lit in the two fireplaces. They would have made little impression on the chill of the great marble hall anyway. They never had.

He nodded affably to the housekeeper and responded to her speech of welcome.

"Where are the ladies?" he asked then.

They were in the drawing room, of course, awaiting his coming. Her ladyship had ordered dinner to be held back until after his arrival, he was informed. They kept country hours at Thornwood. Dinner was already half an hour late. The butler imparted that piece of information with a deferential bow that nevertheless succeeded in putting his master subtly in the wrong.

His lordship raised his eyebrows and regarded his butler in a silence that lasted just a little too long for the servant's comfort.

"It will be held back only a little longer," the earl said. "Give me ten minutes in which to present myself to the ladies, Billings, and then have it announced, if you please." He had been removing his greatcoat as he spoke and handing it with his hat and gloves and cane to a footman who had glided silently from the shadows. He caught the butler's eyes on his traveling clothes, which were certainly not suitable wear for evening dinner at Thornwood Hall—or at any other gentleman's establishment for that matter. He raised his eyebrows once more.

"As you wish, my lord," the butler said and then scurried off toward the grand staircase ahead of his lordship in order that he might be present to turn the handles of the drawing room doors, a feat of strength of which an earl was not expected to be capable. Life as an aristocrat frequently amused, frequently irritated the earl. It was a life not easy to adjust to.

The feeling of dread returned to his lordship as he stepped inside the drawing room, though he despised himself for his cowardice. Actually he was glad the moment had come at last. Soon now it would be in the past and he could forget about it.

There were three ladies in the room, two of whom were getting to their feet even as he entered and curtsying to him. But it was on the third that all his attention, all his strange feeling of dread, was focused, though he did not immediately look directly at her. He was looking at the other two and recognizing his aunt, his father's sister, one of the few figures from his childhood whom he remembered with affection, though she had rarely visited Thornwood. He would not have recognized Margaret though the slender, pretty young lady curtsying to him must be she. She had been just a young child when he had left. She did have the remembered blond curls, though they had been crimped into a mass of ringlets now.

The other lady remained seated. She was dressed all in black, he saw when he turned his eyes upon her as if with great physical effort, from her slippers to her wrists to her throat. Her dark hair was dressed smoothly over her ears, the rest of it invisible beneath a black lacy cap. Her oval Madonna's face was pale and expressionless.

A stranger. A woman without color or youth or vitality. Merely his predecessor's widow, the Countess of Wanstead. And yet not a stranger. Her dark eyes met his for the merest moment before he turned his own away from them, and somehow the girl she had been was there behind the severe facade—the vivid, bright, lovely girl whom he had hated for ten years and more.

And hated still with an unexpected and disturbing vehemence.

He included all three ladies in his bow. "My lady?" he said. "Ma'am—Aunt Hannah, is it not? And Margaret?"

And then the Countess of Wanstead set aside her needle-work, got to her feet with smooth grace, and curtsied deeply to him.

"My lord," she said in her rather low, melodic voice.

She looked quite noticeably older. Thinner, paler—though both impressions might have been attributable to the unrelieved black in which she was clad. She had no wel-coming smiles for him as the other two did—had he ex-pected any? There was no sign of recognition, either, and no embarrassment. But why should there be? She looked proud and haughty and had demonstrated her superiority over the other two by remaining longer in her chair.

This, then, was what he had dreaded so much that he had almost not come to Thornwood at all? Meeting her again after so long? Well, the moment was past, and really there had been nothing to it after all. She was essentially a stranger for whom he felt nothing at all.

Except hatred.

His entrance had not been preceded by the butler, as she had expected. He came in alone, though some unseen hand closed the doors behind him.

Time stood still.

He looked nothing like what she had been expecting. He must have shed his outdoor garments downstairs, but he still looked somewhat travel-worn in clothes that appeared to have been donned more for comfort than for elegance. He was not a particularly tall man. He was not portly, but he had lost the slenderness of youth. He was solidly built. His fair hair was cut short and in the candlelight appeared to be al-most the same color as his bronzed face. His blue eyes looked light in comparison.

He was not a particularly handsome man. And yet there was something about him—a certain air of assurance and command, perhaps—that would surely turn heads wherever he went, particularly female heads. There always had been something . . . But he no longer had a good-humored face, that charisma of charm she remembered so painfully well. There was a hardness about his eyes and his jawline, a certain set to his mouth that suggested a ruthless determination always to have his own way. Perhaps it was a look a successful businessman acquired over ten years.

It was all a momentary impression. But in that moment Christina felt as if she were gazing on a stranger, one for whom she felt an instinctive dislike—and perhaps a certain degree of fear. She and her daughters were dependents of this man, who had very little reason, except common decency, to treat them kindly.

And then his eyes met hers for a brief, timeless moment.

He was so very different, she thought. She might have passed him on a deserted street and not recognized him. And yet he was so very much the same. Her heart pounded its recognition. He might have been hidden at the opposite end of a crowded room and she would have felt his presence.

Gerard.

His bow included all three of them. "My lady?" he said. He had already turned his eyes away from her. "Ma'am— Aunt Hannah, is it not? And Margaret?"

He spoke and behaved as if she were a stranger to him, someone to whom he was paying his formal, distant respects for the first time. And yet for that single moment he had gazed at her surely as she had gazed at him—down the years, pausing and pondering, stripping away layers of change. Stripping away the years.

Aunt Hannah and Margaret were already curtsying and smiling and greeting him. Christina realized in some mortification that she was still seated. She set her work down beside her, got to her feet, and sank into a deep curtsy.

"My lord," she said.

She was in the presence of a stranger, of a man she had never seen before, yet one she had known all her life and perhaps even before that.

The worst was over, she told herself. He was quite simply a stranger.

*   *   *

Christina was thankful for the fact that the other three were inclined to converse at dinner. She did not feel so inclined herself. For one thing, she felt unduly upset by what had happened after the butler had come to the drawing room to announce dinner.

"His lordship has not had time to change yet, Billings," she had said. "Have dinner kept for another half hour, if you please."

"It will be served immediately," the earl had said briskly. "Everyone has waited long enough. May I escort you to the dining room, ma'am?" He had offered his arm to his aunt.

Christina had felt foolish and even a little humiliated— she had given the command without a thought to the fact that she no longer had the right to do so. She should have waited for him to respond to the announcement. But as if that were not bad enough, he had turned his eyes on her and spoken again.

"Unless, that is," he had said, "you take exception to my appearance, my lady?"

Her eyes had swept over him, taking in his slightly creased coat, his loosely tied cravat, his breeches and top boots, which had become filmed with dust at some time during the day.

"Not at all, my lord," she had assured him with all the civility of which she was capable. Gilbert would not have allowed anyone to the *breakfast* table so dressed.

He had said no more and had proceeded to the dining room with Aunt Hannah on his arm—but only after staring at her coolly a little longer than was necessary, an unreadable expression on his face. Mockery? Triumph? Dislike? All three?

He had left Christina with the feeling that she had been subtly but very firmly put in her place. It had left her with the uncomfortable conviction that perhaps the worst was not yet over after all. He had taken the chair at the head of the table, of course. There had been no question of that. But it was where Gilbert had always sat, where she herself had sat since his death. She sat facing him along the length of the table, feeling the full reality of her subordinate, dependent position.

He was very different from what she had expected. She had expected—what? Signs of age? He was only one-and-thirty. He *was* older, but it was no negative thing. He was no longer the slender boy of her memory, but a mature, well-built man. Signs of moody restlessness to replace the eagerness with which he had faced life as a young man? He was a confident, self-assured, even arrogant man. Signs of dissipation? There were none. There was nothing in him—yet, at least—with which to comfort herself and her conscience. Nothing visible with which she might tell herself that yes, she had been wise, she had been right.

She could sense his dislike, as she could feel her own.

"London was more crowded than I expected it to be," he was saying in answer to Margaret's question, "considering the fact it has been only the Little Season and not the spring squeeze."

"Ah." Margaret sighed. "How wonderful that must have been."

"Not as wonderful as your come-out Season was, I daresay," he said. "Did you enjoy it?"

Margaret pulled a face. "*What* come-out Season?" she asked. "I have never been farther than ten miles from Thornwood."

He raised his eyebrows and his eyes met Christina's along the length of the table. She read both surprise and accusation in them.

"Gilbert died last summer, when Meg was but nineteen," she explained. "We were still in mourning this spring. A Season was out of the question." She resented the feeling she had of being on the defensive. She was not giving a true explanation anyway. Why did she not simply tell him the truth?

"Yes," he said curtly. "I see."

"Do tell us about some of the balls and routs and drums you attended, Cousin Gerard," Margaret begged. "Were they very, *very* splendid affairs?"

"I would prefer to hear about your life in Canada, Gerard," Lady Hannah said. "We hear so little about the colonies."

"Oh, yes," Margaret agreed. "Did you live among savages? Did they wear war paint and feathers? Did they shoot at you with arrows?" She laughed at the foolishness of her own questions, a delightful, lighthearted sound so rarely heard at Thornwood.

He told them about Montreal and made it sound like a flourishing, dynamic, but perfectly respectable city. There were families there of taste and education with whom to mingle socially. He told them briefly of his long journeys by canoe inland from Canada to the interior of the continent, where the furs were trapped and traded. He told them about the long, frigid winters spent there.

"I should simply die," Margaret commented, but her cheeks were flushed, her eyes were wide, and she was clearly hanging on his every word.

"Yes." He looked at her with a twinkle in his eye. "I do believe you might, Margaret. No white women ever go inland."

"But white men go there for months, even years at a time?" Lady Hannah said. "Dear me, how lonely they must be."

"Yes, ma'am," he agreed, but his eyes met Christina's again as he said it, and there was a knowing, half amused look in them. She found her cheeks flushing. No *white* women, he had said. It was not quite the same thing as *no women*. Yes, of course there would have been women.

But the conversation inevitably came back to England and London and balls and parties. Margaret had an insatiable hunger to hear about such things.

"I suppose," the Earl of Wanstead said finally, "you have plans for a Season next spring, Margaret? If her ladyship can be persuaded to exert herself to take you to town and sponsor you, of course."

Christina looked sharply at him. What exactly did he mean by that? Was he accusing her of laziness, of unwillingness to exert herself on her sister-in-law's behalf? She was not imagining the antagonism in his manner, she real-

ized. It had not been apparent in anything he had said to the
other two even though he must have found their insatiable
questions tiresome.

"A Season is expensive, my lord," she said tartly.

"And so it is." He raised his eyebrows. "But not beyond
the means of the daughter and sister of an earl, surely?"

She could feel her breath quickening. "That is a question
for you to answer, my lord," she said, "not us."

He looked arrested for a moment until he was distracted
by the appearance of the servants to remove the covers
ready for dessert. He leaned back in his chair.

"You are quite right, my lady," he said. He turned to
smile at his cousin. "But I believe I can offer something for
your amusement sooner than next spring, Margaret. I will be
staying here for Christmas. There—"

"Oh, *will* you?" Margaret leaned forward in her chair, her
hands clasped to her bosom. "I am *so* glad. We feared that
you were coming merely for a few days, just to look around.
But you will stay for Christmas? Perhaps we can invite
some of the neighbors for a party one evening. May we? It
is an age since there was a truly grand occasion at Thornwood."

"Meg—" Christina said.

"Perhaps we should allow Gerard a day or two in which
to catch his breath, Meg," Lady Hannah said with a laugh.
"But we are all delighted, Gerard, that you will be staying
for Christmas. Are we not, Christina?"

"Of course," she said coolly as his eyes met hers again.
That look was back in them—the look that might have been
mockery and was definitely dislike.

"You did not allow me to finish," he said, turning his attention back to Margaret. "I have invited a number of
friends to spend Christmas here with me. There will be a
houseful."

Lady Hannah exclaimed with delight; Margaret was ecstatic; Christina merely stared. House guests? A house
party? Noise and jollity at Thornwood? It seemed like a con-
tradiction in terms. He had invited a houseful of guests for
Christmas—only a week and a half away—without even

consulting her? But why *should* he consult her? She was no longer mistress of Thornwood. Sometimes it was hard to digest that fact.

"I hope this will not upset any of your own plans, my lady?" he asked her.

"I have none, my lord," she said, "beyond the intention of spending a quiet Christmas with Aunt Hannah and Meg, Rachel, and Tess."

He raised his eyebrows.

"My daughters," she explained.

"Ah, yes. Your daughters." There was that disturbing suggestion of a smile again. "There will be other children among my guests. Perhaps yours will enjoy their company for the holiday."

Christina inclined her head but said nothing.

"I believe," he said, looking back at Margaret, "we should organize a ball for Christmas. Not on Christmas evening—most people like to spend the whole of that day with their families. On the evening after, perhaps. Would you like that?"

But Margaret did not respond with quite the ecstasy he might have expected. She darted glances at her sister-in-law and her aunt. "A ball?" she said. "Here, Cousin Gerard?"

"I assume," he said, "that the ballroom has not burned down since my day?"

"No," she said hastily. "No, it is still here. But there has never been a ball here—not since I was a very little girl anyway. Oh, this is *famous*. You do not believe it is wicked to dance?"

"Wicked?" He looked at her with raised eyebrows. "As in evil and sinful? Should I?"

Margaret tittered. "I do not believe dancing is wicked, either," she said. "Is there really going to be a ball here? Promise?"

"Meg—" Christina said, but she felt herself impaled by that cool blue glance.

"There will certainly be a ball," he said. "I suppose that means a great deal of planning. I suppose the whole house party will involve much planning. I had not thought a great deal about it. I will need assistance."

"Oh, I will help," Margaret assured him eagerly. "I will write the invitations."

"And I will certainly help in whatever way I can," Lady Hannah said.

His lordship looked at Christina.

"I suppose, my lord," she said, "the servants have been informed of your plans? It is invariably the servants who do most of the work when their betters set themselves to play." She *knew* that the servants had not been informed—not about the house party, not about the ball. She would have heard. How typically thoughtless of him. He was as foolishly impetuous as ever, then. It was a comforting realization.

He set his elbows on the table, his dessert finished, and rested his chin on his clasped hands. "The servants have not been informed, my lady," he said. "But I suppose having guests arrive here for a week or so of celebration *will* disturb their normal routine, will it not? And yours. You will need to direct them in what is to be done—unless you choose to leave everything to me. Do you feel yourself equal to the task?"

She had no idea. She had lived quietly in the country since her marriage. They had rarely had any guests at all. They had never had a houseful. They had never hosted a house party. They had never hosted a ball. And there was so little notice—only a week. How dared he do this to her!

But he dared, she thought, because he was the Earl of Wanstead. Because he was master of Thornwood. Because he had the right to do here whatever he pleased. And because she was merely a dependent, an encumbrance most of the time, a convenience now. If she said no, he had implied, he would do everything himself. He would humiliate her by ignoring her and behaving as if Thornwood had no mistress at all. As it did not—not by right.

She wondered if he enjoyed the feeling of power he had over her. Or if he simply did not care. He was accustomed to the exercise of power, after all.

"I do, my lord," she said coolly in answer to his question, her hands clenched tightly in her lap.

"We will discuss details in the morning, then," he told her. "Shall we say after breakfast, in the library?"

"I shall be there," she said.

She always spent the mornings with her daughters. She had the household routine organized in such a way that nothing would interfere with that sacred time. And they kept country hours, dining early so that she could spend an hour with the girls before they went to bed. Tonight they had dined late. She got to her feet. "Aunt Hannah? Meg?" she said. "Shall we leave his lordship to his port?"

But he chuckled and got to his feet too. "If his lordship is left alone with the port this evening," he said, "he may well fall asleep over it. I will come to the drawing room with you."

He escorted Lady Hannah again, but when they reached the drawing room, she crossed to the pianoforte with Margaret in order to find suitable music for her to play. Christina seated herself in her usual chair by the fire and reached for her embroidery.

The Earl of Wanstead stood before her. "You were disappointed," he said. "You wished me to stay to imbibe port. Perhaps what you really wished was that I had stayed in London—or Montreal."

She looked up at him, stung. "We dined almost an hour later than usual, my lord," she said. "My daughters are within—five minutes of their bedtime." She had glanced at the clock on the mantel. "And I am not with them."

"And I am stopping you?" he asked her quietly. "By all means go to your children. Why would I wish to detain you? Because your company is so fascinating?"

Or perhaps because as master of the house he might require her to preside over the tea tray when it arrived, she thought. Gilbert had never allowed her to go up to the nursery until his second cup had been poured.

She ignored the insult, the quite open expression of dislike, got to her feet, and curtsied to him. "Thank you, my lord," she said.

She was aware that he watched her as she left the room. Margaret was beginning to play Bach.

If only Rodney had survived, she thought as she climbed the stairs. If only there had been another male cousin between Gilbert and *him*. If only she had not gone to London for that particular Season when she was eighteen. If only she had not attended that particular ball at its start. If only . . .

But life was made up of seemingly small, unimportant, chance events that together created the pattern of one's existence. There was no changing the pattern of hers. It had led her to this very difficult moment. She was a dependent of the Earl of Wanstead—such a familiar title. But the man with the title was no longer Gilbert. He was Gerard Percy.

If only he had been any other man in the world.

But he was not and she was going to have to live with the fact. And with his presence at Thornwood over Christmas.

Chapter 3

The Earl of Wanstead wondered if after all he had not made a mistake. The idea had come to him, or had been presented to him—he still could not clearly remember which—on the spur of the moment. He had proceeded to send out invitations according to the list his friends had helped him draw up. It had all been surprisingly easy—only two refusals, from people who regretted that they already had other plans. But Jeannette and Andrew Campbell had been delighted, as had Colin and Geordie Stewart, two brothers and former partners in the fur-trading company, now both retired. Miss Lizzie Gaynor had been ecstatic, or so her rather gauche younger sister had assured him, and was to come with the sister and their widowed mama. There were to be twenty guests altogether, plus four children.

He had felt rather pleased with the plans for both the house party and the leisurely opportunity it would give him to consider taking a bride—until he had arrived at Thornwood and been oppressed with a sense of gloom.

But it was too late now to regret what he had done.

His lordship rose when it was still dark, having spent a somewhat restless night in the earl's grand bedchamber. The door leading from his dressing room into the countess's was locked, his valet had informed him when he had asked. He had not also asked if the countess still used that dressing room and the chamber beyond it, but the possibility that she did had disturbed him. He had kept thinking of her undressing there, lying in bed there. And he had kept remembering that he had found every opportunity last evening to be rude to her. It was not like him to be uncivil to women, even those he disliked.

He must do better today, he decided, shivering in the morning chill but not bothering to ring for coals to be brought up or for his valet to shave him and help him dress. He was too restless to wait for anyone or anything or even to remain indoors. He dressed in riding clothes and went outside, stepping out into a frosty morning in which he could see his breath but very little else. But he was accustomed to being outdoors in inclement conditions.

He tramped about the inner reaches of the park and noted that everything was kept neat, though the flower beds were now bare, of course. He walked through the trees to the lake at the east of the house. It was not completely frozen over, though the wide bands of ice extending outward from the banks almost met in the middle. If the weather continued cold, the ice would be solid in another week—by Christmas.

He remembered being quite viciously caned once by his uncle for skating before permission had been granted. Gilbert or Rodney had reported him—probably Gilbert. Reporting wrongdoings had been very much in his line, and Gerard's uncle had usually acted with unconsidered wrath on such slight information, just as he had frequently acted with unexpected bursts of generosity, taking his nephew shooting or fishing with him while leaving his sons behind, giving him money over and above his allowance. And then cuffing or caning him again at the slightest provocation— and roaring at and abusing him as the son of a whore. Life had never been tranquil—and never really happy—at Thornwood.

But it was, the earl decided now, a beautiful place, even at this time of the morning at this time of the year. And it was all his. For perhaps the first time he found the thought somewhat exhilarating.

It was a decidedly chilly morning and a brisk breeze cut through the heavy folds of the earl's greatcoat. Nevertheless he stood close to the lake's edge for several minutes, his shoulder propped against the trunk of a tree. The eastern horizon lightened as he stood there, and a gleam of light beamed weakly across the icy water. He had learned in a far-off land to see beauty in the starkness of winter.

But he wanted to see more. He strode away from the lake, back through the trees, and across the long lawn below the house to the stables, where a surprised and rather sleepy groom saddled a horse for him. He rode out to the outer reaches of the park. He made no attempt to go farther, though he was eager now to see everything, to visit both the home farm and all the tenant farms.

He well remembered the forests that surrounded the park on all sides. On the north side, on the hill, they had been cultivated. A scenic walk had been constructed. It was the loveliest part of the park, the part he had always most avoided. He had preferred the wilder reaches of the forest. He had peopled them with dragons and outlaws and smugglers and witches. He had climbed branches and made dens in the hollow trunks of old trees. He had dodged from cover to cover, the hero of every game. And the gamekeepers had been his friends—almost his only friends. Gilbert and Rodney certainly had not been. And though he had been his uncle's unwilling favorite, there had been no real emotional closeness between them.

The branches of most of the trees were bare now. He had never minded bare trees. He could see the sky through them. He had often lain along a stout branch, gazing upward, dreaming of worlds beyond the one he inhabited. He looked about him now as his horse picked its way along well-remembered paths in the gathering daylight. He could see a group of deer off to his left. They looked warily his way for a moment before bolting off out of sight.

He wondered if any of the same gamekeepers were still at Thornwood. He must find out. He wondered if Pinky's hut—Abe Pinkerton had been the gamekeeper's name—was still on the slope above the river north of the lake. Pinky had preferred to make his home there rather than live in greater comfort in the servants' quarters at the house. The boy Gerard had spent many happy hours in that hut, talking, listening, sometimes merely relaxing in a shared silence.

He supposed eventually that he ought to return to the

house. December mornings were dark. Since it was now full daylight, then, he must assume—he had not brought his watch with him—that the morning was well advanced. It must be close to breakfast time.

He was reluctant to return despite the fact that he was both cold and hungry. Despite the fact that there were things to be done and he was not a man to shirk hard work. As he guided his horse out of the trees and headed back toward the stables, he realized, of course, why he did not want to return. His lip curled with self-derision when he realized that a mere woman was making him reluctant to enter his own home.

He wondered for a moment what had happened to the girl he had known. But the answer was obvious. Time had happened to her. And Gilbert had happened to her—for nine years. And she *had* changed. She seemed now to have more ice in her veins than warm blood. She was like a marble statue. She was poised, elegant, beautiful. She was cold, humorless, unpleasant. Unattractive. But then deep down, perhaps she had always been those things. People did not really change, did they?

He could not seem to shake his mind free of her even after the walk and the ride. He must do so. Or at least he must adjust his vision so that he could see her as Gilbert's widow, the woman who must help him prepare for the house party. Wretched thought that he needed her for that! But he did. Well, he thought, she was his dependent now. He had all the power now. Not that he had ever wished to have power over her. But somehow, despite himself, the prospect of a little revenge was sweet.

He dismounted in the stable yard and turned his mount over to the groom, who looked somewhat more wide awake than he had earlier. The earl strode off in the direction of the house. His house. He thought deliberately about Margaret. She was very lovely and lively and amiable. And it was not unheard-of for first cousins to marry.

Late rising had always been considered a vice at Thornwood. Strangely, although Gilbert had been dead for almost a year and a half, they had kept quite rigidly to the daily routine he had insisted upon. It had become like second nature to them, perhaps.

Christina breakfasted with Lady Hannah and Margaret. This morning they did not wait for the earl. Perhaps, Lady Hannah suggested by way of excuse, he was tired after his long journey the day before. He had still not joined them by the end of the meal. Margaret and her aunt went to the morning room to write letters. Christina, happy that after all her morning with her daughters was not to be entirely ruined, went up to the nursery.

She had forgotten about the appointment in the library by the time the earl found her there almost an hour later. While the children's nurse sat in a rocking chair close to the window, knitting them new scarves and mittens for the winter, Christina supervised their morning activities.

Tess was standing before the easel, swathed from neck to ankles in a large apron, a brush almost as long as herself clutched in her right hand. She was dabbing bright paint onto a large sheet of paper. She was only three years old, a plump and pretty little girl, who favored her father rather than her mother. She was producing nothing that was recognizable, but Christina did not care about that. There would be time enough later to teach her to harness her imagination. For now it must be allowed to run free.

Rachel was seated at the table, absorbed in working long columns of arithmetic problems. She never protested at having to do lessons, whatever the subject. The need to win approval by excelling at every task set her was fundamental to her nature. She was seven years old, a thin and serious child with her mother's oval face and dark hair and eyes.

They all looked up when the door opened.

"Ah, here you are," the Earl of Wanstead said. "Good morning." He stepped into the room while Nurse got up from her chair and curtsied.

Christina felt the absurd urge to set her arms protectively about both children. She had that helpless feeling again, the one that had had her tossing and turning all night, sleepless spells intermingled with troubled dreams. They were *all* dependent upon him—and he did not like her. She got to her feet and curtsied to him.

"Good morning, my lord," she said with calm courtesy. And then she felt a wave of fear. She had always despised that feeling in herself, but she had never been able quite to control it—sometimes with good reason. She remembered now that she had had an appointment with him in the library and he had been forced to come and find her. But she could not bring herself to grovel or even simply to apologize. She did what had often brought her to grief and simply confronted him. "You were late for breakfast and I hated to wait idly in the library."

"Late?" His eyebrows shot up. "At what time is breakfast served, pray?"

"At eight o'clock sharp," she said.

"Sharp. I see." He strolled farther into the room, his hands at his back, and circled around the easel so that he could see what was displayed there. "And whose rule is that, my lady?"

"Gil—" She did not complete the name or try to cover up her mistake. It had been Gilbert's rule—the Earl of Wanstead's. The *former* earl's.

The present Earl of Wanstead turned his head to look at her. He said nothing for a few moments—he did not need to. But she would not dip her head or look away from those cold eyes. She had not been mistaken last evening about his hostility toward her, she thought.

"Perhaps," he said, the courtesy in his voice at variance with that look, "you would present me to your daughters?"

He commended Tess on her painting and her choice of bright colors. She beamed happily up at him. He looked down the columns of Rachel's work and commented on its neatness and accuracy.

"You have made only one mistake," he said. "I wonder if you can find it for yourself. It is in the second column."

Far from being offended, Rachel bent her head over the page and began to check her figuring, a look of intense concentration on her face.

Christina resented his interference—quite unreasonably

so. He had not said or done anything that might be called high-handed. But she was very aware that though he had never been named the children's guardian, but that everyone of her acquaintance accepted *her* in that role, nevertheless by law she could not as a woman be their sole guardian. That made him . . .

"Can they be left to their nurse's care?" the earl asked now. "May we adjourn to the library?" He offered his arm.

Christina turned away to give some unnecessary instructions to the girls and their nurse. Then she preceded him from the room, pretending that she had not noticed his arm. She could not bear the thought of touching him.

How foolish! After longer than ten years—a lifetime, an eternity—she was afraid to touch him.

She was still wearing black this morning, from her lacy cap on down to her slippers. He found the fact annoying, though he was not sure why. It seemed excessive, perhaps, to mourn so ostentatiously a man who had been dead for well over a year—even a husband. Yet there was no other sign of brokenhearted grief in her. She bore herself proudly, even arrogantly, with straight spine and lifted chin. But really, he decided as a footman opened the library doors and she preceded him inside the room, how she chose to mourn was none of his business. Nor was the depth of her feelings. She was just Gilbert's widow. Nothing else.

But he felt irritated.

"Take a seat," he said, directing her to one of the chairs beside the fire. He did not immediately take the other. He stood with one arm propped on the mantel, looking down at her.

"Thank you," she said and seated herself. Her spine, he noticed, did not touch the back of the chair. She had sat thus last evening too, both in the dining room and in the drawing room. It must be an uncomfortable posture, but that too was her business. She was looking at him with cool inquiry.

"Well, my lady," he could not resist saying, though he had not intended to do so, "there is a certain irony in this, is there not?"

She did not pretend to misunderstand him. "I suppose you would consider it so," she agreed.

"You chose to marry money," he said. "Yet you find yourself at the end of the day dependent upon the very man you rejected for money—the one who now possesses it all."

If he had intended to disconcert her, he had failed. Her face registered nothing but disdain. "A gentleman," she said, "would not remind a lady of her dependency, my lord."

No, he would not. It was unpardonable of him to have said what he just had. He had not intended to say it. Indeed, he had resolved to treat her differently today. But the desire somehow to hurt her, or at least to gloat over her, was alarmingly difficult to quell.

"A gentleman." He laughed softly. "But the general consensus of opinion at Thornwood has always been that that is something I am not." His father, besotted with an opera dancer, had first taken her for his mistress and then married her less than eight months before he, their only child, had been born. "I am sure you were informed of that even before my subsequent, ah, *career* confirmed the fact."

"Gilbert would not have your name mentioned here," she told him coldly.

He smiled and turned his head to gaze into the coals. She was not without her own desire to hurt, then. Why? Did she regret her decision? Or did she merely resent the way it had turned out? "Was it worth it, Christina?" he asked her. "Marrying for money?"

"Yes," she said. "Yes, it was."

Well. What had he expected her to say? And what had he wanted her to say? That she had made a mistake? That she should have put *love* first? He would have despised her even more than he already did if she had said that. Besides, he had not brought her here in order to vent a bitterness he had not known he felt so rawly or to rake up a past that should have been long forgotten.

"Your younger child is a mere baby," he said. "How old is the elder?"

"Seven," she replied.

"They have a nurse," he said. "Do they also have a governess?"

"No," she told him. "I teach my children myself. It is the way I spend my mornings."

"And I am interrupting this one," he said. "Why have you chosen not to hire a governess?"

She compressed her lips and looked down at the hands she had set in her lap, the back of one resting on the palm of the other. "Governesses cost money, my lord," she said.

"And the estate cannot bear the cost?" he asked her.

She looked up at him with her dark, unreadable eyes. But he read what was in them nonetheless. He understood her though she had said nothing. And he was angry.

"You would not ask?" he said, frowning. "Pride, my lady? Monck would surely not even have questioned the expense."

"Mr. Monck," she said, "has no authority to act on his own. He is merely the steward here."

"And you were afraid," he said, frowning, "that if he had asked me, I would have said no? You must think I have petty notions of revenge, my lady. Or perhaps you enjoy the image of yourself as martyr, your needs spurned by the man *you* spurned years ago. I have recently given Monck far wider powers than he once enjoyed—I understand that Gilbert kept a very tight rein on him. It would be inconvenient for me to do so, when the Atlantic Ocean will soon separate us. You might have asked him for all sorts of things and been granted them. Chances are that I would never even have known."

She did not answer him.

"After Christmas," he said, "you will employ a governess of your own choosing. In future years you will employ drawing teachers, music and dancing teachers, whoever is needed for the education of your children. I shall give instructions to Monck. I daresay the expense will not beggar me."

"Thank you," she said so coolly that he could read no gratitude in the words. But he did not want her gratitude.

He had a sudden thought. It was something he had not noticed in the account books Monck had brought to London, although he had studied them in some depth. But then it was not something he had been looking for.

"What allowance did Gilbert make you?" he asked. "Is it still being paid you?" By God, she would not lay any charge of that sort of spitefulness at his door.

She studied the hands in her lap again, though her chin was still up. "Gilbert paid all my bills for me," she said.

He realized the significance of her words, appalled. It was not that her allowance had been cut off after Gilbert's death and she had been too proud to ask for its restoration. Monck, it seemed, was not the only one who had been kept on a tight rein.

"I see," he said. "Perhaps that would work admirably in a close marital relationship, but I would find such an arrangement distasteful. I have no intention of feeding your hostility by having you run to me—or *not* run to me—with every need. I shall arrange that you have a quarterly allowance sufficient to your needs and those of your children. Do the same conditions apply to Margaret and my aunt?"

"Aunt Hannah was left a small legacy by her husband, I believe, my lord," she said. "I have no idea if it is adequate to her needs. If it is not, she does not complain."

"Tell me," he asked her, changing the subject. "Why has Margaret never had a Season? She is twenty years old. Most young ladies of her age can expect to be already married. Gilbert died when she was nineteen—in the summer. Why had she not made her come-out during the spring? Or the year before, when she was eighteen? Did you not think it important to persuade your husband to take her to town?"

She looked up at him with a strange half-smile on her lips.

"You preferred to stay selfishly at home in the country with your children?" He frowned down at her. "Did *she* not try to persuade her brother?"

"If she did," she said, "she was not successful, was she?"

"Too expensive?" he said, suddenly suspicious. Had Gilbert really been such a nip-farthing? After being a sneak thief in his boyhood? There was some amusement in the thought.

"That was part of it," she said.

"And the other part?"

"Life in town," she said, "is too frivolous, too—ungodly."

"Was that Gilbert's description of it?" he asked her, frowning. "Or yours?"

"My husband and I thought alike," she said stiffly, but she would not look him in the eye and say it, he noticed.

"Frivolous?" he said. "Expensive? Ungodly? *Ungodly,* my lady? Gilbert was never much of a one for God when I knew him. He developed stomachaches and headaches with great regularity on Sunday mornings, as I recall."

"People can change, my lord," she said.

Good God! He gazed at her with distaste. Did this, then, explain the stark black garments, the stiff spine, the lack of smiles, the cold discipline? Was *this* what she had come to? Willingly? He really had never known her at all, had he?

"And so," he said, "there were no balls here during your marriage, no parties, no laughter, no merriment."

"And no vice either," she said tartly.

"Poor Margaret," he said quietly. "Was she at least taught to dance?"

"Country dances, yes," she said. "They are a part of any young lady's education."

"But not often performed in company, at a guess," he said. "I suppose even a mention of the waltz would send you into a fit of the vapors?"

"I have never seen it danced, my lord," she said stiffly. "I have heard about it and have no wish to see it."

"You will do so nevertheless," he said, "in the ballroom here the evening after Christmas." He was feeling more than ever irritated with her.

"I wish you would reconsider, my lord," she said, "and arrange for only country dances. I will not dance at all, of course. I am in mourning, as you may have observed. But—"

"Did you love him so much, then?" he asked. It was none of his business whether she had loved Gilbert or not. It seemed to him that they had deserved each other.

"He was my husband," she said.

"Christina." He sat down at last on the chair opposite hers and sighed. This was not how he had planned for this meeting to proceed. He had meant it to be all business. "I will have house guests arriving next week. They are coming to celebrate Christmas. I am prepared to work hard preparing for their arrival and entertaining them once they are here. Though, as you observed last evening, the servants will bear the brunt of the work. I daresay that between us they and I will be able to do a good enough job. But it would be better if I had a hostess. My aunt would assume the role, but if she is as I remember her, she is a well-meaning ditherer. Margaret is too young. And if I chose one of them, it would appear to be a slight to you, something I would not have happen publicly, no matter what my private feelings may be. Will you do it? Be my hostess, that is, not just a dark wraith hovering in the background, grieving widow of the former earl?"

"I will do whatever you command me to do, my lord," she said.

He found her answer intensely irritating. He had invited some sort of truce, and all he had got for his pains was coldness. "I would advise you, my lady," he said, his eyes narrowing on her, "not to try impertinence on me."

Her mouth opened and shut again. Her eyes widened, and in them for the merest moment he read—what? Fear? *Fear?* She said nothing. She did not remove her eyes from his. Had he been mistaken? Surely he must have been.

He sighed again. "This would all be so much easier if we had never met before last evening, would it not?" he said. "Well, we did meet and fancied ourselves in love. You married Gilbert and I went off to Canada. Now our fates are linked once more—forever, I suppose, though after the holiday we may both forget the fact once more. I will return to Canada; you will remain here. There, it has been set in the open. Can we accept reality now and move on? I think we must both be agreed that young love is a foolish and impermanent thing and that we were fortunate indeed that Gilbert came to town when he did. Will you help me make this a pleasant Christmas for all who will be here?"

"Yes," she said.

"And will you," he asked, his eyes sweeping over her with distaste, "leave off your blacks?"

She licked her lips. He wondered if he understood her hesitation—and if it was something else she had been determined not to ask for. But he refused to give vent to irritation again.

"Is there a dressmaker in the village?" he asked. When she nodded, he swept on. "Make use of her services. I shall instruct Monck to settle the bill."

Her cheeks flushed for the first time. "I am becoming too much of a charge upon you," she said.

But he ignored the remark. "What do you know," he asked her, "about organizing house parties?"

"Very little," she admitted.

It had not occurred to him that after ten years at Thornwood as the countess she might not be up to the task of preparing for his guests. But it seemed that she and Gilbert—and necessarily poor Margaret—had lived a quiet, sober, puritanical existence. Well, it had been their right, he supposed, though he would no longer allow his young cousin to suffer for it.

"Perhaps," he suggested, "we should move over to the desk, get paper and pens ready, and begin to pool our meager resources."

She half smiled at him again, but this time there seemed to be some real amusement in the expression. "At least," she said, "we know that invitations must be sent out for the ball. Meg is going to write them."

It was the first small suggestion of amiability between them. Something to build upon, perhaps? He hoped that at least they could establish some sort of working relationship over the coming days.

If not, it would be a long and possibly disastrous Christmas.

Chapter 4

She was going to have an allowance, sufficient for her own needs and the girls' needs. That was a vague promise, of course. Their combined needs might be judged to be very limited. But even so, *she was going to have an allowance,* money that would be all her own to spend in any way she pleased. Rachel was to have a governess—of Christina's own choosing, and she would be able to spend her own time with her daughters simply being a mother to them. She could have a new dress made by Miss Penny, perhaps even two. What an impossible extravagance.

By the time Christina emerged from the long session at the library desk, her head was spinning with the large number of tasks that lay ahead for the next week—not to mention what would need doing after the arrival of the guests. And yet it was not so much that prospect that lodged in her conscious mind as the fact that she was to have an allowance and a new dress or two. Frivolities.

Freedom!

Whenever she or one of her girls had needed anything, she had had to apply to Gilbert for it. Not just any time she could catch his attention. There had been a set time for such applications, between nine and ten in the morning in his office. She had had to stand before his desk like a supplicant. The baby needed new nappies, she might have told him. No, the ones Rachel had worn would no longer do. They were threadbare and absorbed almost no moisture at all. They were fit only for the kitchen ragbag. Should she go up to the

nursery and bring one down to show him? Very well, then—
she would bring them *all* down.

There were many such memories. Gilbert had been a
careful man with money. He had had a moral revulsion
against waste. There were many thousands of beggars, he
had reminded her on a number of occasions, who would be
only too happy to wear what her ladyship so carelessly dis-
carded. It had been an unjust accusation, she had always
thought—at least after the first year or so. By then she had
become a hoarder. Besides, he had never had much compassion for beggars. As a Justice of the Peace he had rigor-
ously prosecuted any vagrants who had happened into the
neighborhood.

She was not sure now if her excitement over the changes
outweighed her resentment. She hated to be beholden to
him—to the new Earl of Wanstead. She hated his assump-
tion that she had been afraid to ask him for anything—even
though it was *true!*—or that she had been acting the martyr
and deliberately hiding her needs from him.

And she deeply resented *him* and his hostility and sar-
casm—and his very physical presence. She hated his as-
sumption that he knew the whole of it. How simple he made
it sound—she had chosen money over love and so had rejected him for Gilbert. Nothing was ever that simple. But
she scorned to try to explain to him. Besides, there was no
explanation that would satisfy him, for basically that had
been it. She had married Gilbert because he was a wealthy
man. She had rejected Gerard because he was not. But only
basically—there had been a great deal more.

She hated to remember that one particular day in her life.
The memories still had the power to make her feel faint, to
bring the ache of impotent tears to the back of her throat.

She hoped at least after the past hour or so, during which
they had discussed business quite sensibly and without any
personal overtones, that for the rest of his stay they could
treat each other with civility—like a man who had just arrived at his home and met his predecessor's widow for the
first time.

But her feathers were soon ruffled again.

The Earl of Wanstead made an announcement when they were all seated at the dining table partaking of luncheon. It began actually with a question.

"Aunt Hannah," he asked, "do you play the pianoforte as well as you used to? I heard only Margaret last evening."

"I would not say *well*, Gerard," Lady Hannah told him. "I am not sure I ever played *well*, though it is kind of you to say that I did. But I have kept my hand in since returning to Thornwood. Mr. Milne kept only a spinet, which makes pretty enough music, it is true, but I always favored the smoother tones of the pianoforte."

"Good," his lordship said briskly. "You will look through all the sheet music with me afterward, if you would be so good. I wish to find some tune suited to the waltz."

Margaret gaped and returned her attention hurriedly to her plate, as if someone had uttered a profanity that she was pretending not to have heard. Christina's lips thinned.

"Oh, I know several suitable pieces by heart, Gerard," Lady Hannah surprised them all by saying. "I saw it danced once and thought it wonderfully romantic. I never said so to Gilbert, of course. He considered it—well . . ." She glanced at Christina with a smile.

"Ungodly?" the earl suggested.

"Vulgar too," Christina said. *Obscene* might have been a more appropriate word, but Gilbert would never have uttered that word aloud—not, at least, in the hearing of ladies. There were to be waltzes at the Christmas ball after all, then? Despite her specific request to the contrary?

"Splendid," his lordship said. "We will all meet in the ballroom, then, at four o'clock. Margaret and her ladyship will need to learn the steps before Christmas."

No. Oh, no. Absolutely no!

"You are serious," Margaret said, her eyes as wide as saucers. "Caroline Ferris told me that partners have to *clutch* each other when they waltz."

"Only," his lordship told her, "if they do not know the steps and are afraid of falling down—or of treading all over each other's toes. I plan to teach you not to fear either, Margaret."

"Waltzing," she said. Her voice sounded awed. "In the ballroom."

"Precisely," her cousin agreed. "At four o'clock."

Christina ate doggedly on. She would not give him the satisfaction of arguing with him or even commenting, though she could feel his eyes on her for a few moments.

But the earl had not finished with his announcements. "I sent a note to Miss Penny, the village dressmaker, and she sent an immediate reply with my messenger," he said, looking at Christina along the length of the table. "She will be here, my lady, as soon as my carriage has had time to go and fetch her and all the paraphernalia she will need to bring with her. I would be obliged if you will spend a couple of hours with her this afternoon, choosing patterns and fabrics and trimmings and being measured. I have composed a list for her of what I consider your basic needs. If I have forgotten anything, and I daresay I have, feel free to add to the list."

"Oh," Margaret said, turning envious eyes on her, "you are going to have new *clothes,* Christina?"

But Christina scarcely heard her. She had turned icy cold. He had sent for Miss Penny? He had composed a list? A *list*? He dared to assume a knowledge of her *basic needs*? Was she expected to pour out her gratitude?

"Thank you, my lord," she said, "but that was quite unnecessary. I might have called upon Miss Penny myself within the next day or two. She already has some patterns of which she knows I approve. And I need only two dresses."

"But it is excessively kind—" Lady Hannah began.

"*Not* my lady," his lordship said at the same moment, "if you intend to stay at Thornwood to entertain my guests. You will need a whole new wardrobe, I would wager, and a fashionable one to boot. I warned Miss Penny in my note that she will need some assistants if everything is to be ready in time."

"Oh!" Margaret sounded enraptured.

"How wonderful for you, dear," Lady Hannah said. "And it is very fitting that you should do so, Gerard, as well as very generous. Christina is still the Countess of Wanstead, after all, and will remain so until you marry. Which perhaps will not be in the too distant future?"

But Christina was not listening. She knew why he was doing it—and why he was giving her an allowance and the girls a governess. He was demonstrating to her how very wealthy he now was, how very generous he could be even to a woman he disliked, one who had spurned him and his love. He was making very clear to her just how beholden to him she was for everything. He was not trying to make her happy—he was deliberately doing just the opposite.

"I have no immediate plans to marry, Aunt Hannah," he said. "But who knows what the future holds?" He kept his eyes on Christina as he spoke. "You have a concern, my lady?"

"No, my lord." She would look at this list of his. Perhaps she would even add to it. If he was determined to give, then she would take. Heaven knew she needed new clothes and more fashionable ones than the few she possessed. She would put her head together with Miss Penny's and enjoy herself planning a new and colorful wardrobe. But she would not fawn upon him or show him anything like obsequious gratitude. "None at all."

"I shall ask Miss Penny to see you tomorrow, Margaret," he said. "She will be busy with her ladyship's order, but she must make you one garment at least. I daresay you do not own a ballgown?"

Margaret gaped again. "A ballgown?" She clasped her hands to her bosom and gazed adoringly at her cousin. "Oh, Cousin Gerard. Oh, thank you. Aunt Hannah, I am to have a *ballgown*!"

Which would give him a marvelous glimpse, Christina thought bitterly, into what life had been like with Gilbert. If he had not already suspected. She resented his knowing or his discovering. She felt intruded upon. Almost violated.

Ah, Gerard, Gerard, she found herself thinking. *Why could you not have remained simply the golden boy of my memories?* But she would not allow her thoughts to show on her face. She kept her lips tightly pressed together and her expression impassive.

If he *had* been a stranger, she wondered, and had behaved today just as he had, would she be looking upon him as a generous and kind man? Would she have liked him?

But he was not a stranger.

"No," the Earl of Wanstead said. "*Romantic,* ma'am. It is how you yourself described the dance, if you remember."

His aunt lifted her hands from the keyboard. She had been playing with a spirited rhythm more suited to a gallop than a waltz. "Oh, dear, I am so sorry," she said. "Yes, you are quite right, Gerard."

"But it is a lovely tune," he said, lest she think him over-critical, "and you play it well."

She played it again.

"Perfect," he said, interrupting her after a few bars. "Play it just that way, if you please. I am about to discover how good a teacher I am." He grinned at her. He had learned the waltz himself only since his return to England. But it was all the rage in London. His guests would be disappointed if it were not included in the Christmas ball. Or perhaps his determination to have it danced had become firm only when the countess had objected to it.

She had become a Puritan, had she? Well, she would not drag him into her gloom. Or be allowed to continue her stern rule at Thornwood as she had for the past ten years.

"I am sure you will be a splendid teacher," his aunt assured him. "Certainly you will have an eager pupil. Meg has spoken of nothing else since luncheon."

Margaret, he had realized during the past twenty-four hours—not even so long—was an eager, pretty young lady who had no town bronze at all despite her twenty years. She had not even had a Season. She was almost pathetically eager for the house party, for the ball. Life, he was determined, was certainly going to change for his cousin.

He had come to Thornwood half willing to consider her as a bride. Even this morning he had held open the possibility. But he had already put the thought out of his mind. She was still too much the child. But he was her guardian. He would see to it that over Christmas she met and mingled

with some young ladies who were her peers and some gentlemen who would help her to see herself as an attractive, eligible young lady.

She had come into the ballroom with the countess, he noticed. She was wearing last evening's light muslin gown
again, just as if this were some grand occasion. Her eyes
were wide with the anticipation of some treat. He remembered suddenly teaching her as a child to swim and to ride.
Well, now he would teach her to waltz and doubtless cause
Gilbert to turn over in his grave. He strode across the ballroom toward her.

"You are ready, Margaret?" he asked. "It is really not a
difficult dance, you know. It is easier than the simplest of
country dances."

She giggled, a sound that grated on him somewhat. But he
recognized that she was nervous. He reached out a hand for
hers.

"I must ask you, my lord—" the countess said, though she
stopped speaking the moment he looked at her.

"Yes?" he prompted.

"Nothing," she said. "There would be no point, would
there?"

"None whatsoever," he assured her and led Margaret in
the direction of the pianoforte.

The countess was tall, slender to the point of thinness,
tight-lipped, hard-eyed. She was dressed in unrelieved black
from neck to wrists to ankles. Not a single curl showed beneath her black cap. She even *looked* Puritanical, he
thought. She was a woman without joy. He was surprised
that that younger daughter of hers had been allowed bright
colors with which to paint—and that her fair curls had not
been tamed.

She stayed where she was, he noticed, straight-backed,
silent, disapproving. And she would stay too, he guessed, if
only to confirm her own impression that the waltz was a
wicked dance straight from hell. Her silent presence irritated
him. He wished he had suggested that only Margaret and his
aunt come.

"Now, then," he said to Margaret, "we will not try to

move to music yet or take up the correct posture for the waltz." The *clutching* as she had described it at luncheon very much to his amusement. "We will practice the steps first. There are really only three, performed over and over again in a variety of patterns. But you must remember that we will face each other during the dance. Your steps, then, should mirror mine and not copy them exactly."

She stared at his feet, a frown of concentration creasing her brow.

Either he was not a good teacher, he thought several minutes later, or she was a particularly poor pupil. Uncharitably, he thought the latter was the more likely. She kept complaining about running out of feet at critical moments. She tripped over the two she had. She giggled. She pronounced the whole thing impossible. She apologized profusely. But finally she appeared to have grasped the basic three steps of the dance.

The countess watched from just inside the doors without moving a muscle—or offering any comment, criticism, or encouragement. Her silence fairly shouted at the irritated dancing teacher.

"Let us try to set those steps to music," he suggested. "It will be easier, perhaps, once you hear the rhythm."

It was not. Music, it seemed, was the one additional factor that destroyed everything Margaret had learned. She was probably tone deaf, he decided, and lacking in any sense of rhythm. And yet she had played competently enough the evening before. He was the world's worst teacher, then.

"Unclench your teeth," he advised her. "Stop frowning. Listen to the music. Move to it."

Margaret giggled.

But eventually, after Aunt Hannah had started and stopped a score or more times, she had improved quite markedly.

The countess said nothing. Doubtless she was *thinking* a great deal.

"Splendid!" the earl said with an enthusiasm he was far from feeling—what in the name of thunder was he doing in the ballroom at Thornwood of all places, trying to teach the

waltz? He could think of at least a dozen of his Canadian acquaintances who would make very merry indeed with the
fact for a decade or longer if they only knew. "Now let us
try to do it together."

He took a step closer to Margaret and directed her to place
her left hand on his right shoulder while he set his right
against the back of her waist. He took her right hand in his
left. She blushed rosily even though they were the length of
their bent arms apart.

"Start with your left foot," he told her. "Listen to the
music and feel the rhythm. Follow my lead. Aunt Hannah, if
you please?"

His aunt, eternally good-natured and patient, struck up the
tune yet again. Margaret's forehead crashed into his chest at
the very first step.

"Oh, dear," she said and giggled.

"Margaret," he said, trying to emulate his aunt's patience,
"you must not watch my feet. Look at me or over my shoulder. Eventually you must learn to smile and converse while
you dance, but we will not press that point today."

"But how am I to know what your feet are doing unless I
watch them?" she asked.

He sighed. How *was* she to know? But all the partners he
had had in London had seemed to know by instinct. It was,
he supposed, easier to be the man in such a dance than the
woman.

"Trust me," he said. "Try again. Aunt Hannah?"

But they had clearly reached their limit for today, he realized after six or seven more tries, none of which were very
much more successful than the first. Perhaps tomorrow she
would do better or he would have thought of another way to
teach her. If worse came to worst, he supposed she could sit
out the waltzes at the Christmas ball. She would not be able
to perform the dance in London, after all, until one of the pa-
tronesses of Almack's gave her the nod of approval. But she
would be disappointed, he believed, if she were forced to
miss one of the pleasures of the ball over Christmas. And he
did not wish to see her disappointed.

The countess was still standing where she had been for

the past hour. Perhaps she had thought it incumbent upon herself to act as chaperon, he thought unkindly. Perhaps she had imagined that while Aunt Hannah was engrossed in her music he would have been busy seducing Margaret behind the bench.

And then he had one of those sudden memories that had haunted him for a couple of years after he left England, and even in more recent years had come upon him out of the blue, so to speak, often when he had least expected them, to disturb his peace. A memory of dancing the minuet with a young and smiling Christina. Graceful, light of foot, almost ethereal in one of the delicate white ballgowns she had always worn, she had held his eyes and the whole of his attention. There had always been warmth in her sparkling eyes, in her flushed cheeks, in her parted lips.

She had, he had told her once, been born to dance. She had laughed at him and danced on.

She stood now, dark and cold and disapproving just inside the ballroom doors—Christina ten years later. He felt another wave of the growingly familiar dislike.

"Thank you, Aunt Hannah," he said. "And thank you, Margaret. I believe that will do for today. You will learn more, perhaps, from watching the dance performed correctly. You will watch her ladyship and me waltz together." He was leading Margaret across the floor as he spoke—and he had raised his voice.

The countess stared at him with her impassive face, though her lips compressed more if that were possible.

"I cannot waltz, my lord," she said. "And I have informed you that I will not dance at all at the Christmas ball."

"As you will," he told her, shrugging carelessly. "But Margaret needs to watch the steps demonstrated and I need a partner if she is to do that. You are the only one available."

"But I do not know the steps," she said.

"You have been watching them for a full hour," he pointed out.

"And it looks as impossible to me as it seems to Meg," she said. "And it is quite as improper as I had been led to expect."

Because the partners touched and stood face-to-face and very nearly body to body for its duration? And why had he made such a suggestion anyway? he wondered. He would have to touch her. He had no wish to do so. He had the strange impression that he might be turned to ice if he did so.

"Margaret," he said in the bored voice he sometimes affected when he wanted to annoy someone, "I believe her ladyship is a coward."

"Oh, do try it, Christina," Margaret said, sounding somewhat tired and dispirited, "if only to prove to me that it cannot be done."

The countess's chin had lifted a notch.

"She does not even have your courage to try," the earl said. "Doubtless she is afraid of making a cake of herself, Margaret."

The dark eyes darted sparks. "We will see about *that*, my lord," she said, and she gathered the side of her skirt in one hand and swept past them in the direction of the pianoforte. "Are you very tired, Aunt Hannah? Or are you willing to play for a little longer? A *very* little."

"Oh, I am enjoying myself vastly, dear," Lady Hannah assured her.

The Earl of Wanstead raised his eyebrows and winked at Margaret.

Margaret laughed.

But he was not feeling amused, his lordship thought as they crossed the ballroom again and his cousin moved behind the pianoforte bench in order to watch. Good Lord, he did not want to dance with her. He especially did not want to waltz with her.

With a black icicle.

Chapter 5

"It is quite possible, dear Christina," Lady Hannah was saying, beaming her encouragement. "I have seen it done. I have watched several couples twirling about a ballroom without any one of them coming to grief or treading on one another's toes, though quite how they did it I do not know. I never saw anything more delightful in my life."

But Christina was unable to give anything like her full attention to the words. Into what had she allowed herself to be goaded? She should have given in to nothing short of a direct command, but he had not needed to give that. He had called her a coward and she had risen to the bait just like a hot-tempered schoolgirl. And now there was no way back.

She was going to waltz—or try at least. With *him*. She could not bear the thought of touching him, let alone standing face-to-face with him barely an arm's length apart.

And yet for the past hour she had been dancing without ever moving either her feet or her body. She had been dancing with him as she had once done in many London ballrooms. She had danced with numerous partners, but with him it had always been different. With him she had danced on gilt-edged clouds—she had even been foolish enough to tell him that once, and he had taken her hand in his, raised it to his lips, and held her eyes with his own in that intense way he had had. . . .

She had been standing close to the doors of the ballroom, longing and longing to dance—to *waltz*. With him. And asking herself if there really *was* anything so sinful about dancing. It was an activity designed to arouse inappropriate passions, Gilbert had said. Oh, yes, there was at least some truth in that.

He was not going to begin at the beginning with her, she realized in some alarm after he had followed her across the ballroom floor. He stepped close to her even as Margaret moved off to stand behind the pianoforte bench, slipping his arm beneath hers, and spreading his hand against the back of her waist. She felt the shocking heat of it through the wool of her dress, through her shift, against her flesh. And the alarming nearness of him. He seemed suddenly taller, broader, more—male. She raised her left hand and rested it on his shoulder. It was all hard muscle. The bare skin of his throat and jaw seemed very close. So did his face. He took her right hand in his.

She felt flustered beyond bearing and had to concentrate hard on keeping her cool outer bearing. This was far more intimate, far more improper even than it had looked when Meg had stood in her place. No wonder her sister-in-law had been unable to concentrate on the steps.

"Remember the steps," he told her as if he had read her thoughts. "They are grouped in sets of three. You begin with your left foot. After that, you simply follow my lead."

Simply! "Impossible," she said, and then wished she had not spoken at all. The word came out sounding all breathless. She felt as if at least half the air had suddenly seeped out of the ballroom. She felt dizzy with the subtle, musky odor of his cologne. She had never, she suddenly realized, been this close to Gilbert except for their brief encounters in the marriage bed.

"Aunt Hannah, please?" he said. And then he spoke to her again. "Relax, my lady."

He might have instructed her to turn herself into a winged rhinoceros with better hope of success. She was all wooden legs and arms and whirling thoughts. Poor Aunt Hannah, she thought dimly after they had stopped for the third time in quick succession and she had been requested yet again to play the opening bars of the music. This was not working at all.

But he spoke in the seconds before it came time to try

moving again. "Christina," he said softly, "look at me. Feel the rhythm. Feel *my* rhythm."

She was not sure if he had meant the words to sound risqué. She did not immediately think of them that way herself. But she did obey him. For one thing, she felt humiliated that she could not do something as simple as master the steps of a dance. For another, she felt annoyed that he of all people was to be the witness to her failure.

She had been gazing fixedly over his shoulder. She looked now, instead, into his face, which was embarrassingly close. She did not, of course, have to look directly into his eyes. She might have looked at his chin or his mouth. But it was into his eyes she looked, and having once done so, she could not look away again. And this time when she recognized the cue for the dance to begin, she moved off with her left foot, fitting the steps to the rhythm of the music instead of counting determinedly, shutting all else out, including the music and the movements of her partner.

She danced with him step for step and suddenly discovered that she could feel his movements and sense where he would set his feet next. She could match her steps to his. She could feel his rhythm and could relax into it and follow it. She did not need to count, to concentrate on her steps, to wonder if she would get them right. She merely had to let him lead.

Sometimes his eyes could look dreamy. It was when he drooped his eyelids over them as he was doing now. It was a familiar, long-remembered look. His size, his nearness, his body heat, the smell of his cologne no longer seemed threatening. They became like a shelter around her, wrapping her in the sensual pleasure of the present moment, shielding her from everything that threatened from the outside.

His movements had changed, she only half realized after a few moments. He was no longer dancing her back and forth over the same small area of floor. He was taking her around the perimeter of the ballroom, twirling her slowly but perfectly in time to the music. And she felt something she had not felt in years, something she had thought long, long dead in herself.

She felt a great welling of exhilaration. Of joy.

Gerard. Ah, Gerard.

She had no idea how many seconds or minutes passed before he spoke—though they had circled right about the ballroom, she realized then.

"You see?" he said. "It really is possible."

His voice broke the spell, and she realized what she was doing, what was happening. She was dancing. Not only dancing, but *waltzing*. She was waltzing in a man's arms and smiling at him and enjoying every moment and dreaming of him as he had once been—and of herself as she had once been. She was being seduced and she was allowing it to happen just as if she had no will of her own, no character or principles of her own.

Just as if she were that same naive, heedless girl and he was that same flawed golden boy.

She lost the rhythm and they drew to a halt.

But Margaret was applauding and Aunt Hannah joined her after lifting her hands from the keyboard.

"Oh, you waltz beautifully, Christina," Margaret said wistfully. "But how on earth did you know when to twirl about and how to keep your feet from beneath Cousin Gerard's?"

"Now you must admit that I was right," Lady Hannah said. "Is it not the most romantic dance there ever was, Christina?"

"It really is not the thing at all," she said, dropping her left hand, withdrawing her right, and taking a step back. "I daresay our neighbors would be scandalized if it were included in the Christmas ball. It must not be. We would not wish to make anyone uncomfortable, after all." She felt decidedly uncomfortable, remembering how she had forgotten everything but the dance—and her partner.

"I am going to learn it if I must die in the attempt," Margaret said.

"I hardly think it will come to that, dear," her aunt assured her. "Tomorrow you will do better, mark my words."

"Those of the neighbors who know the steps will probably be eager to show off their superior skills," the earl said.

"Those who do not will doubtless enjoy seeing them demonstrated before their eyes. *We* will demonstrate the waltz for them, my lady. You and I."

"But I do not intend to dance at all," she reminded him coolly. His eyes, she noticed, had lost that dreamy, seductive look. They were mocking her. "I shall be your hostess at the ball, my lord, and greet everyone and make sure that all the young ladies have partners. But dancing itself is for young people."

"Precisely," he agreed. "You and I will waltz together."

"Oh yes, Christina," Lady Hannah said. "You really must. You do it exceedingly well, especially when it is remembered that this was your first try. And you are only eight-and-twenty. Of course you are young."

"Gilbert would have disapproved."

"But Gilbert, my lady," the Earl of Wanstead reminded her, his voice almost silky, "is dead." His blue eyes, she saw when she looked into them, had turned hard as steel. He was going to insist that she dance with him, not because he really wished to do so, but simply because he knew *she* did not wish it.

He was no different from any other man, she thought bitterly. He enjoyed exercising power over women, especially any who tried, however feebly, to defy him. He particularly enjoyed his power over her since she had once rejected him.

"It will be as you command, my lord," she said and quelled the twinge of fear she could not help feeling when he narrowed his eyes on her as he had done in the library during the morning—before warning her not to try impertinence on him.

The rest of the week before his guests arrived was an extremely busy one for the Earl of Wanstead. He prepared for their visit in a number of ways, though it was the countess who saw to the hiring of extra servants, and the servants who undertook all the numerous menial tasks, like cleaning and airing every available bedchamber in the house, for example. He undertook a few journeys into the town eight miles away to purchase various supplies, among them a

large box of skates of various sizes. It was his hope that the
ice on the lake would be firm enough to allow skating over
the holiday.

He diligently made the acquaintance of all his neighbors,
calling upon most of them in company with his aunt or Margaret or both. Many of the people he remembered from his
boyhood, of course. He issued verbal invitations to the
Christmas ball even though Margaret had already sent out
cards. It seemed that everyone was planning to attend.

And he spent a good deal of time with his steward, sometimes in the study, more often out of doors about the estate.
He inspected all his farms, which were not very active now
that it was winter. But the relative idleness of the farmers
gave him the opportunity to talk with his tenants and his laborers and listen to their comments and complaints. Most of
the latter concerned repairs that were too slow in getting
done.

It was in the nature of workers and tenants, Charles
Monck explained when questioned afterward, to believe that
they had only to ask for something to have it granted. They
invariably assumed that their employers were made of
money.

He had a point, the earl agreed. He had been a businessman, an employer, long enough to know that a large number
of workers were only too ready to take as much as they
could while giving as little as possible in return. But he
knew too that there was an at least equally large number
who gave an honest day's work in expectation of an honest
day's wage—but who were sometimes not accorded quite
that wage.

He would need more time to assess the situation at Thornwood, he thought, to feel quite satisfied that everything was
running as he would wish if he had the direct oversight of its
operation. Ideally, he would need to observe the working of
his farms over spring and summer and harvest. Since that
would be impossible, he must do the best he could in the
short time available to him.

He tried to resist the impulse to become too involved in
Thornwood affairs.

In his spare time—or so he sometimes described it to himself with wry humor—he gave dancing lessons. He taught the quadrille, the cotillion, the waltz, though sometimes the lack of other couples to make up a set made matters tricky. After that first day, when he had been thoroughly convinced that Margaret must have been born tone deaf and with two left feet, he found that she improved steadily. His cousin might never be a naturally graceful dancer, but she would be proficient enough to acquit herself adequately in the ballroom. She was learning to relax. More important, she was learning to enjoy herself. She sparkled as she danced. She had stopped giggling.

The countess did not attend any more dancing lessons. When he commented on her absence at the dining table one day, she told him that her mornings were necessarily filled with preparations for the house party and that she needed to spend her afternoons with her daughters.

"Bring them to the ballroom with you," he suggested.

Her lips compressed in that way she had of looking severe and disapproving and older than her years. "Is that a command, my lord?" she asked him.

She could be intensely irritating. He hated those words of apparently docile submissiveness, which were always accompanied by her look of ice. For one moment he was tempted to tell her that yes, by God, it *was* a command and that she had better obey it if she knew what was good for her. But he would not give her the satisfaction of being able to look upon herself as a martyr.

"It is a *request,* my lady," he replied with excessive politeness.

She had not come—and he was glad of it. He wanted no repetition of that one afternoon. Somehow he must avoid waltzing with her at the Christmas ball. It should be easy enough. She was quite determined not to dance at all. And there would be plenty of other ladies only too eager to dance.

One day he was so busy that he missed luncheon—and he had breakfasted early. The dancing lesson was to be at four o'clock, as usual. But there was some time left before then that he would steal for himself, his lordship decided, though there were doubtless a thousand and one things he should be doing if he gave thought to the matter. He would not waste part of this stolen time eating. He was not particularly hungry anyway.

He strolled along the wooded bank of the river, which flowed to the east of the house and wound its way behind the hill to the north. He found the gamekeeper's hut in which he had spent so many hours during his youth. It was unlocked. It was clean and tidy inside and kept in readiness for an inhabitant, with logs piled neatly in the corner by the fireplace, though he had discovered a few days earlier that Pinky no longer lived there all the time—he had taken a small cottage in the village. But the hut, empty though it was, brought back memories—happy memories. The earl sat by the window, looking out at trees and the river for all of half an hour.

Not that he had spent the whole time reliving happy memories, he thought ruefully at last. Or not happy memories from his boyhood, anyway. He had been thinking of *her*— of the lovely, eager girl she had been; of the strange something that had happened to her bright, dark eyes when he had first been presented to her, and the corresponding lurching about his own heart; of the way she had always watched eagerly for him at every ball and party after that—she had been too innocent to disguise the fact; of dancing with her until the world receded from around them and there were only the two of them left; of driving her in Hyde Park in a borrowed curricle one afternoon and finding a secluded pathway and kissing her for the first time. She had kissed him back, eagerly, inexpertly—though he had not known the difference at the time—and had rashly gazed into his eyes afterward and told him with passionate conviction that she loved him, that she would always, always love him.

He got up to leave the hut. But he stared for a few more minutes sightlessly through the window to the river below. It had not taken her long to lose her innocence. She had met Gilbert—*he* had introduced them—discovered that he was the Earl of Wanstead, was very wealthy, and was in search of a wife. And if Gerard had ever wondered whether she had bitterly regretted her mercenary decision, he had only to look at her now. She had acquiesced in the type of life Gilbert had decreed for them. She still tried to live it. Except when she had waltzed . . .

Her spine, usually so stiff, had arched gracefully beneath his hand, her feet had seemed scarcely to touch the floor, she had appeared to take the music inside herself. Her eyes had softened, grown dreamy. Her lips had smiled. No—her whole face had smiled.

And the world had receded.

He had wondered immediately afterward if she had done it deliberately as punishment for his insisting that she waltz with him. He thought now that it was more likely he had imagined much of it. She had always been a good dancer. It was to be expected that she would waltz well. He had been dazzled by the simple fact of her nearness and the subtle smell of lavender that had always clung about her.

He left the hut and decided to return to the house a different way. He would take the shortcut through the trees and about the base of the hill. The route would bring him within a relatively short distance of the back of the house. But he could hear voices soon after he had left the trees behind—two of them, one shrieking and one laughing. He soon realized where the sounds were coming from.

The hill was wooded, though a scenic walk had been constructed over it, the path lined with flowering trees and shrubs, with seats and follies at appropriate intervals along it and the occasional carefully revealed vista over the surrounding countryside. One part of the slope had been cleared entirely of trees so that the beholder could look down from the path above over the gardens at the back of the house, over the house itself, and along the cultivated parkland in front of it. It was a breathtaking view. The slope itself was thick and beautiful with wildflowers during the summer. But both summer and winter it had always been out of bounds to walkers. Taking a shortcut either up or down the slope had been strictly forbidden. Its wild beauty was to be preserved at all costs.

But down the whole length of that slope, as the Earl of Wanstead watched from the shelter of the trees a short distance away, sailed seven-year-old Rachel, her legs pumping fast, but almost not fast enough for her body, her arms stretched to the sides. She ran in silence and then turned to begin the laborious climb to the top again. And down the lower half of the slope rolled Tess, over and over, shrieking with mingled fright and glee, until she reached the safe haven of her mother's waiting arms at the bottom. It was the countess who was laughing.

"Caught you!" she said, picking her daughter up and twirling her about, still laughing.

"Again!" The child was all flailing arms and legs. She scrambled upward on all fours as soon as her mother had set her down again.

Ah, his lordship thought, setting one shoulder against a tree trunk, that brought back memories. He had been a sailing ship, a bird, an avenging angel down that slope—until Gilbert had seen him at it one day and had gone off with gleeful haste to report the transgression to his father. One of Uncle's wild rages had followed. The cane had been brought out.

It was a happy family group that he watched now. He had wondered. He had seen them together only one other time, in the nursery, when the children had been quietly at work under their mother's serious supervision. He had wondered if those children were to be pitied. But there could be no mistaking the happiness of the scene before his eyes. She gave her attention to both children. She laughed with them both even though the elder played a seemingly solitary game.

Oh, no, he thought with a curious pang about the heart, he had not imagined it. Somewhere behind the dark, cold, puritanical facade of the Countess of Wanstead lurked the exuberant beauty of that girl he had loved—and then hated. She had appeared briefly in the ballroom while she waltzed with him. She was fully present now with her children.

It was a pang of envy, perhaps. They were family. He was the outsider. Always the outsider.

It was Rachel who spotted him. She had just made her third silent, graceful, solemn descent down the hill and had paused to gaze about her. Her eyes alit on him, and she turned to say something to her mother, who had just caught the younger child again.

He strolled toward them and watched them all change. The intruder was coming into the family group, and the family was closing protectively on itself. He did not even attempt to smile.

The countess had put her children behind her and stood before them as if to protect them from harm. She stood straight and dark and—and what? He sensed some strong emotion. He was given the fleeting impression that it was fear. More likely, he thought cynically, it was annoyance that he had come along to spoil the idyll. He should have walked home the more direct way. He should not have come at all—out on this little afternoon escape, to Thornwood in the first place. He had known that memories would be stirred if he saw her again. He had known, surely, that somehow he would be hurt by them.

"It was my fault," she said quickly and almost defiantly before he could say anything himself. "I did not see any harm in it. Blame me."

Good Lord! She *was* afraid—for her children. Because they had been breaking what must still be a strict rule. Was she afraid he was about to lay about him with a heavy hand? He clasped his hands tightly at his back.

"It is still forbidden?" he asked. "Racing down that hill merited a caning in my day—bent over the desk in the earl's study. One hoped to avoid having to sit down for an hour or so afterward." He leaned a little closer to her when she did not crack even the semblance of a smile or show any other sign of relaxing. "But I have just remembered that I am the one who now makes the rules at Thornwood. Let me exercise my authority, then. This particular rule is rescinded—completely, for all time. The hill is no longer out of bounds to runners or rollers."

But if he had expected a smile this time, a look of relief, a thank-you, he was doomed to disappointment. "It was made," she said, "to protect the wildflowers."

For the space of an hour or two in the library that first

morning, when they had planned the house party, there had been some semblance of amiability between them. But there had been none since—he would not count their waltz in that category. She would not allow any pleasantness.

The younger child was clinging to her mother's cloak and then reaching up both arms. The countess bent to pick her up. The other child stood where she was, not moving, not smiling. She was a thin, plain, solemn little girl. He looked at her, tipping his head slightly to one side so that he could see her around her mother.

"What were you?" he asked her. "A sailing ship?"

"A swan, sir," she said.

Ah. Imagining herself graceful and beautiful? Strangely, she had looked both though she was not a pretty child. But she would perhaps grow up to resemble her mother.

"With this cloak," he told her, "I believe I would make a magnificent crow." He spread his arms, grasping the edges of his cloak with his hands.

There was a little wobble of a smile at the edges of her mouth.

"Shall we see whether the swan or the crow flies the faster—and the more gracefully?" he suggested.

"Yes, sir," she said and turned to climb the slope silently beside him. The countess stood below, holding Tess.

The crow flew faster though far less gracefully. And it did not reach the bottom—at least, not propelled by its billowing black wings. It tripped over its top boots halfway down and rolled clumsily the rest of the way, roaring with alarm. Rachel was smiling, he could see as he got to his feet and brushed himself off. The younger child was giggling helplessly in her mother's arms.

"I believe," he said, "the swan won on all counts."

"You did it on purpose, sir," Rachel accused, but her eyes were bright with merriment.

"I?" He raised his eyebrows. "I have murdered my boots, for which my valet will scold me roundly. Would I do such a thing deliberately?"

But he had interfered in the family outing for long

enough. "I have to return to the house for a dancing lesson," he said. "Do continue playing." He made them all a bow.

But Rachel took a step toward him. "*Dancing?*" she said, and he could see suddenly from her luminous eyes that she would indeed inherit her mother's beauty. "Oh, sir, may I come and watch?"

"Rachel!" the countess said sharply even as his eyes flew to her face. She closed her eyes briefly and set Tess down on the ground. "His lordship is busy."

"But not too busy to allow of an audience," he said. "If you will permit it, my lady."

She bit her lip.

"If *you* will permit it," he said again quietly. "Not otherwise."

"Please, Mama!"

"I believe," he said, "it is the minuet that is on the agenda this afternoon—not the waltz."

"I will bring both children to watch, then," she said. "I shall keep them out of your way, my lord. Rachel has a passionate interest in dancing, though she has been told repeatedly that it is—" She bit her lip again and did not complete the sentence.

Frivolous? Evil? Ungodly? *Who* had first told her that? Gilbert? Christina? Both?

"Allow me to escort you back to the house, then," he said, offering her his arm.

She looked at it, and he thought for a few moments that she would refuse to take it. But she did so and began to walk with him. Rachel walked silently at his other side. The younger child skipped along ahead of them, humming to herself.

A family group, he thought. Or what would look like a family group to a stranger. He and Christina—Gilbert's widow. And Gilbert's children. They had nothing to say to each other, he discovered, he and the Countess of Wanstead, though it took them all of ten silent minutes to reach the house.

He was an outsider.

And had no wish to be an insider, surely.

Chapter 6

All had been made ready for the arrival of the house guests four days before Christmas.

A number of extra servants had been hired. Every room in the house had been swept and dusted and polished until it sparkled. Every bedchamber had been prepared and assigned. All the extra leaves had been added to the dining room table so that it extended to its fullest possible length. Great quantities of food and other supplies had been ordered and what had already arrived had been stored away—or already cooked. Crates of wine and other liquors had been hauled into the cellar. One sitting room, which had almost never been used for the past ten years, had been restored to its original function when a crew of hefty servants carried down the old billiard table from the attic and set it up for two maids to clean. The attic had also been denuded of boxes of toys that had been deemed unsuitable for girls and had therefore never been brought down for Rachel and Tess. The nursery had been filled with these new treasures and the adjoining rooms set up as children's bedchambers. Even the wintry park had been raked clear of leaves and other signs of neglect.

There was really nothing left to do except await the arrivals, Christina thought finally as she wandered from day room to day room after luncheon. And change her clothes, of course. Indeed, Aunt Hannah and Margaret and even the earl had already gone to their rooms in order to get ready.

She recognized a reluctance in herself. A reluctance, perhaps, to begin what she had worked hard for during the past week. Life had changed so much already. It would surely change even more drastically in the coming days. There was a certain attraction in the thought, she was forced to admit. She had loved her come-out Season and yet that had been years ago. She had been only a girl. Life had been so very quiet since. And so very dull, a deep inner voice added.

But her chief reluctance, she knew, had nothing to do with the imminent arrival of the guests, who would change Thornwood and the daily life there beyond recognition. Her real reason for delaying going to her room was that she knew what her maid would have laid out for her there. A new afternoon dress of bright royal blue. It was so beautiful that she could scarcely bear to look at it. The thought of actually wearing it was almost painful.

She would be different, she thought. The unrelieved black she had worn for the last year and a half was not so very different from the drab, serviceable colors she had worn for years before that. They had come to feel like safe colors, something behind which she had been able to hide. Though she had never thought of them that way until her new clothes had started to arrive and she had tried them on and imagined herself wearing them in public.

For *him* to see.

How foolish she was being, she thought, setting out resolutely for the staircase and her rooms. If she did not hurry she would be late. He had asked her to be his hostess. She must be ready to meet the first arrivals, then.

She was standing in front of a full-length pier glass in her dressing room a little more than half an hour later while her maid hung up the garments she had worn during the morning. Perhaps, Christina thought, she should wear black just for today after all. It would make her look more elegant for receiving visitors. It would make more obvious to them her role in the household as the widow of the former earl. And perhaps . . .

But the door from the corridor was flung back after the briefest of knocks and Margaret rushed inside.

"There is a carriage approaching," she said, her voice

breathless with excitement. "Much earlier than any of us expected. And I am not *ready*, Christina. Just look at my hair."

She was wearing a pale blue dress, a color that became her well. But true enough, her hair was a disaster. Her maid was of the unfortunate belief that the more ringlets and curls she coaxed into her mistress's hair, the more elegant the resulting creation would be. She had outdone herself on this occasion.

"Perhaps a brush through the ringlets would create soft curls that would look very well for the afternoon," Christina suggested even as her heart pounded with the news that the first of the guests were fast approaching. "You have such pretty hair, Meg. Sophie will do it for you, will you not, Sophie?"

Her maid looked dubiously at Margaret's head. "Sit down on the stool, Lady Meg," she directed, "and I will see what I can do."

"It really is not essential that you be downstairs for everyone's arrival, anyway, Meg," Christina assured her. "You will meet everyone at tea. However, I promised his lordship that I would go down. I had better go without further delay."

But Margaret, the promise of Sophie's superior services having calmed her somewhat overwrought nerves, was staring wide-eyed at her sister-in-law.

"Oh, Christina," she exclaimed. "You look *beautiful!*"

It was a dress deceptively simple in design, only slightly scooped at the neck with slim long sleeves. It flared into soft pleats to the ankle from its fashionable high waistline. It was quite unadorned. It was without question the most elegant dress in her pattern book, Miss Penny had declared, and Christina had agreed with her. But she felt herself flushing now. Beautiful? But all beauty was vanity, Gilbert had been fond of saying, and trying to look beautiful was playing into the devil's hands. Had she been trying?

But there was no time now to change back to the comfortable black. Or to change her mind about wearing a cap. Sophie had dressed her hair in a smooth chignon, but it was too high on the crown to allow for a cap.

The countess's rooms overlooked the terrace and the front

lawns. Before she could rush from the room she heard the distinctive rumble of carriage wheels moving from the paved driveway onto the cobbled terrace. There was no time even to think further. She left the room and hurried along the corridor and down the grand staircase. The front doors, she could see as soon as she stepped through the stairway arch into the hall, were already open. The Earl of Wanstead was standing near them, about to step outside. He turned to watch her approach.

He dressed usually for comfort, she guessed. But today, in a form-fitting coat of blue superfine, gray pantaloons, shining Hessians, and gleaming white linen, he looked very elegant indeed. Handsome.

But the impression, barely formed in her mind, was soon driven out by acute embarrassment. He stood very still, and his eyes moved with slow deliberation down her body from head to toe. Without her customary blacks she felt naked. He made her a formal bow, which was quite unnecessary since they had seen each other at luncheon.

"My lady," was all he said, but there was something in his eyes that brought heat to her cheeks.

She wished—oh, how she longed for her blacks!

The Earl of Wanstead had several times over the past week regretted his decision to host a house party. As a bachelor he had rarely entertained on any grand scale even for a single evening. But all the preparations appeared to have gone smoothly, thanks, he admitted, to the servants—and thanks to the countess. Now that the time had come he was feeling rather excited if the truth were known.

It was impossible to tell who was arriving in the first carriage, but since it was not a private coach but a hired conveyance, he guessed that it might be Andrew Campbell and Jeannette. It would be like them to come early. He hoped they *would* be first. They reminded him of home—or of what had been home for ten years—and they were particularly close friends of his. He had missed them. It seemed much longer than a week since he had seen them last.

By sheer good fortune the day was bright and sunny. Nevertheless it was cold—the grass and the bare branches of the trees had been white with frost when he had gone riding just before dawn. He certainly did not want to stand around on the terrace longer than was necessary. Even so, he was about to step outside when a movement to his left alerted him to the fact that the countess had come downstairs to help with the greetings, as she had promised to do. He turned his head to look at her.

She looked so startlingly different without her mourning clothes that he forgot all about good manners and stared. No, he did worse than stare. He let his eyes roam over her. Both the design and the color of her dress were inspired, he thought. They emphasized the tall, slim elegance of her figure and accentuated the darkness of her hair and eyes. She looked sheerly elegant. More than elegant. She looked stunningly beautiful.

"My lady," he said, making her a deep bow just as if it were she who was the one arriving.

"Someone has come?" she asked in her usual imperturbable cool manner. He immediately felt foolish.

"The Campbells, if I am not mistaken," he said. "Shall we go outside to greet them?"

She preceded him through the double doors and down the horseshoe steps without another word. A groom had just opened the door of the carriage and put down the steps, and a young man was vaulting out, not making use of them. He was smiling cheerfully and looking about him with open appreciation. Yes, Andrew, of course.

"Gerard!" he called, looking beyond the countess's shoulder. "*This* is Thornwood? Should I salaam?"

It was good to see him again, to hear his slight Scottish accent. "A simple kiss on my signet ring will suffice," the earl said with a laugh. But he had spotted Jeannette, who in typically independent fashion was about to descend the steps unassisted. She looked delightfully familiar and fetchingly pretty in a green velvet carriage dress. He hurried forward to offer her a hand.

But he changed his mind when she looked up and smiled at him, all sunshine and dimples and red hair and green eyes—and freckles. He set his hands instead on either side of her small waist and lifted her down bodily. The poke of her bonnet reached barely to his chin when her feet touched the cobbles. She was such a little thing, but she was always a perfect bundle of energy. She laughed up at him.

"Gerard," she said, "we have been speechless with awe for the last few minutes. It is a veritable *palace!*"

He grinned at her and lowered his head to kiss her impulsively first on one cheek and then on the other. "Welcome to Thornwood," he said. "How good it is to see you again—to see both of you." But especially Jeannette. They had always been the best of friends, able to talk easily to each other on almost any subject under the sun.

But he became aware of the silent presence of the countess, and suddenly and for no discernible reason it seemed important to him that she should like his friends—and that they should like her.

"May I present the Countess of Wanstead?" he said. "My dear friends from Montreal, Christina—Jeannette and Andrew Campbell, brother and sister as I am sure you can tell from their similar coloring."

Jeannette turned her head sharply to gaze at Christina and Andrew looked startled. The earl knew what was coming even before either of them spoke, but he was powerless to stop it. He should have been more careful in his introductions.

"The countess?" Andrew said, his voice all astonishment. "You have *married,* Gerard? But this is—"

The countess clasped her hands together, lifted her chin, and thinned her lips.

"Her ladyship is my cousin's widow," the earl explained hastily. "She still bears the title, Andrew, as I do not yet have a wife of my own."

It was an embarrassing moment, but Andrew merely chuckled and bowed over her hand.

"Lady Wanstead," he said, "I am pleased to make your acquaintance."

"And I yours," she said, smiling at them both, the perfectly courteous hostess.

"You must forgive us, Lady Wanstead," Jeannette said, extending her own hand. "We knew of your existence but we expected an aged dowager. We should have remembered, of course, that your husband was Gerard's *cousin*."

Christina smiled as she took Jeannette's hand in her own. "Do come inside where it is warmer, Miss Campbell," she said. "And you too, sir. You will be eager to settle in your rooms and freshen up after your journey. Perhaps you would even like to rest before tea. There will be plenty of time. You are the first to arrive."

"Are we?" Andrew Campbell grimaced. "It is a family failing, I am afraid."

"I hope," the earl said, "your journey down here was less eventful than mine. I had to stop to have a wheel repaired." He was walking up the steps beside Andrew, the two ladies ahead of them. They were a marked contrast to each other, he thought, both lovely but in quite different ways. It seemed strange seeing them together, his past and his present—and perhaps his future? He had felt a more than usually strong rush of affection at seeing Jeannette again.

And being the Earl of Wanstead, he had realized with some reluctance during the past week, really had set a certain burden of responsibility on his shoulders.

But he would not think of that at present. He would consider it at greater leisure over Christmas.

There was a great flurry of arrivals after that. There was a constant to-ing and fro-ing from the terrace to the hall and up the staircase to the various guest chambers. And then mingled with it there was a steady descent of guests making for the drawing room even before it was teatime. A swell of sound came from the room as acquaintances greeted one another and exchanged observations on their journey and comments on the weather and on the beauty of Thornwood.

Lady Hannah and a brightly flustered Lady Margaret were acting as hostesses in there, Christina knew. Aunt Hannah was in her element as she had an acquaintance with several of the guests and was quite capable of greeting even those she did not know and making them comfortable. Lady Hannah and Mr. Milne, her late husband, had mingled a great deal with society right up to the time of his death. Though she had never grumbled since straitened circumstances after her widowhood had brought her back to Thornwood, Christina had always been aware that she found the absence of social life at her nephew's home somewhat trying.

Margaret was clearly nervous.

"But I know no one in there except Aunt Hannah," she had protested when Christina had found her hovering outside the door, unwilling to go in even though only three or four of the guests had descended at that point.

"But of course," Christina had said. "How could you know anyone, Meg? Smile and go to Aunt Hannah. She will present you, and then you must simply keep on smiling and answer any questions you are asked and think of some to ask in your turn. It will all be far easier than you expect. Your hair now looks very becoming, by the way."

Poor Meg—so unpracticed in the social arts despite her age and rank. Christina felt a familiar twinge of guilt. She had not been able to help matters while Gilbert was alive, of course, or for the year following his death. But she had made no effort during the past five months or so to make life more interesting for her sister-in-law. It was almost as if she had been lulled into a sleep long ago and had been hovering on the brink of waking but had resisted doing so. Sometimes it was more comfortable to remain asleep than to be awake.

Margaret, she saw twenty minutes later when she had a moment to peep into the drawing room, was in the very midst of a group of young people, both ladies and gentlemen, looking flushed and animated and very pretty indeed. If only Gerard really meant to give her a Season during the coming spring, Christina thought. If only he did not forget once Christmas was over and his thoughts turned back to Canada. She would forgive him a great deal if he would just do that for Meg.

But there was no time to dwell upon thoughts of her sister-in-law. There were guests to welcome and names to remember. She thought she remembered Sir Michael and Lady Milchip from her own come-out Season. She certainly remembered their elder son, Mr. Ralph Milchip, who had been a friend of Gerard's. They had their younger son with them too, Mr. Jeremy Milchip, and their young daughter, Winifred, who blushed shyly as soon as she stepped down from her papa's carriage and saw the earl and the countess standing there. Meg must be given the task of seeing that she was drawn into every activity over the coming days, Christina thought. And at the same time Meg could learn from the girl something of the wisdom of dressing and styling her hair with reasonable simplicity.

Lady Gaynor, a handsome widow in her forties, and her two young daughters, who were introduced as Lizzie and Susan, arrived at almost the same moment as the darkly handsome young Mr. Samuel Radway and his sister, Clara. And then, before Christina could be quite sure she would remember which name went with which face, Mr. and Mrs. John Cannadine arrived with their two young children, the younger of whom was fast asleep in his father's arms while four-year-old Alice was cross and loudly wailing.

"She has missed her afternoon sleep," Laura Cannadine explained apologetically. "I do beg your pardon, Lady Wanstead. Just when one wishes one's offspring to be on their best behavior, they embarrass one beyond bearing."

"I know," Christina said, smiling in sympathy. "I have two of my own. Let me take you straight up to the nursery. Ah, your nurse is in the other carriage, I see. I shall show you where to set Alice down and my children's nurse will help yours get settled. I know just how important a regular routine is for children."

"How kind you are," Laura said as her husband, grinning, transferred his sleeping son to the nurse's arms.

Christina descended from the nursery ten minutes later in time to greet Lord and Lady Langan, who also had two children with them, both boys, both a little older than the other two. They would surely be splendid companions for Rachel.

Two gentlemen had arrived together while she was upstairs, she learned. She tried to remember from the list she had conned over the past few days who was still missing, and discovered to her dismay that she could no longer remember who had already come. After ten years of marriage, she thought ruefully, this sort of thing should be second nature to her.

The remaining two guests arrived just as she was about to give orders for the tea tray to be taken to the drawing room before going there herself to preside. They were two gentlemen, both in their forties, Christina estimated. Like the first arrivals, they were business associates of the earl's, retired partners in his own fur-trading company. They were brothers, clearly gentlemen, whose Scottish accents would have betrayed their origins even if their names had not.

"Mr. Colin Stewart, my lady," his lordship said, presenting them to her. "And Mr. Geordie Stewart, his brother."

And that was everyone, she thought in bewildered relief. Now all she had to do was learn the trick of calling everyone by the correct name.

"Welcome to Thornwood," she said. "I hope we can make your stay happy here over Christmas. Do come inside where it is warmer."

At least, she thought as she entered the drawing room and set about pouring the tea, she did not have to face the task of making strangers comfortable with one another. With a few exceptions everyone seemed to know everyone else well enough—as was to be expected of people of the *ton*. It was she who was the peculiar one, though she had been happy enough, especially at first, to withdraw from society after her marriage. And she had been ready enough to believe that the world of polite society was without merit, even wicked.

But there was something strangely seductive about this gathering of smiling, chattering people. Everyone looked amiable and harmless enough. And there was something delightful about looking around and seeing people dressed colorfully and fashionably. Perhaps she had been wrong. . . .

She listened to a snippet of conversation during a few moments while she was alone at the tea tray. It involved Margaret and three gentlemen. One of them was Mr. Ralph Milchip. The other two must be the gentlemen who had arrived while Christina was in the nursery. She remembered one of them by sight and thought he must be Viscount Luttrell. At least his name was on the list of guests, yet she could not remember having been presented to him.

"What I want to know, Lady Margaret," the third young gentleman was saying, "is why we have never yet seen you in London. It is a crime pure and simple, if you were to ask me."

"Perhaps, sir," Margaret replied, sounding downright coquettish, "because I have been too busy and too merry in the country to be able to spare a moment for London. Have I missed something of importance by not going there?"

Gilbert would have been horrified. The tone of the conversation was clearly flirtatious. Christina merely smiled to herself. *Good for you, Meg,* she said silently.

"One is made to think of flowers blooming unseen in deserts," Mr. Milchip said.

"Except that the countryside is no desert, sir," Margaret retorted.

"Have you missed something of importance, Lady Margaret?" the gentleman who was probably Viscount Luttrell said, his voice languid. He had a quizzing glass in his hand, Christina noticed, though he had not raised it all the way to his eye. "Certainly you have. You have missed me."

Margaret's delighted laughter mingled with the deeper guffaws of his companions.

"How absurd, my lord," she said.

It was harmless stuff, Christina thought. Surely it was all harmless. And then she looked up to find the viscount turning around, his quizzing glass all the way to his eye now, and looking directly at her.

"Ah," he said, "I have just realized that I am parched. And that I must be in the presence of the countess, for whose absence on the terrace earlier Wanstead apologized most profusely."

Christina inclined her head and lifted the teapot to pour him a cup. "I am," she said.

He made her a formal and elegant bow. "Harry Vane, Viscount Luttrell, very much at your service, my lady," he said.

"I am pleased to make your acquaintance, my lord," she

said. Yes, definitely, he too had been one of Gerard's friends.

Mr. Frederick Cannadine, younger brother of the married John Cannadine, also introduced himself and accepted a cup of tea while Mr. Milchip continued to converse with Margaret.

Perhaps not quite so harmless after all, Christina was thinking. For a few moments Viscount Luttrell had surveyed her through his quizzing glass. In those few moments she had felt as if all her clothes were being expertly stripped away from her body. And in his lazy eyes after he had lowered his glass and made his bow and presented himself she read a deep, knowing appreciation.

She felt a thrill of very feminine gratification. And then she despised her own pleasure.

Chapter 7

An hour or more passed before the guests began to drift off back to their rooms to rest before getting ready for dinner, or to supervise the unpacking of their luggage, or to write a letter or two. It was dizzyingly pleasant, the earl found, despite his earlier misgivings, to see Thornwood filled with cheerful, chattering people, to know that they would all be there over Christmas. A house party had been an inspired idea by whoever it was who had first thought of it.

He had amused himself while mingling with his guests and making sure that they were all well supplied with tea and dainties in trying to imagine one of the young ladies present as his countess, as his hostess for any future entertainment of this sort. There were only two real possibilities, of course, since he had already ruled out Margaret. He would definitely feel more comfortable with Jeannette as his wife, he thought as he watched her conversing and laughing with people she had not met until today. And yet perhaps Lizzie Gaynor would fit more naturally into the role of countess—if he were to stay in England. If he went back to Canada, of course . . .

If?

He tried not to let his imaginings distract him. He certainly was not going to make anyone an impulsive offer. He was going to take his time deciding—whom to ask, and whether to ask anyone at all. One thing was clear: he was going to have to be careful. Educated guesses must have been made about the motives of a bachelor earl in hosting a

Christmas house party at which several of the guests were unattached young ladies.

"We were most obliged for the invitation, my lord," Lady Gaynor said to him. "We would have spent Christmas with my late husband's family as usual, of course, but Lizzie wished to come here instead, because some of her particular friends were to be here, you know, and it is important to young people to be with others their own age."

"I am honored that you came, ma'am," he told her.

"Thornwood is perfectly splendid, my lord," Lizzie said, touching her fingertips to his sleeve for a moment and gazing into his eyes. "I do so look forward to seeing all over the house. Do tell me that you will conduct a tour."

"Tomorrow morning if that will suit you," he replied.

"I shall think of nothing else from the moment I awake," she assured him.

He felt almost as if a clandestine assignation had been made.

And all the time, while he imagined the possible future, he was aware of the woman who was at present the countess and his hostess. She had done superlatively well at making his guests feel welcome and at home. She had shown unexpected warmth and charm, especially to poor Laura Cannadine, who had arrived flustered and embarrassed by her screeching infant. And of course she looked unusually beautiful.

He almost resented the fact that her beauty and warmth and charm had been assumed for the sake of his guests as they were frequently donned in private for her daughters. She was becoming something of an enigma to him. But he did not wish to unravel the mystery. He kept his mind and his eyes off her during tea—or tried to, at least.

Finally everyone had wandered off, most people to their rooms, Lady Langan and Mrs. Cannadine to the nursery with the countess. Only Viscount Luttrell remained.

"Come into the billiard room," the earl suggested, "and have a drink. I need a few minutes in which to relax."

"Grand!" the viscount said, looking about appreciatively

when they got there. "A masculine domain. Every man needs one, especially if he has females living with him."

"The table was gathering moths and dust in the attic," the earl told him as he crossed the room to the sideboard, where he poured them both a drink. "It was hauled up there some time during my predecessor's time. Playing billiards was a sinful pastime apparently." He grinned as he handed the viscount a glass.

"Sinful!" Viscount Luttrell whistled. "Are you serious, Gerard? Your cousin? I always thought he was a peculiar fish, I must confess, even though I never knew him well. I never even saw him after his marriage. A killjoy, was he?"

"One might say so," his lordship said.

"Poor Lady Wanstead." Viscount Luttrell chuckled. "One hopes for her sake that there were certain pastimes considered less likely to, er, plunge them both into hell."

The earl preferred not to pursue that topic. He ran one palm over the velvet of the tabletop. "The servants made a good job of cleaning it," he said. While still looking faded with age, it did not look either spotty or dusty. Neither did it smell musty.

"Well," the viscount said, fingering the cues and then taking one down from the wall and feeling its balance in his hand, "have you made your choice yet, Gerard?"

His lordship winced. "Devil take it, Harry," he said, "have I walked into a trap of my own making? Am I obliged to choose a wife during the coming week? Is it expected?"

The viscount laughed. "You have been away too long," he said, "or you have been titled for too short a time. Men like you and me are always being expected to choose a wife. One attends a ball and dances with a chit and smiles at her and her papa is drawing up the marriage papers and her mama the list of wedding guests. One has to learn how to depress expectations."

"How?" The earl chuckled with him.

"By never being too particular in one's attention to any one particular lady," his friend advised him, "even if—heaven forbid—one really is considering paying one's addresses to her. By cultivating one's reputation as something of a rake. In your case you might take care to preface a number of remarks with phrases like—'When I return to Canada . . .' "

They were standing at the long windows, sipping their drinks and looking out over sloping lawns to the forest beyond. The lake was hidden from view.

"That would probably be fair warning," the earl agreed. "I never did intend to stay in England, you know. I am still planning to return to Montreal in the spring. And yet—"

"And yet old England exerts a pull on the heartstrings, especially when a little piece of it is one's own," the viscount said. "I feel it whenever I go home—which is as infrequently as I can make it because my mother and the girls are always after me to marry and settle down and my father is always reminding me of his mortality and of my future responsibilities. Fortunately he is hale and hearty and not even sixty yet. But sometimes, when I am there and realize that one day it will all be mine, I—well, I am dashed nearly tempted to rush off and get myself a leg shackle and an heir so that I can be sure it will always be in the family. The urge soon passes, let me add."

They both laughed.

"But you are right," the earl admitted. "Knowing while I was still in Montreal that I was Earl of Wanstead and owner of Thornwood Hall was one thing. Actually being here and having to live the part is another thing altogether. Sometimes I think I should not have come at all. I was perfectly contented as I was. I had made a life for myself."

"What about Miss Campbell for a bride, then?" the viscount asked. "Too low on the social scale, Ger?"

"Hardly." He felt a twinge of anger on Jeannette's behalf, but he did not let it show. Birth was of more importance than almost any attribute of character or fortune with the *ton,* and Luttrell was very definitely one of its members. "She is a gentleman's daughter, Harry—and a gentlewoman's. Which is more than can be said of me, after all. Perhaps I would be too low on the social scale for her."

"She is deuced pretty, I grant you," his friend said.

"I am exceedingly fond of her," he said.

"Which is not a particularly ardent thing to say," Viscount Luttrell pointed out. "Shall I replenish our glasses?"

"Help yourself," the earl told him, but he held on to his own almost-empty glass. "I am not looking for ardor, Harry, or romantic love or anything like that. I outgrew that nonsense long ago. And I am not sure I am looking for anything or anyone even *without* ardor."

"You have been taking life altogether too seriously, Ger," his friend told him, downing his fresh drink in two swallows. "What you need is a mistress. Or at the very least a flirt. But you don't want to flirt too particularly with the likes of Lizzie Gaynor or you will find yourself with a leg shackle before the new year is even slightly tarnished. Widows are often the best bet. They enjoy their freedom and independence and frequently do not want to give up either one to another husband, yet unlike their maiden sisters they know what they are missing in the way of bed sports."

"I'll put an advertisement in the *Morning Post,* then," the earl said with a grin. "I had better go up and get changed. It would not do to be late down for dinner in my own home when I have guests, would it? Her ladyship would not stop glowering for a week."

"The countess?" Viscount Luttrell raised his eyebrows in surprise. "Is she capable of glowering? She is a devilish attractive woman. More so now than when she was younger, though you were quite taken with her then, if I remember rightly. I daresay we all were. It is a damned shame that Wanstead—your cousin, that is—was a killjoy, Gerard. Dampened her spirits, no doubt."

"That, I suppose," the earl said, unaccountably irritated by the turn the conversation was taking, "was their business." He set down his glass and moved in the direction of the door.

"It makes one feel one would be rendering an invaluable service to lighten those spirits again, does it not?" Viscount Luttrell said. "She is remarkably easy on the eyes—no doubt on the body too, though perhaps *easy* would not be quite the word. The lady is eminently bedable. Those long legs—ah, the mind boggles. Oh, sorry, old chap, do you object to such plain speaking about your cousin's widow?"

He did. For a moment he saw red. He had to repress an impulse to whirl about and plant his friend a facer.

"She does live under my roof," he said rather stiffly. "She is under my protection here since Gilbert made no separate provision for her. Have a care."

The viscount chuckled. "I always have a care for my women, Ger," he said. "I don't raise expectations and I don't break hearts. I do give pleasure where I take it. And I do make sure that partings are amicable. You will not have a distraught widow on your hands when Christmas is over, old chap. Gentleman's honor."

The urge to answer with both fists was still almost irresistible—almost, but not quite. She was adult and she was free. She was nothing to him except a constant annoyance. If she chose to dally with Harry over Christmas, then that was up to her. Though the very thought of them together, Harry and Christina . . .

"I will not have any scandal in the house with respectable guests present," he said curtly.

But Viscount Luttrell merely raised his eyebrows and his quizzing glass at the same moment. "Scandal, Wanstead?" he said. "I? When Christmas is over, old chap, even you will not know for sure whether I have bedded the widow or not." He lowered his glass and smiled dazzlingly. "Though you may wager upon it that I will have."

The earl opened the door with a vengeful jerk. "We are going to be late," he said.

"What about your young cousin?" his friend asked, preceding him through the door. "Are you considering a courtship with her, Gerard? A pretty little thing. It is the easiest and the most delightful thing in the world to make her blush and to watch her eyes sparkle."

"Hands off!" the earl commanded. "Lady Margaret is a mere child, Harry. Not in years so much, perhaps, but definitely in experience. She has never been from home and is almost dangerously innocent. She is not nearly up to your expertise. And she is my ward."

The viscount laughed. "I do not seduce infants," he said. "And I certainly do not marry 'em, old chap. Relax!"

If Luttrell should so much as attempt . . .

The Earl of Wanstead climbed the stairs to his room without saying another word on the subject. If Luttrell should attempt what? Seducing Margaret? He simply would not do so. Seducing Christina, then? She was a widow of close to thirty years. If it happened, it would not be seduction. It would be her free choice.

But it made him feel savage to imagine that she might choose to engage in a discreet affair with Luttrell. Discretion or no discretion, it would be happening beneath his roof— beneath the roof shared by her children. But that, he was honest enough to admit, was not his real objection.

He rang impatiently for his valet, who should have been in his dressing room long before now. His happy mood at the arrival of his house guests appeared to have evaporated somewhere between here and the drawing room. The devil! he thought, snatching at his neckcloth, too impatient to await the arrival of his man. All this talk of marriage and avoiding marriage had thoroughly blue-deviled him.

Would she fall prey to Harry's experienced charm?

Had he led Lizzie Gaynor and her mama into believing that an offer of marriage was imminent?

Had Jeannette ever thought of him as anything other than a friend?

Could he simply return to Montreal in the spring, pick up the threads of his life as it had been before the arrival of that fateful letter by last spring's first ship, and forget about the burdens of being the Earl of Wanstead?

Would she go as far as to allow Harry to bed her? Hardly—she was cold and Puritanical. Not a promising mix for a would-be seducer. But she had not been that way this afternoon with his guests. And she was not that way with her children. And she waltzed as if the music and the rhythm were a part of her very soul.

"You have taken your time," he snapped irritably as his valet entered the dressing room in answer to his ring.

"You just rang, sir," his valet of longstanding pointed out quite reasonably.

Yes, and so he had. It would certainly not say much for his character if he started taking out his bad moods on servants.

"And you brought my shaving water with you?" he said. "Good man."

Christina had spent longer than she ought in the nursery. Not that she need worry about her children feeling neglected for the next week, she had realized. Although there were only four other children there, their presence was likely to prove endlessly fascinating to Rachel and Tess, who had never had many playmates apart from each other. But her daughters had wanted to tell her everything there was to be told about their new friends, and then those children had wanted to tell her everything about themselves. And of course there were their mothers with whom to get acquainted.

There was barely time to dress for dinner and have her hair redone. But perhaps the shortage of time was just as well, she thought as she hurried downstairs. She was wearing an evening gown of emerald green satin, and Sophie had piled her hair higher than it had been during the day. She felt alarmingly exposed to view. Black clothes, she thought again, formed a marvelous mask behind which to hide.

She was not reassured by the greeting awaiting her in the drawing room.

"My dear Lady Wanstead," Lady Milchip said, coming forward and taking one of Christina's hands in her own, "I do wish you would tell me who your modiste is. Though I daresay it is a secret. All the most elegant ladies of my acquaintance have secret modistes." She sighed and then laughed. "You certainly know what to wear to complement your dark coloring."

"My modiste, ma'am," Christina assured her, "is the village dressmaker. I will pass on your compliment to her."

Viscount Luttrell, she noticed without looking directly at him, was surveying her through his quizzing glass again.

She remembered suddenly that long-forgotten mingling of excitement and embarrassment at being the object of a gentleman's notice. He was, she suspected, the type of gentleman Gilbert had always most despised. A rake, no less.

Well, she thought, there was surely no harm in feeling feminine again.

The earl, she saw when she glanced across the room, was dressed with extreme elegance in black and white. He was smiling at something Miss Lizzie Gaynor was saying to him. The girl's hand was resting on his sleeve and she was looking up at him with a somewhat proprietary air.

Christina remembered again what had struck her earlier in the afternoon when she had watched him lift Miss Campbell down from her carriage and then kiss her on both cheeks. It was something she should have thought of a week or more ago, she supposed, but she had been too wrapped up with painful memory, uncomfortable reality.

He was an earl, a propertied gentleman, a man with two vast fortunes, if it was true that fur-trading was as profitable as she had heard it was. He was one-and-thirty years old, a single man. He had succeeded to his property and title a little over a year ago. He had arrived back in England only a few months ago. What could be more natural than the fact that he was in search of a wife? And what more leisurely way to do it than to invite a number of eligible young ladies to his own home so that he could become acquainted with them in the environment a wife would occupy with him?

It was clear to see that Miss Gaynor was very eligible indeed. So were Miss Susan Gaynor, Miss Clara Radway, and Miss Winifred Milchip. And if Jeannette Campbell was not quite so eligible by *ton* standards, her father being in business though he was a gentleman, she was certainly not ineligible. And she appeared to have the advantage of Gerard's regard in addition to good looks and pleasing manners. And of course she came from the world with which he had been familiar for the past ten years. Even Margaret was not an impossibility, though Christina felt a nasty lurching of the stomach at the very thought. Surely not Meg!

Soon, then, he might be expected to marry. And if he did

so, unless his bride was Miss Campbell, he could be expected to remain in England and make Thornwood his home. That would relegate her, Christina, to the rank of dowager countess. She would be even more of an encumbrance than she was now. She would be a hanger-on in the home he shared with his wife.

The prospect was enough to make her feel somewhat light-headed.

Lady Milchip and a few of the other guests had been conversing around her unheard. She had merely been smiling and giving mechanical answers to any question directed her way. But she suddenly heard one question quite clearly.

"Lady Wanstead," Lady Milchip said, "I can remember your come-out year. You are Lord Pickering's daughter, are you not?"

"Yes," Christina said. "Yes, I am."

"Ah, I was sure of it," Lady Milchip said. She smiled about the group, including everyone in her remarks. "Such a very charming gentleman he was. And so very dashing and handsome as a young man—you have inherited his dark good looks, Lady Wanstead. There was scarce a young lady in my time—myself included—who did not have a soft spot for him, though he was an unconscionable rogue."

There was general mirth over her admission. Christina laughed with everyone else.

"I could tell a story or two about Lord Pickering," Lady Milchip said, wagging one finger. "And I would do so too if I did not think the telling would put Lady Wanstead to the blush. I have not seen him in an age. Whatever has become of him? And I do hope that is not a dreadfully tactless question."

"Not at all," Christina assured her. "He is still alive and in good health. But he lives quietly at home most of the time now."

"Ah, a shame." Lady Milchip sighed. "Though I am glad to hear that he is alive and well. Perhaps you would send him my regards the next time you write to him. Though maybe he will be coming here for Christmas?" She looked hopefully at the countess.

"No, ma'am, unfortunately not." Christina smiled. "He has other plans, I am afraid."

Lady Milchip proceeded to reminisce about her youth for the amusement of her audience. She had grown up in an age when young people had known how to enjoy themselves, she would have them know.

He had been alive at least when she had written a year ago and again six months ago, Christina was thinking. Her father's name was another that Gilbert had forbidden her to mention after their marriage. More than that, he had forbidden her to write or to receive letters or otherwise to communicate with him. Again she had not argued or felt any inclination to do so for a long time. But the ties of blood were stronger than she had ever suspected—she had discovered that even before Gilbert's death. Her father was alive and living quietly at home, just as she had just told Lady Milchip. Or so the replies to her letters had stated without adding any explanatory detail. Both replies had been written in the same strange hand and signed "Horrocks." There had been no explanation of who Horrocks was. She had not tried to find out.

And then she caught the eye of the earl across the room. He was looking intently at her almost as if he could read her thoughts. For a moment, caught unawares, she felt the connection there had always used to be between them. She felt breathless. And then he raised his eyebrows and she recognized his look as a signal. The butler had come into the room to announce dinner, and according to a prearranged plan he was to lead Lady Milchip in tonight while she was to take the arm of Sir Michael.

How foolish of her to have fallen into a dream. She was the Countess of Wanstead, his cousin's widow. And for this week only, his hostess.

Chapter 8

The seating arrangement at the dinner table was to change each evening. That had been decided and planned at one of the meetings with the earl. Christina, in her permanent place at the foot of the table, had Sir Michael Milchip on her right for this evening and Mr. Geordie Stewart on her left. The table was too long and the guests far too many for the conversation to be general. She set herself to leading the conversation at her end of the table.

Mr. Stewart she found to be an interesting gentleman. He and his brother had lived in Montreal for several years before retiring from active involvement in the fur trade. He was a widower, whose wife had not long survived their return from Canada. He was a pleasant-looking gentleman whose sandy hair was thinning and receding from his forehead. Without in any way committing the social error of dominating the conversation, he entertained Christina and some of the other guests at their end of the table with stories about Canada and about the year-long, arduous journey into the interior and back that all partners were expected to make at least once in their lives.

"Though Percy—the Earl of Wanstead, that is," he said, "has done it three times in all, I believe. But then he was always a man to do his duty twice over and once more for luck."

Was he? Was that what Gerard had *always* been like? Christina had grown so accustomed to thinking just the opposite of him—she had *needed* to believe the opposite. Had she misjudged him all those years? She looked down the length of the table to see him conversing politely with his neighbors.

When the last cover had been removed Christina stood to signal the ladies that it was time to adjourn to the drawing room and leave the gentlemen to their port.

The evening was going rather well, she thought by the time the gentlemen joined the ladies half an hour later. She had hated the prospect of the house party at first, partly because she had no experience at organizing such events, but mainly because she had feared that the earl's guests would be as wild and rakish as he. It had not taken her long, of course, to realize that he was no longer either wild or rakish himself. He had changed. He had matured. And he had prospered. They were all somewhat bitter realizations.

Or perhaps he never had been irresponsibly wild. Perhaps she had only needed to believe that he was. Perhaps she had rationalized her own decision. She felt almost ashamed of the fact that just over a week before, when she had been awaiting his arrival, she had hoped to see evidence that she had been right to do what she had done.

The guests were a pleasant group of people, she thought now. And the young people were eager for some gaiety. Margaret, who at Christina's suggestion had taken the shy Miss Milchip under her wing, was turning the pages of the sheet music while that young lady played the pianoforte, and the elder Miss Gaynor and Miss Radway had joined them at the instrument. Lady Gaynor and Lady Milchip had settled on either side of the fire at Aunt Hannah's bidding.

"We will set up the card tables," the earl announced as soon as everyone was gathered in the drawing room.

"Splendid, dear," Lady Hannah said.

"Ah." Baron Langan rubbed his hands together and smiled genially at his host. "You fleeced me of a fortune just two weeks ago, Wanstead. I shall have it back with interest tonight, I'll wager."

"No!" Christina spoke sharply before she had time to think. "No cards at Thornwood. There will be no gambling beneath my roof." She listened, appalled, to her own words and the arrested silence that succeeded them, but it was too late to recall them. All eyes had turned her way, including the icy blue ones of the earl. She smiled before the moment could turn from awkwardness to disaster. "Not tonight, I beg you, my lord. We ladies have been waiting with as much patience as we could muster for the gentlemen to come and dance with us. Shall we have the carpet rolled back? Aunt Hannah, can you be prevailed upon to play for us?"

Fortunately she appeared to have hit upon just the right form of entertainment for this first evening. There was a general murmuring of enthusiasm and Miss Lizzie Gaynor clapped her hands.

"Oh, yes, please, my lord," she said, addressing herself to the earl. "Do say we may dance. And do say there are enough willing gentlemen to partner us."

"I claim Lady Margaret's hand," Mr. Frederick Cannadine said, "provided it is a country dance and the steps not too difficult."

There was general laughter, and Margaret flushed with pleasure.

His lordship inclined his head to Miss Gaynor. "Then dancing it will be," he said, "and we will reserve cards for another evening. You will honor me, Miss Gaynor?"

In no time at all, it seemed, the carpet had been rolled back to clear a space large enough to accommodate a set of dancers. Lady Hannah had taken her place at the pianoforte and the gentlemen had chosen their partners. The chairs had been arranged so that those who chose not to dance could watch.

"Oh, thank you, no," Christina said when Viscount Luttrell solicited her hand. "I do not dance, sir."

Inevitably he raised his quizzing glass to his eye. "Ah, pardon me, ma'am," he said, surveying her through it. "Now that I can see you better, your reason for refusing is instantly apparent. Your advanced years have given you a stiffness in the joints, I gather? Do say yes. One would hate to have to conclude that there is something objectionable about one's person."

Christina laughed. "How absurd you are, my lord," she said. "I am quite sure any one of the young ladies would be quite delighted to be partnered by you. And indeed I *am* a woman of advanced years."

"Dear me," he said, his glass sweeping over her before he lowered it. "If it were not ungentlemanly to say so, ma'am, I would be forced to declare that you lie. Come and sit by me, then, if you will not dance with me. I shall lend a sympathetic ear to a recitation of all your aches and other elderly woes."

She sat beside him while the music began and the dancers performed the intricate steps of a country dance. They kept up a flow of easy chatter, all of it nonsense, all of it blatant flirtation on his part and laughing banter on hers.

She should be feeling annoyed, she thought, to have been made the object of a rake's gallantry. But she could feel only genuine amusement and even pleasure. The days of her youth seemed so very long ago. She really did feel quite elderly in comparison with all the ladies who were dancing. Ten years—almost eleven—had passed since that one come-out Season she had had. How she had enjoyed it, she remembered now. How exhilarating it had felt to be young and passably pretty, to participate in all the busy whirl of a Season, to be admired and flirted with and—loved.

Her eyes watched the Earl of Wanstead as he made an arch with Lizzie Gaynor's hands clasped in his and the other dancers passed beneath it.

He *had* loved her as she had loved him. A foolish youthful emotion that was as insubstantial as a dream—and that left enough pain in its wake to cripple one for a lifetime. Gerard. Could she ever have imagined in those few golden months that one day they would be in a room together, separated as if by a thousand miles?

"It would be a challenge worth undertaking, I do declare," Viscount Luttrell said, "to rid your face of that look of longing, ma'am, and to replace it with a look of—something else."

She turned her head sharply toward him. Light flirtation was in danger of giving way to something less comfortable. But before she could think of a suitable rejoinder to set him in his place, he spoke again.

"Of course," he said, "any of my friends would tell you, ma'am, that I am far too indolent to undertake anything as challenging as a challenge." His eyes laughed lazily at her.

Christina pitied any raw young girl on whom he chose to turn that practiced charm. She would stand no chance at all. But then, she realized with a flash of insight, he would not behave thus with any raw girl. He thought she was his equal in experience with flirtation and dalliance. She was eight-and-twenty, after all, and a widow after a nine-year marriage. He could not know that she had lived in a cocoon for ten years and was just beginning, very tentatively, to break free of it.

But for all that she would not be easy prey. To light flirtation, perhaps. To anything else—well, surely he could not seriously mean anything else.

"Then perhaps, my lord," she said, "I should give thanks in my prayers tonight for your indolence."

He laughed appreciatively. "I must at least exert myself to dance," he said as the music ended and there was a smattering of applause from dancers and spectators alike. "Perhaps your young sister-in-law will not claim creaking bones as an excuse for refusing me."

Margaret clearly claimed no such infirmity. Already flushed and smiling, she fairly sparkled when Viscount Luttrell bowed elegantly before her.

The Thornwood drawing room looked like a different room from the one with which she was long familiar, Christina thought over the next hour as she watched the dancing and conversed with those who did not participate. She had always thought it a gloomy, oppressive room, too large for family gatherings, though they had dutifully sat in it every afternoon and evening of her married life rather than in a smaller, cozier salon. Now it looked bright and cheerful and almost too small for the impromptu dance with which they were amusing themselves.

The tea tray arrived far too early for the liking of the young people, who protested that it could not possibly be almost time for bed yet. The earl assured them that they were welcome to stay up all night if they wished and if they could persuade his aunt to continue playing that long. But Lady Gaynor reminded her daughters, and in the process everyone else, that there were still three days to go before Christmas, not to mention the days of Christmas itself. They must not recklessly use up all their energies on the very first evening.

"Oh, yes," Susan Gaynor agreed, though with obvious reluctance. "And I look positively *hagged* if I do not have a good night's sleep."

"I do not believe you could look hagged," her partner, Mr. Radway, said gallantly, "if you tried from now until doomsday, Miss Susan."

But Lady Hannah had been summoned from the pianoforte to drink her tea, and it was generally agreed that it had been a long, busy day and that it was time to retire for the night.

"Perhaps tomorrow evening," Christina said as she bade everyone good night, "we will have dancing again."

But her own day was not yet quite at an end, she discovered as she was about to leave the drawing room, the last of the ladies to do so. The earl had moved close to her and laid a hand on her arm.

"I will have a word with you in the library before you retire, my lady," he said quietly in her ear. "There is a fire in there and candles burning. Wait for me there, please. I will not be long."

There was nothing in his voice to indicate the purpose of such a meeting. It was very likely that some plans needed to be discussed for the morrow. But her stomach muscles knotted and she felt breathless. Suddenly and quite unreasonably she was terrified. It had not been a request, after all. It had been a command.

"Very well, my lord," she replied coolly.

Several of the gentlemen settled in the drawing room for a last drink and some male conversation before bed. Fifteen minutes passed before the earl could decently leave them and go to the library. He half expected when he arrived there that Christina would be gone. But she was not. She was standing close to the fire, facing the door. She took a few steps toward him when he entered the room and closed the door behind him.

She looked quite stunningly beautiful in that emerald green gown, was his first foolish thought. His next was even more foolish. If things had been different, he might have been coming to her now in her boudoir, ten years of marriage behind them. That slender, shapely body and the very essence of her might have been as familiar to him now as his own person. He repressed the wayward thoughts and strode across the room until he was within arm's length of her.

"No cards at Thornwood," he said softly, quoting her. *"There will be no gambling beneath my roof."*

He raised his right arm to gesture to the chair behind her, intending to instruct her to be seated. But both her hands shot up, palms out, to shield her face, which she turned sharply to one side. He froze, his arm still upraised. She lowered her own arms slowly and looked warily at him.

"I beg your pardon, my lord," she said.

He continued to stare at her for several moments. "My God, Christina," he said at last, "did you believe I meant you violence?"

She merely stared back at him and shook her head almost imperceptibly.

He had been feeling angry for most of the evening—angry at what she had said, angry that she would not dance, though he had not asked her himself, angry that her shimmering satin gown and the elegant figure inside it had made it impossible for him to concentrate his attention on anyone else, angry that she had sat talking with the older guests just as if she were a staid dowager and not a young and lovely woman. And angry that she had sat out the first set with Luttrell, clearly eating up his flatteries and giving as good as she had got—as if she were anything but a staid dowager. She had looked smiling and young and carefree—as she had never looked for him, except when they had waltzed. He had come to the library with a biting speech to deliver. But it seemed to have disintegrated in his mind. Did she think *that* badly of him that she feared he might strike her? How dared she!

"Sit down," he told her curtly. "Would you like to ring for more tea?"

"No," she said, seating herself with her usual uncompromising straight-backed posture. "No, thank you, my lord."

He sat opposite her instead of remaining on his feet, looming over her, as he had intended.

"Gilbert would not allow card playing?" he asked her.

"*Gambling*," she said. "He would not allow gambling. Neither would I." Her chin lifted a notch.

"Or dancing," he said quietly, "or any sort of socializing during which guests might have been in danger of enjoying themselves. And he was a nip-farthing. Life here must have been intolerably dull."

"I daresay you would have found it so," she said, looking at him with the hard expression she seemed to reserve for him.

"And you did not?" He frowned. "You were happy with such a life? Have you changed so much, then, Christina, from the girl I remember whose eyes and whole aspect always glowed with an eagerness to taste life to the full?"

"No," my lord," she said, "I have not changed except to have grown older, wiser, more mature. I still value what I have always valued—safety, security, dependability."

He gazed at her, unable again to see the girl in the cold, beautiful, disciplined face of the woman. "And those things," he said, "I was unable to give you? Because added to them there would have been a sense of adventure? I was not wealthy, heaven knows, but I could have supported you."

"I believe we have already agreed, my lord," she said, the scorn back in her face, "that we both had a fortunate escape when I married Gilbert."

"Yes, of course," he said, and he felt mortified that he had tried yet again to make sense of what had happened within a twenty-four-hour span over ten years before.

She had been at Vauxhall Gardens one evening, a member of a party that had included him. They had known each other for a few months by then. Although she had almost always been correctly chaperoned, they had contrived within the limits of the rules to see enough of each other and to converse enough beyond the hearing of others to have built what had seemed to be a close friendship. They had fallen deeply in love. But surrounded as they had been by the magical splendor of Vauxhall that night, their relationship had reached a peak of emotion.

They had danced together, walked together, watched the fireworks display together. And they had succeeded in losing the rest of their group for just long enough to kiss in a secluded alley—not their first kiss, but definitely their most passionate. It had almost gone too far. But that had no longer seemed to matter. They had murmured their love for each other. As they strolled afterward, they had talked about things they would do, places they would see after they were married. She had been bright and warm with happiness and love and hope. He had begun that same night to compose in his mind a suitable speech to deliver when he called upon her father.

"I have not changed," she said now. "I never was the heedless woman you thought I was."

The next evening when he had arrived at a ball, one of the grand squeezes of the Season, eager as he always was to see her again, he had caught sight of her across the room, her hand on Gilbert's wrist, a small crowd gathered about them. And then he had heard the news, which had been fast spreading among the guests—the news of the betrothal of the Earl of Wanstead to the Honorable Miss Christina Spense.

She had refused to speak privately with him from that night on. She had refused to receive him when he called at her father's house. She had returned both his letters unopened. Gilbert, to whom he had reluctantly introduced her just three weeks before the night of that ball, had sneered at him.

"Did you seriously expect Miss Spense to marry *you*, Gerard?" he had asked. "When you have no title or property or fortune beyond the merest competence? When you have not even *birth* to recommend you? As a wise young lady she has chosen the Wanstead title and fortune, and Thornwood. I take it you will not expect an invitation to the wedding, cousin?"

Gilbert and Christina had been married within a month. And within a month Gerard Percy had been on his way to Canada to seek his fortune and ease for a bruised heart— both of which he had found there. He had been happy there until word of Gilbert's death had reached him and with it the news that he was now in possession of those very things for which she had rejected him ten years before.

"No," he said now in answer to what she had just said. "I liked the woman I thought you were, but I was deceived. I was too young and naive, I suppose, to understand that people are not always what they seem to be. Some people can amuse themselves with flirtations as if they were real love while at the same time conceiving calculating and mercenary plans for their own advancement."

He watched her lips thin, but she said nothing.

"There will be card games in the drawing room tomorrow evening," he said, "and most other evenings, I daresay. It is a favored amusement among members of the *ton*, as perhaps you are aware. I suppose money will change hands—small sums. It would be in grossly bad taste to play for high stakes at a party of this nature. Did you believe that Langan was serious in what he said about a fortune? I believe I won five pounds from him two weeks ago. Does that seem dreadfully depraved to you?"

"No," she said stiffly. "I beg your pardon, my lord. I spoke without thinking."

"Yes, I believe you did," he said. "Especially when you referred to this house, or the roof of it, at least, as your own. I must advise you in future to think before you speak."

She flushed and looked down at her hands. "I beg your pardon, my lord," she said again.

He had come in order to make that point. He had come, he supposed, to see her look thus and speak thus—totally cowed. But having won the victory, he felt unaccountably irritated. Was that *all* she had to say? No arguments? No anger? He wished she would fight him. He would like nothing better than a shouting match with Christina. He resented her docility. It weakened his victory.

"Thornwood is mine, Christina," he said. "If I choose to make it into a gaming hell over Christmas, that would be my right. If I chose to conduct an orgy here, that too would be my right. Would you not agree?"

She looked up at him. "Oh, assuredly," she said. "But I believe one or two of your guests would have something to say about either of those uses of Thornwood, my lord."

"But it would be my *right*?"

"Yes, my lord, it would be your right." The scorn was in her face as well as her voice now.

"You must trust me, then, as a gentleman," he said, "not to do anything here unbecoming my position and my responsibility to the ladies and the children in my care."

Her nostrils flared and for the first time he had the satisfaction of knowing that she was angry.

"Oh, yes," she said, "I must trust you. Just as all my life I have had to trust the men who have had the *care* of me. It is one of the great benefits of being a woman. One always has a man—a *gentleman*—to take responsibility for one's care. All a woman has to do is what she is told to do and she will be eternally happy. What could be easier? How gratifying it is to know that I am not to fear either a gaming hell or an orgy here over Christmas."

"You have had choices," he said harshly. "You are not as much a prisoner of your gender as you would like to believe when you are in this self-pitying mood. Ten years ago you had a choice between Gilbert and me—between wealth and position on the one hand and love and adventure on the other. You made your choice. Is it my fault that both Gilbert and Rodney died young and left you to my charge after all?"

"Choices!" She almost spat out the word. "You know nothing about *choices*, my lord."

"And you still have choices," he told her, though the idea was new to him even as he spoke it. "You can remain here with your children as my dependent for the rest of your life, feeding your sense of martyrdom whenever I do or say anything that the sainted Gilbert would not have done or said. Or you can marry again. Have you considered that option? You are still young and beautiful—and desirable. You are probably aware that men of Luttrell's caliber do not direct their gallantries to undesirable women."

She stared at him, and he could see that she was white with fury. "So!" she said. "This is how you discharge your responsibilities, as you call them, my lord. You foist them upon some other man. And of course I am almost certain to be flattered into making what you wish me to believe is a *choice.* What woman, after all, would not melt with gratification at being described with those three words—young, beautiful, desirable? Am I really those things? But I must be if Viscount Luttrell has deigned to exchange a dozen words or so with me. Then it is truly amazing you do not desire me yourself. But perhaps you do. Perhaps this is why you have lured me alone to the library at such a late hour. *Do* you desire me?"

"I do not believe, my lady," he said coldly, "I would want you if you were the last woman left on earth." He might at least, he thought, have found a more original way of uttering the setdown. "Why should I be aroused by a woman who can moan with desire and talk with passionate conviction of love one day and discover the next that there is someone wealthier to be hooked in exchange for similar moans? No, thank you, Christina. I find such calculating femininity distinctly unappealing."

She was smiling—not at all pleasantly—and she spoke huskily. "But I doubt, my lord," she said, her eyes mocking him, "I would be able to find anyone wealthier than you are now."

And now, he thought as they stared at each other, there was nothing left for either of them to say. Now perhaps they were both satisfied. They had exchanged anger and spite and irritability, and where had it led them?

To desiring each other, that was where.

For although the husky voice had been deliberately assumed, and although he had declared that even her lone female presence on this earth would not entice him, they were gazing at each other with anger and dislike and unmistakable lust. He wondered if she was honest enough with herself to admit that last.

"Perhaps," he said, getting to his feet, "you can find someone here at the house party *almost* as wealthy, my lady. I would not, incidentally, advise you to set your cap at Luttrell though he has dazzling expectations. He is more interested in bedding you than wedding you. And I, unfortunately, am not on the market. Not for you, at least."

"No," she said, placing her hand in his when he offered it and rising from her chair. "It is all too easy to see at whose doors you are shopping, my lord. Someone young and biddable and not too clever will suit you admirably. She will bend easily to your autocratic will."

"And perhaps," he said, "she will be less bitter about the simple fact that she was born a woman. Shall we go to bed?"

He could have bitten his tongue out as soon as he said it, as soon as he read her interpretation of his words in her startled eyes. He closed his own eyes briefly and smiled ruefully, his anger disintegrating.

"Christina," he said, "we must somehow cry truce. For at least a week, perhaps longer, we have to exist side by side in this house. Can we do it, do you suppose, without constantly crossing swords, often deliberately?"

"I believe it should be possible, my lord," she said.

"Well, then." He squeezed her hand, which for some reason he was still holding. "Tomorrow we will try to do better. Though today the house party made a good beginning, did it not? Everyone seems happy to be here." Say *good night*, he told himself. *Make an end of this.*

"Gerard—" she said.

It was the sound of his name on her lips that did it. Spoken softly. He did not wait to hear what she was going to say, or even if she intended to add anything. Perhaps his name was all she had to say. He dipped his head and set his mouth to hers.

Soft, warm, sweet, lips parted, as were his own, and pressing back against his own. Moist flesh, taste, heat. And the flaring of a need to delve deeper, to plunge beneath the surface of her, to drink at the well of her femininity.

He lifted his head hastily.

"Well, at least," he said, "we know that some of what we spoke in anger was lies."

"Yes," she agreed and she slid her hand from his. "Good night, my lord."

"Good night, my lady," he said and watched her cross the room unhurriedly, with her customary lithe grace. She opened the door without jerking on it and closed it quietly after she had passed through it. He wondered how much of an effort of will it had cost her to act as if nothing untoward had happened.

Hell! His hands closed into fists at his sides. He was fighting full-blown arousal.

Damnation!

Chapter 9

Never once had Christina thought of remarrying. She had found a guilty sense of freedom and peace in her widowhood, even during the year of deep mourning with all the restrictions it had imposed upon her appearance and activities, even during the months since when she had continued to live in much the same way she had lived for nine years before Gilbert died—as if asleep or in that dazed state between sleeping and waking.

But she was not free. And there was no peace. She did not even have the limited freedom of knowing herself mistress of Thornwood.

Thornwood is mine, Christina.

There had been intense satisfaction in his voice when he had spoken the words. They had repeated themselves in her mind over and over again during a night of disturbed sleep.

You can remain here with your children as my dependent for the rest of your life . . . Or you can marry again.

He wanted to be rid of her. Was it surprising? She wanted to be rid of him. And there was only one way of doing it.

The following morning, the first full day of the house party, was as bright and sunny as the day before. He was eager to grant Miss Lizzie Gaynor's request and give a tour of the house, the Earl of Wanstead said at breakfast, but how could they possibly waste such glorious sunshine when his head gardener, apparently renowned as a forecaster of weather, was predicting snow within the next day or two?

There was a flurry of excitement about the table. White Christmases were rare, everyone agreed. It was rarer still to find oneself on a country estate when one of them happened along.

Perhaps they would change plans, then, his lordship suggested, and take a walk in the park while they might do so without the danger of breaking their necks at every step. There would be time enough later for him to show off his house.

And so almost all of them walked about the long lawn before the house, stopping to view its architectural splendor from various angles, and then they had proceeded on the scenic walk over the hill north of the house. The earl had Miss Gaynor on his arm the whole way. If she was disappointed at the postponed tour of the house, she was certainly not showing it. Her face glowed with rosy color beneath the fur-trimmed hood of her cloak, and she stopped the whole party far more often than seemed necessary in order to exclaim with delight over the beauty of various picturesque views.

There was a young lady, Christina thought, who had set her cap for a title and a fortune and a grand estate and a young and handsome husband. Just as she herself had been accused of doing when she married Gilbert. She wondered if Gerard was making the parallel in his mind.

Christina moved from group to group, making sure that everyone saw the best prospects and was not too cold or breathless or footsore to continue. Margaret was walking arm in arm with Winifred Milchip, though they were flanked by Frederick Cannadine and Viscount Luttrell and appeared to be very merry indeed. Christina steered clear of them and found herself during the final stage of the walk beside Mr. Geordie Stewart.

"This is a grand estate, Lady Wanstead," he said to her, offering his arm. "It is enough to make any man who owned it forget about returning to the rigors of life in the New World."

It had been her one hope during the night, Christina thought, that Gerard would *not* forget, that he would return to Canada in the spring and having returned would never come back again.

"You will like the house too, sir," she said. "The state apartments are rarely used, but they are glorious to gaze at. And his lordship *does* intend to use the state dining room and the ballroom over Christmas. There is a lovely portrait gallery too for anyone interested in family histories."

"I shall look forward to the tour," he assured her.

But their conversation soon became more personal. He sympathized with her over her loss of a husband so recently and so young, and she asked him about his late wife. Mrs. Stewart had been a native woman with whom he had lived during his winter in the interior of the continent beyond Canada.

"Such arrangements are quite respectable, ma'am," he explained to her, "else I would not have sullied your ears by mentioning it. There are no white women in that part of the world, you see, yet many white men live there for years at a time. Such arrangements with native women are known as country marriages. They are monogamous relationships and are frequently happy unions for both partners. Sometimes they last beyond the term of a man's stay in the Northwest. I brought my country wife out with me and married her in Montreal. She died a year after that when I brought her here. There were diseases to which she had never been exposed."

"I am sorry," Christina said.

"Yes." He smiled. "I was fond of her, ma'am, and she was good to me. I wish we had had children. I understand that you have?"

"Two daughters," she said and mentioned their names and ages to him.

"They must have been a comfort to you," he said, "when you lost your husband."

"Yes," she agreed. "They have been the chief source of joy in my life since their births."

"I hope," he said, "you will allow me the pleasure of meeting them. Colin is a bachelor and I am a childless widower, but we have a sister in Scotland who has ten children and a number of grandchildren too. I have had some experience in amusing children."

The idea of remarriage, new to her and quite abhorrent in

many ways, had persisted through the morning. And it focused itself now on the unsuspecting person of Mr. Geordie Stewart. He was a man of mature years, a kindly man, or so it seemed, and one with wealth enough if her guess was correct to offer a wife perfect security. But it seemed unpleasantly calculating to be thinking of marrying a man who had done nothing more than be courteous to her. She had been accused last night of being calculating.

But if he stayed in England, she thought—*Gerard,* that was—then she simply must find some way of escaping an intolerable situation. And there was only one way.

She expected that the earl would be as eager to avoid her this morning as she was to avoid him. *That kiss!* The memory of it, brief as it had been, so consumed her with embarrassment that her mind shied away from it altogether—and could think of nothing else. Not just the kiss, but the mortifying knowledge that she had burned for him, that her womb had throbbed with the need to feel him there. Mortifying indeed!

But seemingly he did not share her embarrassment. As soon as they had all returned to the house and most of the guests were on their way upstairs to change from their outdoor clothes, he summoned her to the library. She wished it might have been anywhere else if they must talk. She felt embarrassed just to see the room again and to remember that just *there* before the hearth, close to the chair on which she had been sitting . . .

She crossed the room to the large oak desk, and ran her palm over the smooth top of it as if testing it for dust.

"Christina," he said, closing the door behind him. His voice was brisk and businesslike, she noticed. "Last night I suggested that we try to do better today, that we try to be more civil to each other. It is something I still hope we can do, but it has been very clear to me that I also owe you an apology."

She turned her head to look at him.

"You hurt me once," he said in the same impersonal tone. "It was long ago. We were both young, very different people from what we are now. But the ignoble urge to hurt where we have been hurt is hard to resist, I have found to my chagrin. I have been trying to hurt you ever since I arrived here over a week ago."

She could acknowledge what he said only with a brief nod—and with inner surprise at his honesty. It seemed somehow to set her at a disadvantage.

"I beg your pardon," he said. She heard him draw breath. "And for the disrespect I showed you last night by kissing you."

She felt heat in her cheeks and hoped that her blush was masked by the heightened color the outdoor chill must have whipped into her face.

"It was nothing," she said, and her eyes locked on his for just a few moments too long. She lowered her gaze. What a patent and foolish lie to have uttered in the face of his honesty.

"I am a wealthy man," he said, his voice brisk again. "When I marry, I will make a settlement on you and your daughters. Included in it will be a home of your choice and the upkeep of that home. There is no need for you to consider a marriage of your own unless it is your wish to do so."

Despite herself—she *knew* he was trying to be conciliatory—she felt a flaring of anger. *When I marry . . .* "You are determined, then," she said, "to consider me a heavy millstone about your neck and to keep me constantly aware of the fact. Is this sugar-coated revenge, Gerard?"

He stared at her, hard-eyed and tight-jawed.

"Before I forget—" He strode toward her so that for a moment she felt a resurgence of last evening's blind terror. But he was looking at something on the desk rather than at her. She stepped smartly aside and he picked up a sealed letter from the top of a pile and handed it to her. "This came with the morning post. I beg your pardon, I should have handed it to you before we went outside."

Christina did not receive many letters and looked down curiously at the one he had just given her. It was addressed in a somewhat shaky hand, as if it had been written by an elderly person. It was handwriting she had not seen in many a long year, but she recognized it instantly. And then doubted the evidence of her own eyes. Lady Milchip's words in the drawing room last evening had planted the idea in her mind. It would be too much of a coincidence. . . .

But a second glance at the letter confirmed her first impression. It was from her father.

"Are you all right?" a voice asked her, and she looked up blankly, a buzzing in her ears.

"Oh," she said. "Yes. Yes, thank you."

He glanced down at the letter in her hand and up into her face again. "Why do you not sit down by the fire and read it?" he suggested. "I can come back later."

But she had noticed the pile of letters on his desk that doubtless he had hoped to deal with while his guests were busy about their own business.

"Please do not feel obliged to leave," she said, crossing the room and taking the chair in which she had sat last evening—though she was scarcely aware of the fact. It was only later that she thought she ought to have taken her letter to the privacy of her own room. She broke the seal.

He had heard that the new Earl of Wanstead was in England. He wondered if he was at Thornwood. He wondered if he should send his compliments. The words were difficult to read, written as they were in the same shaky hand that had addressed the outside. Christina scanned the letter quickly, hungry for news of her father, for the expression of some personal concern for her or the granddaughters he had never seen. There were words of affection, quite lavishly expressed, much as she had expected. But affection was clearly not what had motivated him to write.

She folded the letter carefully after she was finished, set it down on her lap, and stared into the fire.

"Not bad news, I hope?"

"No."

Only memories—of an uncertain and frequently unhappy childhood, of a mother she had loved and grown to despise, of a father she had loved and come to hate. Of that contempt and that hatred turned against herself. How could she despise the mother who had always shielded and protected her? How could she love the father whose weaknesses had them all living constantly on the brink of hell? How could she conspire with both her mother and her father—though no single word of conspiracy was ever spoken among them—to live a lie?

Everyone had thought them a perfectly happy family. It was the mask they had all put on for the world. Everyone had loved her sociable, charming, handsome father. Everyone had admired her serene, dignified, loyal mother. Everyone had envied her as the focus of their love.

As she grew up, loving and hating them, she had dreamed of a different life for herself than the one she had always known. And she had planned it, intending to let sense and reason and wisdom determine her choices.

A hand appeared in front of her face suddenly. It held a glass half full of some brown liquor.

"Drink this," the Earl of Wanstead said. "It will make you feel better."

"I do not drink," she said, turning her head away.

"No, of course not." He set the glass down on the mantel. "It is sinful, no doubt."

And then she wished she had taken the glass and at least pretended to sip from it. He came down on his haunches in front of her and took both her hands in a firm clasp. She had not realized how like ice blocks her own were.

"How may I be of service to you?" he asked.

By telling her how she might be wise—she never had learned the trick. By telling her how to stop loving people who had not earned her love—quite the contrary, in fact. How could she possibly *still* love her father? How could she read a letter that was so predictable in its selfish, self-absorbed contents that she might as easily have written it herself and saved him the effort—and feel her heart yearn toward him?

"You cannot," she said. "It is a—a petty debt is all. Yes, perhaps you can help. I told Mr. Monck that it would be more convenient for everyone if he started paying the allowance you so generously granted me in the first quarter of the New Year. May I—may I ask him to pay it to me now instead? I will not ask for more before the second quarter, of course."

She thought she might well die of humiliation. She kept her eyes on the dancing flames of the fire.

"Of course," he said, tightening his hold on her hands. "I shall speak to him myself today. He will pay you a quarter's allowance now and another in January. Will it be sufficient to cover your debt? Tell me now if it will not. I will not have you anxious over money."

But his kindness, over which she should be feeling nothing but deep gratitude, only succeeded in suffocating and irritating her.

"It will be sufficient." She withdrew her hands from his and looked at him. "And you will *not* pay me again in January. You will *not*, Gerard." Her humiliation was complete when she found herself having to blink back tears.

He stood up and looked silently down at her. "This house is just not going to be big enough for the two of us, is it, Christina?" he said. "I must return to Montreal. Or if I marry and remain in England, I must house you some distance from Thornwood. Or you must marry." He ran the fingers of one hand through his hair.

"It would be just like you," she said hotly, "to go away again and leave me here to be plagued by the guilt of having driven you away from your own home."

"Would it?" He clasped his hands behind his back. "Would it be just like me, Christina? To go away rather than live where I might see you again? Would guilt at having driven me away plague you? Did it the last time?"

She did not answer him. But she would not look away from his eyes either.

"You need not so burden yourself," he said. "If it was you who drove me to go to Canada, Christina, then I must thank you. I found activity there to satisfy my restless yearning for adventure. I prospered there. And I was happy there. If you have believed all these years that I have been lonely and pining for you or for a wasted life, you have been much mistaken. It is only a sense of duty that has me thinking now of possibly staying. If you make the next week or so here as intolerable to me as the last week has been, then perhaps you will be doing me a similar favor to the one you did me before. I shall go back home and be happy again."

"Then I wish you would go tomorrow," she said. *"Today."*

"Do you?" He smiled. "At least I have brought you back from the brink of fainting. I have my uses, my lady. Pardon me, I must summon Monck. I imagine you would rather not be present to hear yourself spoken of as if you were a child without a voice of your own."

She rose hastily to her feet, grasping her letter in one hand. How rude she had been. She was beholden to him. He had been kind and he had been generous and she had hated him for it and ripped up at him without any just cause.

"Thank you," she said. "Thank you for granting my request."

"If it is any comfort to you, Christina," he said, crossing the room ahead of her and holding the door open for her, "I find your financial dependence upon me as suffocating as you. I would dearly like you to feel free to invite me to go to hell without suffering pangs of guilt at the thought that you owe me allegiance. For God's sake if you must hate me, do so wholeheartedly. You were Gilbert's wife. You are the mother of his daughters. As such you have every right to the support of this estate. As much right to it as I have. In future when you want something of it, *tell* me so. You do not need to *ask*. Much less do you need to thank me."

"Oh," she said, pausing to look at him, "how you enjoyed that. And how very true your words are. I have a *right* to the support of this estate. Not to your support, but to *its* support. I wish I had realized that before. But it is true. And now I may hate you with my whole heart."

"Yes," he said curtly, but there was the merest suggestion of a smile lurking behind his tight-jawed glare.

She smiled dazzlingly at him as she passed through the door.

It did not take long to instruct Charles Monck to pay her ladyship a quarter's allowance without delay and to talk with him about a few other items of business. It did not take much longer to go through the morning post and dispose of the bulk of it and set aside the few items that would need more attention when he had the time to spare.

He needed to think.

She had not had money of her own since her marriage. Monck had confirmed her claim that Gilbert had paid all her bills, and those bills had been few. The earl had looked himself through the account books for the past six years and had discovered incredibly few entries relating to clothes or jewels—there were none at all of the latter, in fact—or other personal items for either the countess or her children.

She had had no spending money since Gilbert's death. She had submitted the bills for her few mourning clothes but had never asked for money.

What debt could she have incurred now that she would not merely submit as a bill for payment? There was no evidence that she had ever been extravagant—quite the contrary. Her spontaneous reaction to the proposed card games last evening, which she had expected to be gambling games, had demonstrated her puritanical horror of wagering.

It was no trifling debt despite her description of it as such. She had come very close to fainting. Even before she had opened the letter her pallor had been apparent—it had shown up shockingly in contrast to the two bright spots of color that remained high on her cheeks from the outdoor chill. She had recognized the handwriting and had known what debt was being called in.

What debt?

It was none of his business, he told himself. He would willingly pay it, whatever it was, but she had rejected any more help than an advance on next quarter's allowance.

It had looked like the handwriting of an old or sick person.

He was prevented from further thought on the subject by a light tap on the library door followed by its opening. A head peered cautiously around it.

"Oh," Jeannette Campbell said, looking mortified, "there *is* someone in here. I am so sorry for disturbing you, Gerard.

I was told I might find a book here, but I can come back another time."

"Come in." He strode toward her, smiling. "I cannot imagine anyone by whom I would more prefer to be disturbed. There are shelves of books, some few of them even readable, I believe. But can your choosing one wait, Jeannette? Will you put your cloak and bonnet back on and come outside with me again?"

She looked at him in some surprise, but she shared his love of the outdoors, he knew. They had agreed long ago that it was the best place in which to do one's thinking and relaxing.

"Of course," she said. "Give me two minutes."

They were striding off in the direction of the lake five minutes later. They did not talk. That was one thing he liked about Jeannette. She did not need either to chatter constantly or to be chattered to. They could be perfectly comfortable together in silence.

"There," he said at last after they had threaded their way through dense trees. "It is rather large, but it is quite hidden from the house."

"Ah," she said, gazing at the lake, which was completely iced over now. It was surrounded by trees, many of them evergreens, most with bare branches. "The sight makes me feel homesick. There is a vastness and a starkness about the scene untypical of what I have seen of England. It is lovely."

"Yes," he said.

She looked at him after they had stood side by side in silence for a while. "Do you wish to talk about it?" she asked.

He chuckled softly. That was another thing about his friendship with Jeannette. They could sometimes sense each other's mood. "Not really," he said. "I am not even quite sure what *it* is. Have you ever hated anyone, Jeannette?"

She gave the question some consideration. "You do not mean just the flashes of intense dislike and anger we feel against people sometimes, do you?" she said. "You mean something deep-rooted and long-lasting, something that eats away at you."

"Yes." That was it exactly.

"No," she said. "I have never hated like that. Is it something fairly recent, Gerard? Perhaps it will pass off and you will forget about it. Does it hurt badly?"

"I thought I had forgotten," he said. "But maybe I just pushed it deep and denied it and let it fester."

"And coming home has brought it all back to you," she said. She added quietly. "Coming *here*. You did not have a happy childhood here, did you? I remember your telling me about your uncle's volatile temper, about his openly favoring you over his own sons and causing them to hate you. But they are all dead, and it is not the place you hate, is it? It is someone. I am sorry. I do not wish to—"

"She accepted Wanstead's marriage offer on a three-week acquaintance," he said, "because he was an earl and had property and a vast fortune."

"Gerard," she said, touching his arm, "many women marry for such security. It is not easy being a woman. The prospect of being left destitute is more frightening for us than for men. We are so limited in the ways we can provide for ourselves."

"Mmm," he said. He did not want her making excuses for Christina.

"Perhaps," she said, "she was fond of him or grew fond of him. You cannot know unless she has told you differently. You have been far away. She has two very sweet little children—I met them this morning."

He smiled at her. "You are too easy to talk to, Jeannette," he said. "I did not intend to burden you with my problems— certainly not with the specifics. Do you think you are going to enjoy being here?"

"Of course," she said. "We expected, Andrew and I, that we would spend Christmas alone together in London. We were already feeling rather sorry for ourselves, far from home and family and particular friends. And then you invited us here. It was extremely kind of you. And yes, we are both already enjoying ourselves. It is a beautiful place and our fellow guests are amiable."

"I suppose," he said, only because she was Jeannette and it was not in the nature of their friendship to keep anything secret that concerned them both, "you have some idea of the reason behind this house party? Apart from the celebration of Christmas, that is."

Her eyes wavered from his for just a moment. "Andrew suggested it," she said, "and I have seen since yesterday that it is probably true."

"Well," he said, "my dear friend. Any comments?"

"Yes." She set her head to one side and regarded him closely. "You have a great deal of energy, Gerard—*restless* energy. You have always been in search of something, I believe, and have still not found it. Don't settle for anything less than that something even if you still do not know what it is. Don't force yourself into believing that Miss Gaynor is the wife for you—unless you *know* she is. You would end up unhappy and bound for life to your unhappiness."

"Perhaps," he said, "it is of you I think more than of Lizzie Gaynor."

She shook her head. "We have known each other for many years, Gerard," she said. "Ever since I was a schoolgirl. You would have *known* by now."

"And yet," he said, "you are one of the dearest friends I have ever had, Jeannette, man or woman."

"You need more than friendship of your life's partner," she said. "I have never seen it in action, but I sense deep passion in your nature. Just as there is in mine, though perhaps very few people realize it. One day I am going to share the sort of love with a man that poets write of." She smiled impishly.

"I envy him," he said.

"No, you do not," she said. "You need only my friendship, Gerard, as I need yours. It is said, you know, that hatred is very akin to love."

"There is too much dislike," he told her. "There are too many irritants. There is too much bitterness and lack of trust. There is too much—"

"Passion?" she suggested. "My feet are cold. Are you going to take me walking, or are we to stay here until I am standing on two lumps of ice?"

He offered her his arm. "Shall we walk?" he suggested.

Chapter 10

The rest of the day was filled with various activities. The earl gave a tour of the house after luncheon and then took most of the younger guests out riding while the countess ordered around the carriage and the gig and went into the village with another group. There were a few shops there at which some modest purchases might be made, as well as a Norman church to explore, and an inn at which to take a pot of tea before the return home. Christina, Lady Langan, and Mr. and Mrs. John Cannadine then took their children outside for a game of chasing across the wide lawns and a vigorous game of hide-and-seek among the trees. In the evening, after dinner, the card tables were set up and most of the guests settled to play. Clara Radway won the grand sum of five shillings and everyone else boasted lesser wins or lamented lesser losses. Not by any stretch of the imagination could the drawing room have been called a den of vice.

Although a few of the gentlemen ended the day with a game of billiards, most of the guests retired for a respectably early night in anticipation of another busy day on the morrow. Their services would be required for the gathering of greenery with which to decorate the house for Christmas, the earl had announced at dinner, and no one was to be excused. Sir Michael Milchip had complained halfheartedly about his gout until Lady Milchip had declared for everyone at the table to hear that it was the first *she* had heard of his suffering with any such malady. The baronet had looked sheepish as he winked at Margaret seated opposite him, there had been a general burst of laughter at his expense, and that had been the end of any attempt to shirk the hard labor.

The mood at breakfast the next morning might have been gloomy, given the fact that the daylight beyond the windows of the breakfast room looked almost as murky as the night that had preceded it. But as Viscount Luttrell remarked, standing at the window with his quizzing glass to his eye, those were snow clouds not so very far up there if he was not very much mistaken.

"All the more reason why we should go outside without delay once breakfast is over," the earl said. "The snow will be falling by noon or very soon afterward. I have it on the authority of the head gardener, who made the prediction in the hearing of my valet. Sit down and eat, Harry, or you are going to have to work on an empty stomach."

"Dear me," the viscount said, lowering his glass and turning toward the warming plates on the sideboard. "Work—whatever is that, Gerard? It sounds decidedly nasty."

"It means scouring the countryside for holly and ivy and pine boughs and mistletoe," Mr. Ralph Milchip said. "It means chopping and tearing and climbing and suffering bleeding fingers, Harry. And then it means dragging heavy loads to the house. And, as a reward when one has done all that, it means the pleasure of climbing and balancing and pinning all over the house merely so that one may see indoors a meager shadow of what one can see outdoors any day of the week without any effort at all. It is for this pleasure that Gerard has invited us all here."

Margaret laughed.

"Mistletoe?" Viscount Luttrell had brightened visibly. "If I really must work in order that you will continue to feed me, then, Gerard, I will volunteer to lead that party. Provided, of course, I may choose my own workers and test the efficacy of the product after I have found it." He turned lazy eyes on Christina and took a seat some distance from her.

Despite all the grumbling and complaining that ensued, it was clearly understood by everyone that the gathering of the greenery was to be the highlight of the house party so far. It felt surprisingly good, Christina thought as she made her

way up to the nursery a short time later to get the children
ready for the outdoors, to hear people teasing and laughing
and even insulting one another in a purely lighthearted way.
And to see people openly willing to enjoy themselves. The
house had never been decorated for Christmas. It was a heathen custom, Gilbert had always said, unsuited to the solemnity of a Christian observance.

Sobriety might be very worthy, but it was also very dull.
This year the children were going to have a *happy* Christmas. She would see to that.

Fifteen minutes later Christina was back downstairs with
her two daughters, all of them dressed warmly against the
windy chill of a December day that promised snow at any
moment. The hall was already abuzz with the merry sound
of voices.

"Lady Wanstead." Mr. Geordie Stewart strode toward
them as soon as they appeared in the stairway arch, and
swept off his tall beaver hat. He beamed first at Christina
and then at each of the girls. "I finally have the pleasure of
seeing your daughters. Will you do me the honor of presenting me?"

He bowed formally to Rachel, who curtsied gravely, and
took her hand in his to raise to his lips.

"My pleasure, ma'am," he said.

He smiled genially at Tess.

"I have two broad shoulders, just made for carrying little
boys or girls," he said to her. "My nieces and nephews often
make use of them. Would you like to ride up on one when
we step outside?"

"Yes, please, sir," Tess said. "We are going to have a bonfire and chocolate down by the lake."

"After we have helped gather greenery, Tess," her sister
reminded her. "We are going to decorate the house with it,"
she explained to Mr. Stewart. "Mama bought yards of red
ribbon in the village yesterday. I am excited."

She spoke so very solemnly, Christina thought. Those
words were strangely touching—*I am excited.* Would
Rachel ever learn to show excitement as well as to feel it?
Had irreparable harm been done . . . But no. Rachel would

see during the coming days and for all the years to come while Christina had any influence over her that brightness and gaiety and excitement were not necessarily evil in themselves.

"Well, and so am I," Mr. Stewart said with answering solemnity. "Very excited. There is a magic about Christmas that is always there no matter how old one grows. Last year I helped my nieces make a kissing bough—though they did most of the work and I did most of the watching, it must be admitted."

"What is a kissing bough?" Rachel asked.

When the whole party left the house a few minutes later, to the accompaniment of much noise and laughter, Tess rode on Mr. Stewart's shoulder while Christina walked on one side of him and Rachel on the other. And he conversed with the girls with practiced ease, avoiding the unfortunate tendency many adults had with children of being either overhearty or condescending.

It seemed almost, Christina thought, testing the feeling rather guiltily in her mind, like being a family.

The earl, she could see, was walking at the head of the group with Jeannette Campbell's arm drawn through his. Their heads were bent close together and they were laughing at something. They looked good together, she admitted reluctantly. There was nothing of the coquette about Miss Campbell and nothing flirtatious in the manner of either of them. But they were clearly very fond of each other.

She forced her mind and her eyes away from them.

She was going to enjoy the morning. After so many years the decision simply to enjoy had to be consciously made. She had come, she realized, to accept the notion that enjoyment and sin were synonymous terms. She felt almost as if she had been drugged for ten years and was only now beginning to withdraw to reality.

"Now, ma'am," Viscount Luttrell said to her when they had all arrived at the lake, "you are to be my lieutenant in this mission of ours to provide the gentlemen with endless excuse to kiss the ladies over Christmas. You live here and must therefore know where all the best mistletoe is to be found."

"I really do not, my lord," she said, laughing.

"Then we must hunt for it together," he told her. "And if we are not sure when we find it that what we have discovered is the real thing, then we must simply put it to the test. Mistletoe, it is said, makes the lips tingle when set to someone else's. A poor imitation of mistletoe has the unfortunate effect of making one feel nothing at all."

Christina merely laughed as the viscount added Frederick Cannadine and Margaret to his team.

And she laughed half an hour later when Viscount Luttrell spotted mistletoe high on the trunk of an ancient oak tree and clambered up to gather some. He was far fitter and more agile than his habitual indolent manner might lead one to suppose, she realized. He was soon safely on the ground again.

"Now," he said, "to put the product to the test. I do hope, ma'am, that I did not expend all that energy in vain. There is only a limited supply of it. Dare we find out if this is real mistletoe?"

She smiled at him.

But his teasing manner did not extend to the way he kissed her. He did something with his lips against her own so that hers parted without any protest at all—and he pressed his tongue deep into her mouth. Christina was breathless with shock and indignation.

"I believe, ma'am," he said, gazing into her eyes from a mere few inches away, his own half closed, "we have discovered the real thing."

Which were ambiguous words if ever she had heard any.

"But I feel severely hampered," he said, "by the fact that I must keep one arm suspended above your head and by the fact that other persons are likely to hove into sight at any moment and might be shocked by the sight of anything more ardent. Perhaps I can make off with one small sprig of this mistletoe when we return to the house and suspend it in a private place known only to you and me—preferably a place with a comfortable horizontal surface beneath it."

Could he possibly mean what she thought he meant?

But he smiled slowly, and the lazy, teasing look was back in his eyes. "Or perhaps," he said, "you would like to slap my face without further ado."

"The thought has crossed my mind, I must confess," she said, smiling back.

"One hates," he said, "to rush headlong through any game that is worth playing, though sometimes, of course, one is tempted to be gauche."

He was not just flirting with her, she realized. He was bent on seducing her—just as Gerard had warned he might. It seemed rather incredible after the way she had lived for the past ten years. She should be both terrified and outraged. He wanted to go to bed with her! But she could feel only amusement and a guilty sort of pleasure in knowing that she was still desirable.

"I believe, my lord," she said, "my best move in this game would be to effect a hasty retreat. I shall go and see that my children are safe."

"And I believe, ma'am," he said, "I shall allow you to evade my clutches—for now."

Three or four servants could probably have done a far more efficient job than he and his guests did, and in half the time, the Earl of Wanstead reflected an hour or so after they had begun. The piles of holly and pine boughs on the bank of the lake had grown respectably high, but all the gatherers had done at least as much playing as working. And they accomplished whatever they did with a great deal of noise and laughter.

The earl himself did not set a good example. After setting down his second load of pine boughs, he paused to watch Jeremy Milchip and Samuel Radway make a long slide over the firm ice at the edge of the lake while Susan Gaynor and Winifred Milchip looked on, Susan squealing with mingled admiration and fright. And then his lordship, about to turn back to his work, spotted Rachel watching solemnly from a short distance away.

She was a strange child—grave and quiet and unnaturally

self-contained. And yet on two occasions when she had come to the ballroom to watch the dancing lessons he had seen yearning in her eyes. The second time he had invited her to dance to the music while he practiced steps with Margaret. She had looked anxiously at her mother, but Christina, tight-lipped, had nodded her assent. The child had moved with spread arms and half-closed eyes perfectly in tune to the music just as if—as if she had been a free, graceful creature of the wild.

"It looks like fun?" he asked, strolling up to her now and nodding in the direction of the sliders on the lake.

She did not look away from them. "It must be the loveliest feeling in the world to move like the wind," she said.

"Why do you not try it?" he suggested.

She shook her head slowly. "I would not be allowed."

He did not believe Christina would forbid it. She had not forbidden the racing down the hill or the dancing in the ballroom, though she had given only reluctant acquiescence to that. But she had expected him to be angry about the hill incident. She had tried to protect her children from punishment. He frowned. What sort of a bastard had Gilbert been as a father and husband? What sort of a hold did he still have over his family?

"But I am the one who sets the rules here, remember?" the earl said. "I say you *are* allowed, and I will tell your mama so if she should wonder. Shall we try it together? I cannot seem to stay on my feet on hillsides, but perhaps I can do better on ice."

She reached for his hand and walked solemnly with him to the long, shining slide the two men had made. The earl went first. He had had plenty of experience with ice and kept his balance with no trouble at all. Susan and Winifred clapped their hands while Jeremy whistled.

Rachel fell at the first two attempts, but she refused help and she would not give up. After a few more tries she was zooming along the ice, her arms outstretched, her face tight with concentration. But finally, after one particularly long run, she turned her head to look at the earl and smiled radiantly at him.

His heart turned over. She was like a butterfly being released from its cocoon, he thought. Perhaps just in time. Quietness and even solemnity were probably part of her nature. But so was her capacity for joy in the self-expression of movement. Plain as she was at the age of seven, he thought, she was going to grow into a beauty, just like her mother. And her beauty could be vibrant if she was allowed to be spontaneously herself and if she was secure in the love of those around her.

He had had very little to do with children. He had no experience with paternal feelings. He had never before felt a child tug at his heartstrings.

He lifted one hand in acknowledgment, grinned at her, and turned back to the task at hand, as did the other four truants, while Langan and his wife and children were approaching to find out what all the noise and excitement were about.

But finally a couple of gardeners arrived to build the promised bonfire, and everyone was quite happy to accept its lighting as a signal that the work was at an end. It looked, after all, Mr. Colin Stewart declared, as if they could decorate a dozen mansions with everything that was piled up waiting to be carried to the house. Several servants were on their way to the fire with steaming jugs of chocolate and enough cups for everyone.

"What a splendid idea, Wanstead," Sir Michael Milchip said, rubbing his gloved hands together, "to bring a fire and warm drinks to us instead of leading us back to find both at the house. It prolongs the atmosphere of festivity."

"Oh," Lizzie Gaynor said, gazing upward and taking the earl's arm so that he might lead her to the fire, "do you think it really *will* snow, my lord? I can think of nothing more exciting for Christmas except that it might well confine me to the indoors. I never could discover how anyone can walk on snow without falling at every step. I would need a secure arm to which to cling."

"I cannot imagine, Miss Gaynor," he said, "that you will be confined to the indoors." He patted her hand and looked into her eyes.

"How kind you are," she murmured.

The cold air and exercise had brought a becoming sparkle of vitality to her face. She was a young lady who knew what she wanted of life, he thought, and was actively seeking it out. She wanted a good marriage—preferably not with a sixty-year-old duke who suffered from gout. At the moment she believed she wanted a marriage with him. She was pretty, accomplished, well-bred, good-natured. She would, if he decided to remain in England, be the perfect countess for him. She knew the world of *ton* far better than he. She had been brought up to the kind of duties that would be required of her. He did not love her, but then love was no longer something he looked for in marriage.

He thought of Jeannette's warning. He should not marry Lizzie Gaynor or anyone else, she had said, unless he was sure that she was the one he had been waiting for. There was a passion in his nature, she had told him, that needed to be satisfied. Was she right? He did not believe so. His life had been ruled by reason for the past ten years and longer, and he had been the happier for it.

"It *is* going to snow," he said, holding out one hand and looking at the dark surface of his glove. A white flake landed even as he watched. "Not even future tense, in fact."

Everyone gazed upward.

Christina was not at the fire. The earl made as accurate a count as was possible with so many people milling about the servants and the chocolate pots. Everyone else was present except her and Tess. The child had been playing earlier with the other children. Christina had been gathering mistletoe with Luttrell, who was now flirting with Susan. Perhaps Tess had grown cold and Christina had taken her back to the house.

But none of the other children appeared to be noticing the cold.

He stood a little apart from everyone else and peered among the trees to see if he could spot them. It did not take much effort. He caught a glimpse of red in the distance—Tess was wearing a red cloak. Perhaps she was not interested in bonfires and chocolate and the company of other children. Perhaps her mother was playing with her.

"Excuse me a moment," he said and strode away from the lake.

At first he thought they really were playing. Certainly they were both laughing. He always felt a pang of something—anger? bitterness? loneliness?—when he heard Christina laugh. She seemed able to do it with everyone except him.

"I will have this all worked out in a minute," she was saying, and they both laughed again.

They were sitting side by side on the branch of an old tree, Christina's arm protectively about her daughter's shoulders. They were not very high off the ground, but it was clear that they were stuck. The Earl of Wanstead strolled toward them.

The countess openly winced. "Oh, dear," she said, "I was just trying to persuade myself to swallow my pride and yell for help. I would have done so in a moment if I had known *you* were about to come to our rescue."

"Stuck, Tess?" he asked. "You are trying to rescue your mama?"

"I would not jump," Tess told him and laughed with apparent glee. "Mama said jump and I would not. And then she climbed up to get me and now we both cannot get down." But such was her childhood trust in the security of a mother's arm that she did not look at all alarmed.

"She was just out of arm's reach," the countess explained, "both when I was standing on the ground and when I climbed the trunk. But now I seem to have no way of getting her to the trunk short of lifting her across my body. I am quite reluctant to try that. This branch is higher than it looks from down there."

She was wearing half boots with a drab gray cloak—part of her old wardrobe, he had guessed when he saw her earlier. But the flush of cold and embarrassment in her cheeks added becoming color to her appearance—and the inch or two of bare flesh between the top of her boots and the hem of her cloak added definite allure. He wondered if she was aware of that glimpse of leg she was showing.

"I am taller," he said, stepping closer and raising his arms. "I can almost reach your ankles, Tess. Will you trust me and jump into my arms? I will not drop you, I promise." He winked at her. "On my honor as a gentleman."

"If I hold her under the arms and lower her a little—" the countess began, but Tess had simply leaned forward and dropped straight into his waiting arms. He was aware of baby curls and a soft little cheek and small clinging arms and feather lightness—and a delighted little laugh as his arms closed tightly about her.

"There," he said. "One rescued princess."

"And I, I suppose," Christina said crossly, "am the dragon."

"Breathing fire and brimstone," he agreed, grinning up at her before setting the child's feet on the ground and letting her go with surprising reluctance. "There is a bonfire through the trees there, Tess. You can see it from here. You will miss the chocolate and the fun if you do not hurry."

She went skipping off without a backward glance.

The earl folded his arms. "I assume," he said, looking up at Christina, "that *you* are not in need of rescuing."

She was still sitting on the branch, glancing uneasily at the trunk a foot or so distant with its very easy hand- and toeholds.

"Oh, dear," she said and laughed. "This should be easy."

"If you are," he said, "just say the word."

"Oh!" She glared accusingly down at him and then spoiled the effect by dissolving into laughter again. "You are enjoying this."

"Especially," he said, "the inch or perhaps the inch and a half of space between the tops of your boots and your hem."

She shrieked.

He stepped closer again and reached up his arms. "You had better do what your daughter just did, Christina."

"I'll climb down on my own, thank you," she told him, on her dignity. "Go away!"

But when he turned obediently to leave she shrieked at

him again. She hurtled downward almost before he was ready for her. He went staggering back under the impact of her weight and turned only just in time to brace his back against the tree trunk and save them both from falling to the ground.

She was laughing helplessly—no, *giggling*—against the capes of his greatcoat, and was pressed to him from her forehead to her knees. He guessed that she was not fully aware of that fact yet. He was—uncomfortably aware of it despite the protective layers of both indoor and outdoor garments between them. He could smell lavender.

"I have never had much of a head for heights," she said.

"And I suppose," he said, "it never occurred to you to summon someone else to rescue Tess even though there were any number of persons with steady heads all about you?"

She laughed. And then stopped laughing and stood very still against him. And then tipped back her head and looked up at him. It did not seem to occur to either of them at that moment to release the death hold they had on each other.

They gazed at each other. She drew breath and her lips moved, but she did not say what she had been about to say. He did not even try to speak.

He had held her thus that night at Vauxhall, folded against himself, almost into himself. She had been heart of his heart, almost flesh of his flesh. Had he not loved her quite so dearly, perhaps he would have made her just that among the denser trees beyond the dark path. She would not have resisted. She would have opened for him, received him, trusted him. The human soul yearned always for completeness. He had been within a heartbeat of finding wholeness on that evening. But honor had held him back.

And so the restless yearning, the incompleteness, unrecognized, firmly denied, had driven him like a scourge ever since.

Had he been so deceived on that evening? Had she known even then. . . .

"Did you know on that night," he found himself whispering to her, "that the very next day you would betroth yourself to him?"

"No." She was whispering too. "It is as well we cannot know when the world will end or when we will die—or when everything that makes the world a beautiful place or life worth living will come crashing down about us. No, I did not know."

It had not been an act, then, her tenderness and her ardor on that evening. It had been real. She really had loved him.

"Christina." There was nothing else to say. Just her name and all the pain of its utterance.

"I did not know," she said again and tipped her head to rest her forehead beneath his chin again.

But she had still chosen money rather than love. Temptation had come in the form of an offer from Gilbert just the day after she had very nearly committed herself to him in the ultimate way—and she had been dazzled. There could have been no other motive than greed for what she had done. Her father, a genial, well-liked man, who was the very antithesis of a tyrant, had always been indulgent of her wishes. He had always liked Gerard and welcomed his visits and smiled kindly on his suit, though no formal offer had been made. Perhaps she had expected that after her politic marriage to Gilbert and the birth of an heir, she would be able to have her lover too.

Perhaps he had surprised her by taking himself off to Canada and staying there. Perhaps he had even succeeded in hurting her.

And there had been no heir—only two daughters.

Perhaps now, he thought suddenly, she was beginning to imagine that opportunity had come knocking again. Perhaps she had detected the weakness in him that was undoubtedly there. Perhaps she was indeed scheming for a second marriage.

"If you have recovered from your fright," he said coolly, "I believe I would like to return to my guests at the fire. I certainly do not believe either of us would like to be seen like this, would we? Looking as if we are embracing?"

She pushed away from him hurriedly and turned her back

on him before he could see her face. Her voice matched his own when she spoke.

"Thank you," she said. "I *was* weak-kneed for a moment. I am quite recovered now." And she strode on ahead of him toward the fire.

And that had been a ridiculous notion, he thought. If she was scheming for anything, it was to get herself as far away from him as possible as soon as possible. For whatever reason—whether it were guilt or something else—she certainly hated him as much as he hated her.

He pushed away from the tree and followed her.

Chapter 11

The ballroom was not to be decorated until the day after Christmas. It was to be done by the servants under Christina's supervision. That had all been arranged beforehand. Nevertheless, it was a busy place two afternoons before Christmas. All the greenery had been piled in there ready for use in other parts of the house, and so there was a constant to-ing and fro-ing once the task of decorating had begun. And it was a conveniently large room in which to make the kissing boughs.

Lizzie Gaynor was the self-proclaimed expert in their construction. She organized two groups, one consisting of Christina, Laura Cannadine, and the children, and the other consisting of her mother, Lady Milchip, and Lady Hannah Milne. She skipped gaily back and forth between groups, doing nothing herself, but freely advising, criticizing, praising, and generally, Christina thought with some amusement, getting in the way. But she was the one who claimed the credit when the children's elaborate creation was carried to the drawing room to be hung from the ceiling close to the pianoforte.

"See how clever I am at designing kissing boughs?" she called, laughing and twirling about with exuberance and succeeding in looking very pretty indeed.

The drawing room had been transformed into a garden of pine-scented greenery and red bows and bells, which the housekeeper had discovered in some corner of the attic. The guests responsible for the room's decoration, including the earl himself, who was in his shirtsleeves and looking generally somewhat disheveled, all stopped what they were doing in order to admire and exclaim over the kissing bough.

"You are greatly to be commended, Miss Gaynor," his lordship said. "It looks like the finest specimen of kissing boughhood I have ever set eyes upon. Congratulations are due the workers too."

He grinned at the children, and for one moment his eye caught Christina's. She looked away. She did not care to remember that foolish incident during the morning, when she had jumped from the branch and landed in his arms and had stayed there far longer than was necessary. For a few dazed moments she had quite forgotten . . . For all the changes ten years had wrought in his physique, she had been caught up in very physical memories. And in the sort of yearning that self-discipline had suppressed in her for so many years that she had thought it quite dead.

"Does it work?" Mr. John Cannadine asked.

"The kissing bough?" Lizzie asked, her voice still determinedly gay. "Of course it works, sir, and once it has been hung up, I shall be delighted to prove the point with whoever chooses to test it with me."

"Since I will be doing the hanging," the earl said, taking the bough from Rachel and Paul Langan, "then I claim the right to do the testing too." He looked at Lizzie, raised his eyebrows, and chuckled.

And so, ten minutes later, to the accompaniment of laughter and applause and whistles, the Earl of Wanstead was kissing Lizzie Gaynor beneath the kissing bough and taking his time about it too.

Christina was appalled at her reaction. She watched, smiling as everyone else was doing. And she saw his head bent to another woman's, his lips claiming hers, his hands spread on either side of her waist while hers came to his shoulders. And she knew exactly how he would feel and smell to the other woman—just as if the sensations were happening to *her* body. Lizzie Gaynor was surely the favorite to become his wife. Aunt Hannah and Lady Milchip had speculated quite openly about it on the walk back from the lake. And they looked like a courting couple.

Christina wanted to bawl. She wanted to scream. She wanted to make a noisy, undignified scene. She was—she was jealous! She *hated* Lizzie Gaynor. And she hated him—perhaps the more so because there was no reason for her hatred. Quite the contrary. She was the one who had wronged him. He had told her that her desertion had hurt him and driven him to Canada. His own dislike of her was a result of what she had done to him. And she knew now that the way she had justified her behavior all those years ago had been all wrong. There had been no justification.

She had lost all that was most precious in her life.

She turned blindly and hurried from the room, colliding with Mr. Radway as she did so and then dislodging a ribbon-bedecked bough from the door as she jerked it open. She fled up the stairs to her room. But her room did not provide sanctuary enough. She needed to be quite alone. She needed to be somewhere where she could recollect herself and find some peace.

There was only one place. She had not been there since . . . That had been three years ago. It was three years since she had last been there, but the yearning to go now, to be away from the house where his presence was suffocating her to death, was overpowering.

She crossed to the window and gazed out. The snow was falling thickly and already settling in a white blanket on the lawns. It looked beautiful in the early twilight. They had all been watching it throughout the afternoon and hoping that tomorrow they would be able to go outside and enjoy it. They had all expressed the hope that it would remain for Christmas.

It should hinder her from going out. She set her forehead against the glass of the window. But she could not go back downstairs. Not yet. She just could not. The calm that she had imposed upon herself like a heavy armor for years past, the calm that had helped her cope with her life, had deserted her to be replaced with a wild, unpredictable swing of emotions over which she seemed to have no control whatsoever.

It was the third day of the house party. Her presence at tea was no longer essential. Rachel and Tess were downstairs, but there were other children for them to play with and plenty of adults to make much of them. When the time came, they would go back to the nursery with the other children. She need not worry about them. But if she stayed in her room, someone was going to come knocking at the door sooner or later. She could not face anyone at present.

A short while later Christina was hurrying down the servants' staircase and letting herself out of a side door. She approached the trees from the back of the house, lest someone should spot her through the drawing room windows. The snow was powdery underfoot and not very slippery. Neither was it very deep yet. She found her way through the trees to the river and turned north along its bank. It did not matter that the paths were no longer visible. She knew the way well enough.

She had found the gamekeeper's hut first when Mr. Pinkerton still lived there. She had used to go there sometimes to sit and talk with him, even to take tea with him. After he had moved to the village, though he came back sometimes and always kept the hut clean and ready for use, she used to go there alone. Not often. She had duties at home. Every minute of her day had been regulated. She was answerable to her husband for every one of those minutes. But sometimes she had found time to be alone, to seek peace, to seek the remnants of herself. They had been among the most precious interludes of her married life— until Gilbert had discovered her there one day and had put an end to them.

The door was unlocked. She went inside and shut it. She might have lit a candle with the tinderbox that was in its accustomed place on a shelf. She might have lit the fire that was built ready in the small hearth. But instead she took off her boots and curled her feet under her on the bed in the corner by the window, wrapping about herself her cloak and the sheepskin blanket that had been rolled there. She chose to sit in the semidarkness and in the cold. She twined her arms about her knees, rested her cheek on them, and closed her eyes.

She tried not to think. She tried to allow the quietness and the dusk to soothe her and heal her.

The Earl of Wanstead timed the kiss carefully. He did not want it to be so short that it might seem insulting. But he did not want it to be so long that it would raise expectations. And yet even as he tried to make it just the right kiss for the occasion, it struck him as odd that his mental processes should be so sharp when he was kissing the young lady to whom he was considering paying his addresses. He was concentrating so hard on kissing her in just the right way and for just the right length of time that he was scarcely aware of what it felt like to kiss her.

The drawing room door banged shut and one of the pine boughs pinned to it thudded to the floor just as he lifted his head and smiled. He was planning to turn to Rachel and little Alice Cannadine, who had helped make the kissing bough, and draw each of them beneath it for a kiss too.

"Is Lady Wanstead unwell?" John Cannadine asked, frowning in the direction of the door. "She seemed in a prodigious hurry."

"She has been unusually busy during the past few days," Lady Hannah said—she was holding the other kissing bough, which was destined for the hall below. "Perhaps she has gone to her room for a rest."

Nothing else was said about the countess's hasty exit. It was time for tea, and everyone was quick to tidy the room and summon those who were still busy in other rooms. The kissing bough was being made much of.

Why had she left? the earl asked himself. She had gone in a hurry while he was kissing Lizzie Gaynor beneath the mistletoe. The answer to his question was obvious, of course, and it irritated him no end. Kissing boughs were doubtless heathen creations, and kissing in public—perhaps even in private!—was the work of the devil. It was a good thing he had not got around to pecking Rachel on the cheek, he thought grimly. He might have found himself accused of all manner of atrocities.

He was glad she did not come back down for tea. He did

not want to see her thin-lipped, disapproving face again any time soon. It was a discourtesy not to put in an appearance, of course, but that was her problem, not his. She was not his wife, for which blessing he would be eternally thankful. Tess, who had been playing with Alice and the younger Langan boy all through tea, came and stood before him when Laura Cannadine was about to herd all the children back to the nursery, and wanted to know where her mama was. He went down on his haunches before her.

"I believe Mama is being a sleepyhead," he told her. "You exhausted her this morning, Tess, by making her climb trees and getting her stuck."

She giggled.

"You go on up with the others," he told her, patting her plump cheek. "Mama will come and see you later. And, Tess? Thank you for helping with the kissing bough. It is really lovely."

She smiled sunnily and skipped off to join the other children.

Where *was* Christina? She had not told anyone she was unwell. It was unlike her to abandon her duties or to lie down in the middle of the day.

"Ask her ladyship's maid if she is in her room, Billings," he instructed the butler after stepping out of the drawing room. "And if she is well."

But the message came back that her ladyship was not in her room at all. One of the scullery maids, who had been shaking a cloth outside the kitchen door an hour earlier, had seen her walking up behind the house, going in the direction of the woods.

At twilight? When it was snowing rather heavily? If she had been going for a stroll in order to get some fresh air— but was that likely after all the air and exercise she had got during the morning?—would she not have mentioned the fact to someone? Would she not have asked if anyone wished to accompany her? At the very least her children?

What the devil?

Everyone had dispersed after tea to amuse themselves at various informal activities or to rest after the exertions of the day. There were a few hours to spare before it would be necessary to dress for dinner.

She had been gone for longer than an hour. Without a word to anyone. And she was still not back. It was heavy dusk outside now. Not that the night was going to be a dark one with all the light snow clouds that were still disgorging their load. But even so it was a strange time to go out for a prolonged stroll—alone.

Damn the woman, he thought. He had been going to suggest a game of billiards with Harry and Ralph and anyone else who cared to join them. There was a cozy fire in the billiard room. He had had enough of the outdoors and of physical exertion for one day. If she had gone off alone, it was because she wanted to be alone. There was no danger to her. Despite the snow, there was no blizzard, and she must know her way about the park. He would certainly be the last person she would want to see.

But he knew he would not be able to rest again until he was sure she was safe. And since it had never been in his nature to wait passively for something to happen if he could possibly help it, he knew that he was going to go out there looking for her. Just to see annoyance, even contempt, in her eyes for his pains, no doubt.

The marks of her bootprints were not quite obliterated, he discovered when he went outside. Slight depressions in the snow revealed that she had indeed gone toward the forest in a diagonal line, heading north. It was too dark when he finally got among the trees to find any sign still remaining that she had passed this way, but if she had not swerved out of the direction she had taken, she would have reached the river eventually. And if she had been headed there at such an angle, the chances were that she would not then have turned south. If she had gone north along the riverbank, it seemed probable that her destination was Pinky's hut. She had been living at Thornwood long enough, after all, to have discovered it ages ago.

Why would she decide to go to Pinky's hut today of all days? And at this time of day? And during a heavy snowfall? One answer was obvious to him. It was so that she might enjoy some privacy. He waded onward nevertheless, feeling somewhat murderous. Though she was not to blame, he supposed, if he was foolish enough to follow her, unbidden.

At first he thought he had been mistaken. There was no sign of a light in the window, not even the flickering light of a fire. And there was no smoke coming from the chimney. But he climbed the slope to the cottage anyway and opened the door.

He thought there was no one in there. Certainly there was no light, no sound, no movement. But there was something lighter than the surrounding darkness on the bed, and he stepped closer in order to have a clearer view. He left the door open behind him.

His eyes registered the fact that it was indeed she who was sitting silently there at the same moment as she moved. She jerked closer to the wall farthest from where he stood, and her arms came free of the sheepskin blanket in which she had been wrapped in order to cover her face protectively. She made a guttural sound in her throat.

He froze.

And then he turned to cross the single room of the hut again in order to shut the door. He found the tinderbox by touch alone—he knew where it had always been kept—and lit the single candle that stood in a holder on the table. He knelt in front of the hearth and set a light to the kindling so that the fire would burn and bring some warmth to the room.

"I am not going to hit you," he said quietly.

She had been almost relaxed, almost warm, almost at peace. She had been in a half dream, though still awake. She had not heard anyone approach—but how could she have when any footfall would be deadened by the blanket of snow? When the door had opened and she had seen the silhouette of a man, first standing there and then stepping inside, she had been paralyzed with terror. Not of strangers. It had not for a moment occurred to her that some dangerous vagrant or fugitive might have found his way to the shelter of the hut.

She had acted from sheer instinct. She had tried to duck out of his reach. She had tried to protect her face. She had thought he was. . . .

But he had not touched her. And even as he walked away and closed the door and groped for the tinderbox, even before she saw him clearly, she knew that she had been disoriented. Dead men did not walk. She knew who he was. The light from the candle, suddenly illumining his face as he bent over it, merely confirmed the fact. He did not look at her. He proceeded to light the fire. Only then did he speak.

"I am not going to hit you," he said.

"I did not know who you were," she said. It seemed that there was warmth in the room already. Perhaps it was just the light and the crackling sounds of the fire catching hold that gave the illusion.

"No," he said. "I suppose you did not."

He came to stand before the window beside the bed, though he did not look at her at all. He stood gazing out. Probably, she thought, with the light inside the room he could see nothing out there. But he stood there for a long time, not moving. She could have reached out and touched him if she had wanted to do so. She stayed where she was and did not move at all.

Why had he come? How had he known where to find her?

The answers did not seem important. Neither, for that matter, did the questions. He had come. It had been somehow inevitable.

She had been aware from the beginning of her marriage that it was here at Thornwood that he had grown up. She had never tried to place him anywhere in the house or park. She had never wondered which bedchamber had been his, which rooms he had spent most of his time in, which parts of the outdoors had been his favorite playgrounds. She had not wanted to know. But she had known, though neither she nor Mr. Pinkerton had ever mentioned his name, that this hut had been a haunt of his, that it had been a special place for him. How had she known? There was no answer to the question. She simply had.

And she knew now that she had been right. He belonged

in this cozy little room. It breathed his presence. She had never consciously admitted to herself that she had come here through the years in order to allow herself the very small comfort of that knowledge.

"We left something unfinished at Vauxhall," he said at last without turning from the window.

"Yes," she said.

"We should have finished it and been done with it," he said.

"Yes."

He turned from the window but still did not look at her. He went to stand in front of the fire and gazed down into the flames, which were dancing about the logs piled in the hearth. He stood there for a long time before taking off his hat and gloves and greatcoat and setting them on the rocking chair where Mr. Pinkerton had loved to sit. He shrugged out of his coat and stood for a few moments in his shirt-sleeves before starting to unbutton his waistcoat.

And so it would be ended, Christina thought as she watched him undress until he stood before the fire wearing only his breeches and stockings. It was a strange moment, beyond time. It was unreasonable, what was happening, what was about to happen, but it was a moment beyond reason. It did not need to be talked about, discussed, argued upon. It did not even need the spark of passion.

Something had not been finished. And so they would finish it now. There was no looking to the future. It was a moment without future.

He turned to her then, his expression blank, as she supposed her own was. Nothing needed to be said. She got off the bed and spread the sheepskin blanket over the woolen ones. She turned them all back to reveal white sheets. She took off her cloak. There was no need to spread it over everything else. The room was not large—it already felt almost cozily warm. She reached up her arms to undo the buttons at the back of her dress, but he turned her with his hands on her shoulders and did it for her. She drew off her dress, removed her stockings and undergarments, and turned to him, wearing only her shift.

She stepped against him, breathed in the warm, distinctive, musky smell of him before spreading her hands over his bare chest and lifting her face to his.

There was something to finish. They had both acknowledged that with a quiet sort of resignation. There had been no passion in their decision. But it was passion that had not been completed between them, the passionate desire—no, the passionate *need*—to give and to take, to share all that was themselves—bodies, minds, hearts, souls. To rid themselves of the brokenness, the incompleteness of their separate selves in order to make one whole.

That was what had never been finished. And never forgotten. It was a hidden fire that had needed only a spark in order to ignite again and blaze to its finish.

A kiss was not enough—that was soon apparent. Not even when they were wrapped in each other's arms, straining together, their mouths wide over each other's, their tongues touching, circling, deeply exploring. Not even when their hands pressed hungrily over bare flesh and beneath their few remaining garments.

"Lie down," he told her harshly, but he held her up long enough to peel her shift off over her head. He tossed it aside. He unbuttoned his breeches as she lay down, pulled them off hastily with his stockings, cast them onto the floor, and came down on top of her.

It was not an encounter for pleasure, for subtlety, for the erotic building of desire, for intimate play. Something needed to be finished, and that something was a passion that had smoldered for longer than ten years.

He thrust her legs wide with his knees, pressed his hands beneath her buttocks, held her firm while she lifted her knees and braced her feet against the mattress, and plunged deep. They both cried out.

A little sanity returned after that. He lay still on her and in her, pressed deep, his hands unyielding beneath her. She tilted and strained upward to draw him even deeper into herself. They were both panting audibly.

He withdrew his hands, braced himself on his elbows, and

lifted himself enough that he could look down into her face from a mere few inches distant.

They gazed deeply into each other's eyes.

"Oh, yes," he whispered, "it will be finished between us."

The passion in his face might have been love, might have been hate, might have been both.

And this, she thought, disoriented again, was not the marriage act with which she was long familiar. This was not passive endurance. This was not repugnant to her. This was the culmination of the dream she had dreamed at Vauxhall.

He lowered his head until his forehead was against the hair that had pulled loose from her chignon, and began to move.

At first there was merely an awareness of impossible intimacy, of incredible pleasure. But very soon there was only passion again—raw, mindless, heavy, panting, aching passion. And a frightening pain that was beyond either pleasure or passion, and yet was not quite pain, until—ah, then . . .

She heard someone cry out—two persons. And then terror and peace clashed strangely together, leaving her with the sudden clear awareness that it had happened—that she was no longer herself, that he was no longer himself. That they were another being, a single entity that was the two of them and yet was different from either of them separately.

They had become one.

For the merest heartbeat of a moment.

Even as the awareness was speaking itself to her mind it was gone, beyond her grasp, beyond recall. A little flash of heaven, which was a something or a state of being beyond either place or time or the ability to be expressed in words and was therefore to be sensed fleetingly but never to be grasped.

But for a moment there had been heaven. Not for her. Not for him. For *them*. And then it was gone, and they were a man and a woman on a bed in a gamekeeper's hut, at the end of a sexual coupling, their bodies still joined.

When he withdrew from her, moved to her side, and pulled the blankets over both of them, she felt relaxed, happy, and sadder than she had ever felt in her life before.

She turned her head to look at him. He gazed back at her. She could see his eyes, but she could not see into them. His face was blank. So, she guessed, was hers. Reason and time had come back and so had the future. There was too much to be lost by *not* looking blank.

They were two very separate people again.

They had finished what they had started long ago. Without understanding quite why, they had completed something that had haunted them both, something that had prevented them from moving happily along with their lives. Now it had been done. And everything was in the past.

"At last," he said, echoing her thoughts, "it is finished."

"Yes," she said and closed her eyes.

Yes, it was finished. Now, everything was finished.

Everything.

She hit the frightening bottom of despair.

Chapter 12

"I am glad," he said, "that I came back—back to England and back to Thornwood. I thought it was all over but it was not. Now it is."

"Yes," she said.

He caught her elbow and steadied her. The snow was still falling. It was deeper now than when he had first come outside. "When walking in snow or on ice, you know," he told her, "you need to keep your center of gravity over your feet. You will slip less, and when you do, you will fall less."

"Thank you," she said, turning from the riverbank and moving into the trees, removing her elbow from his hand as she did so. "I can manage."

As he had guessed, it was not a dark night. It was a good thing too since he had not thought of bringing a lantern with him.

"Now I can go back to Montreal, where I belong," he said. "And I will have the satisfaction of knowing that I live there from choice. There will be no more fear of coming here, though I will not come again. You can live in peace here with your daughters. You need not consider remarriage unless you really wish to do so."

"No," she said.

"We can be free of each other." The foolish words kept spilling from his mouth, though they seemed to have come from nowhere. Had his brain really processed them? Did it really believe them? Did *he* really believe them? Did she?

"Yes," she said.

This whole strange episode was like some sort of bizarre

dream. He could scarcely believe what had just happened. There had been no thought behind it, no reasoning, no sense. The strangest thing of all, perhaps, was that the blame, or the explanation, could not even be laid at the door of passion. It had not started as a passionate encounter—though it had very quickly become that.

Had some part of his mind really believed that if he could just bed her he would then be able to forget her?

"All this might have been avoided," he said irritably, "if one of your daughters had only been a son."

She stopped walking suddenly, and he almost collided with her from behind. He had said and done some remarkably stupid things during the past couple of hours, but this really surpassed everything.

"Forgive me," he said. "Your daughters are perfect. They really are, Christina."

"I had two sons," she said. "The one was born early and never breathed. The other was fully developed and seemed perfect. I held him for maybe an hour until he died. Strangely, Gerard, for the weeks and even months that followed the deaths of both my sons, I did not once dwell upon the annoyance of the fact that you were still Gilbert's heir."

Oh, hell!

He set his hands on her shoulders. She shrugged, but she did not shake him off. He knew so little of her life for the past ten and a half years. She had been a wife. She had borne four children and known the agony of losing two of them. She had been widowed.

"What I said was unpardonable," he said. It was. He could not ask her forgiveness again.

"Gilbert never loved them," she said softly. "Rachel and Tess, I mean. They were merely *girls.*"

He squeezed her shoulders tightly and drew her back against him. She rested her head against his shoulder for a few moments. Her eyes were closed, he could see.

"I have not had much to do with children," he said. "I do not have an easy rapport with them. But I have an affection for both of yours, Christina. You have done well with them."

She drew away from him and trudged on ahead of him. Soon they drew clear of the trees and could walk side by side. They did so, not talking, though when he took her elbow again to help keep her feet in the soft snow, she did not withdraw it as she had earlier.

He had held her naked in his arms, he thought. He had been inside her body. Twice. That had been the maddest thing of all. Passion had driven them fast through that first encounter, the one that he had told her immediately afterward had finished everything. And then some time after that, after they had lain quietly side by side, not talking, not touching, not sleeping, he had turned to her again, and she had turned to him, and they had come together in a slow coupling, almost—almost as if they had been making love.

He knew her thoroughly in the biblical sense. And suddenly he felt that he knew her as a person far better than he had during the week and a half of being at Thornwood—or at least that there *was* a person to be known, not just the girl he had once loved. Her brief mention of the two sons who had not survived had given him a powerful awareness of the fact that she had *lived* the past ten years, just as he had. She had suffered—and perhaps in other ways than just the loss of two babies. From what he could piece together of her marriage to Gilbert, it had not been a happy union. And yet she had come through those years with her dignity intact. Margaret and his aunt loved her and deferred to her judgment. The servants respected her. And she was a warm and loving mother.

"You will be marrying Miss Campbell, then, I suppose?" she said, breaking the silence abruptly. "She will be the wise choice if you are returning to Canada. Miss Gaynor would not take kindly to being taken away from England."

But he had realized something that perhaps she had not thought of yet. "I will not be able to sail until spring," he said, "though I will probably return to London next week. Before I leave England, you will know if you are with child or not. If you are, then I will be marrying you, Christina."

Even in the darkness he could see that he had startled her. She turned her head sharply in his direction. She drew breath to speak but said nothing. She skidded in the snow, and he gave her the full support of his arm. They were very close to the house, he could see.

"I will not be offering for anyone over Christmas," he said. "You will not be trying to fix the interest of either Luttrell or Geordie Stewart. It may not be finished between us after all, Christina. It may be just beginning."

She shook her head but still said nothing.

"It seems as if we have been gone a month," he said as they approached a side door of the house. "In reality I suppose it is only a couple of hours. I hope at least we are not late for dinner."

He held the door open, and she preceded him through it without a word.

It would be the final irony, he thought as she hurried on ahead of him, if he had got her with child. In Pinky's hut, where he had spent some of his happiest hours. At Christmas time, when one's thoughts turned to children and love and the impossible.

Hatred, Jeannette had said, was very akin to love. At the moment he felt neither for Christina. He felt only an unwilling pull toward her, a need to know the woman who had haunted him for longer than ten years, to know what those missing years had held for her, to understand why she had made it impossible for him ever to marry anyone else, to understand why he both dreaded and hoped that his seed, inside her now, had impregnated her and bound them together for life.

No, he decided, striding off in the direction of the staircase, he surely could not have believed for one single moment that it really was all finished between them.

Christmas Eve. It was surely the dream of all Christmas Eves, Christina thought the following morning, setting one knee on the low sill of the window in her bedchamber after pushing aside the curtains, and gazing out on a white world, just beginning to sparkle in the early light of day.

She shivered. The fire had been built up and lit, but it had not had time to warm the room. Yet the shiver was not entirely from the cold. Partly it was excitement. Christmas would surely come this year in full glory, not merely slip on by as it had done through most of her life, it seemed. Partly it was memory, which she might have dismissed as a strange dream if she had not been able to feel the unmistakable physical effects of tender breasts and a slight soreness inside, where he had joined his body with hers. Partly it was indecision—she still had every penny of the money Mr. Monck had given her on Gerard's instructions tucked into a cubbyhole of the escritoire in her private sitting room. She still had not even written a reply to her father's letter.

It was a heady mixture of emotions for the morning of Christmas Eve. And over and above them all, the constant awareness, humming through her consciousness, as it had all night, even weaving itself through her dreams, that now, at this very moment, she might have the beginnings of his child in her womb. A part of her for nine months. And binding her to him for the rest of her life.

Perhaps something had begun, not ended last night, he had said. She rested her forehead against the window glass.

But her thoughts and her wonder at the sight of the snow were interrupted by the sound of someone opening the door of her bedchamber without first knocking. Rachel hurried inside, barefoot and clad only in her long flannel nightgown, her long, dark hair hanging loose down her back. And on her face, such a bright look of excitement that Christina felt her heart turn over. She had not seen Rachel look thus since . . . Oh, for a very long time.

"Mama, look!" she said, hurrying toward the window. "Have you *seen*?"

"The snow?" Christina smiled and crossed to the bed to drag free a blanket to wrap about her daughter. She lifted her to stand on the sill, just as if she had been a tiny child again, and kept her arms about her as well as the blanket. "Have you ever seen anything more wonderful in your life?"

"No," Rachel said, and her voice sounded almost like an agony.

The sun was just rising in the clear east. There were still

clouds overhead, but they were moving off. The snow had stopped falling.

"See how the sun sparkles off the snow?" Christina said.

"Like hundreds and thousands of jewels," Rachel said with a sigh.

She snuggled against Christina, who reveled in the feeling. For a long time Rachel had not been a child for physical closeness.

"Mama," she said, "Paul and Matthew said last night that their mama and papa are going to take them out to play in the snow today. May I go too? Would it be wrong?"

Wrong! Christina closed her eyes and hugged her daughter more tightly. Wrong to play? To have fun and exercise?

"I will not make a loud noise or run around too fast," Rachel promised. "I will not get under anyone's feet. Please, Mama?"

Christina swallowed against a gurgling in her throat. "I am coming out to play too," she said. "So is Tess. So are all the other children and most of the grown-ups too if my guess is correct. And I am going to make all the noise in the world. I am going to laugh and shriek and dash about just as if I were—what?"

"A puppy?" Rachel suggested.

"A whole litter of the most unruly puppies in the world," Christina said. "You will need to press your mittens against your ears once I get started. And I am going to get under *everyone's* feet."

"Mama?" Rachel dipped her head sideways to rest on her mother's shoulder. "I am glad Lord Wanstead came here and brought everyone else with him. I like him."

"Do you?" Christina kissed the sleek dark hair with its crooked part.

"He does not frown and say no all the time," Rachel said. "He dances and slides and smiles. He is not an evil man, is he?"

"No, he is not evil, sweetheart," Christina said.

"I am glad." Rachel sighed. "Because I like him. I hope he stays here forever and ever."

No. Rachel had always needed a hero. But heroes could

bring pain, especially to children, who could not distinguish between worthy and unworthy heroes.

"I believe he must go away again," Christina said gently. "He does not really belong to us, you see, and he has a home elsewhere. But he likes you. He told me so himself. And he will be here for Christmas. He is going to make Christmas happy for all of us. It will be something to remember and talk about after he has gone."

"May I build a snowman?" Rachel asked.

"Ten, if you wish." Christina hugged her and kissed her before lifting her down and releasing her. "But if we stand here talking all morning, not even one will get made. Shall we go and wake Tess?"

Yes, they would have him for Christmas, she thought as she went up to the nursery with Rachel after pulling on a dressing gown over her nightgown. And it was going to be a happy Christmas—for all three of them. She was determined on that.

And after he was gone, there would be memories to live on. But she would not think of that yet.

A few of the older people had remained indoors as well as Laura Cannadine, who was in a delicate way and was afraid of sustaining a heavy fall. Everyone else, including the six children, were outside soon after breakfast. There were no decorations to gather today and no errands to be run. The park had already been quite thoroughly explored. There was only one thing to do outdoors, then, and they did it with unabashed enthusiasm.

They frolicked.

Inevitably it all began with a snowball fight, disorganized at first, everyone pelting whoever else happened to be within range, somewhat better organized later after the earl had bellowed for a ceasefire and had announced that he and the countess would choose teams, picking alternately, and then be given five minutes during which to discuss strategy with their respective regiments.

Christina took the first round without any argument, he was forced to admit when the five minutes were up and he emerged from a huddle with his warriors. She, it was clear, had not spent the time discussing strategy with some semblance of democracy, but had played tyrant and issued swift orders to her company. Some had been set to rolling and stockpiling as many snowballs as it was possible to make in five minutes while others had been directed to push the snow into a waist-high bulwark, behind which they were all crouched, fully armed, by the time the signal for war was given.

It all looked more impressive than it was, of course. Most of the prepared snowballs felled the enemy on the first glorious barrage, but since the weapons were not lethal, the enemy rebounded with a shriek and a roar and came on undaunted. And since the victors had stood up to cheer their victory instead of preparing for the next assault, the momentum quickly shifted. And since the bulwark had been built in a long, moderately straight line, a single small breach meant the collapse of the whole structure.

Once the breach had been accomplished, the battle degenerated into chaos and shouts and screeches and giggles. Most of the contestants resumed the old method of forming and hurling snowballs indiscriminately at friend and foe— indeed, very few could remember which was which. Viscount Luttrell threw himself in front of the countess and defended her with great show and gallantry in an imaginary sword fight with Samuel Radway; Geordie Stewart collapsed full-length on the snow under the impact of one tiny shower of snow and groaned pitifully as he tried unsuccessfully to defend himself against a hail of balls from Tess, the Langan boys, and Alice Cannadine; Jeremy Milchip and Frederick Cannadine had captured a shrieking Margaret between them and were ungallantly trying to stuff snow down the back of her neck; Lizzie Gaynor was hovering close to the earl, occasionally clinging to his arm, with a nice show of timidity and unsteadiness of foot, though she showed a glowing, laughing face whenever it was turned up to him; Rachel was pelting him with remarkably accurate aim—and laughing gleefully at every hit and looking anything but her usual plain, rather sad self.

He was busy, being the focus of much of the attack and for very pride's sake making quite sure that he gave as good as he got. But he was not too busy to notice the transformation in Christina. It had not been apparent at breakfast. She had been quiet and dressed in gray—not part of her new wardrobe, he had guessed—with her hair combed back severely from her face and brow and dressed in coiled plaits at her neck. She was still dressed in gray now. But there was nothing dull about her demeanor. She fought with energy, laughing and yelling, her cheeks and nose bright with the winter chill, her eyes dancing with merriment.

What a contrast, he thought, with the mental picture he had of the woman who had greeted him in the drawing room on the evening of his arrival at Thornwood less than two weeks before—dark, severe, and joyless. It might have been better for him if she had remained that way. He could not keep his mind, either, away from an image of her as she had been early last evening in the cozy warmth of Pinky's hut, naked beneath him on the bed, her eyes heavy with passion, her lips swollen from his kisses.

"Arrghh!" he exclaimed in disgust as a large, soft snowball collided with his nose and splattered over his whole face. That was what he got for lowering his guard and going off into a dream for a moment. He scraped away snow with his gloves and looked around quickly to see if he could identify his assailant. She was laughing in gloating triumph—Christina.

He roared and dived for her. She went down beneath his weight and landed on her back in the deep, soft snow. She laughed at him when he lifted his head and looked down at her.

"Unfair!" she said. "Snowballs are allowed. Wrestling is not."

"But who makes the rules here?" he asked, grinning at her. "Do I have to remind you constantly?"

But both her laughter and his grin quickly died. He could smell lavender, he thought foolishly. Her lips had parted and her gaze had lowered to his mouth. They were also surrounded by family and friends. He adjusted his weight, flipped her over before she realized his intent, pressed her face-down into the snow for a moment, and then grasped her flailing arms and pinioned them by the wrists behind her back.

"Ho!" he bellowed. "I demand the surrender of the count-ess's forces. Else I shall have her eating snow for the rest of the morning."

She was laughing again.

"Egad," Viscount Luttrell said, executing a piece of ele-gant swordplay over the two of them. "I have just finished carving up one man who dared threaten her ladyship's per-son. You want to be next, Wanstead? On guard!"

"I will wager," John Cannadine said, "that my children and I can build a better snowman than any other three peo-ple here present can do—within the next hour, shall we say?"

"A wager?" The viscount spun about. "With what as the prize, pray?"

"The first to be served with chocolate and mince pies when we go back inside?" the earl suggested, getting to his feet and reaching down a hand to help Christina to hers.

"Ah, a wager not to be resisted," Viscount Luttrell said. "My lady?" He bowed elegantly to Christina, who was try-ing to slap the snow off her cloak with equally snowy gloves. "You look like someone who knows a thing or two about the construction of snowmen. Will you join me? And Miss Campbell? You have not a hope in a million, John, my lad."

The earl had Lizzie and Rachel on his team; Geordie Stewart had Tess and the younger Langan boy; the older boy was with his parents; Jeremy and Frederick and Margaret took up the challenge. Ralph Milchip pronounced himself judge and jury. Everyone else wandered about, giving ad-vice and encouragement. Clara Radway and Susan Gaynor waded off to the kitchen to beg coals and carrots.

Milchip made a grand moment out of the judging after he had pronounced the hour at an end. He moved from one snowman to another, his hands clasped at his back, a frown of concentration wrinkling his brow, his lips pursed. The children, the earl noticed in some amusement, watched his face, tense with suspense. Now how was Ralph going to avoid disappointing several of them? he wondered. Rachel had stepped closer so that the brim of her bonnet was almost brushing his arm. He cupped her shoulder with one hand and smiled down at her. She had thrown herself into the task with energy and solemn concentration. She wanted very badly to win.

"Well," the judge began, speaking at last, "a difficult decision. Difficult indeed." He shook his head. "But one must make a decision. Very well, then. I award a prize to the Cannadines for the squattest, fattest snowman I have ever seen."

John laughed, Alice jumped up and down in glee, and young Jonathan sucked the thumb of his mitten. The other children looked disconsolate. Some of the adults applauded; some jeered. Ralph held up both arms.

"And I must award a prize to the Countess of Wanstead's trio for the tallest snowman," he said; "and to Lady Margaret's for the snowman whose head has fallen off more often than anyone else's; and to Mr. Stewart's for the snowman with the broadest smile; and to Lord Langan's for the only snowman with arms, though one has just this moment dropped off, it is true; and to the Earl of Wanstead's for working the hardest and producing the overall largest snowman."

Rachel looked up at his lordship with bright eyes, and he winked at her. Had Ralph thought of how the prize was to be claimed? he wondered.

The judge imposed silence by raising both arms again, and proved himself worthy of his position of authority. "As for the prize," he said and paused for effect. He looked about at the group of builders. "The first cup of chocolate and the first mince pie go to—the first one back at the house." And he turned and raced off in the direction of the main doors, laughing like an imbecile and leaving a cloud of snow in his wake.

"We had the biggest snowman and worked the hardest," Rachel said in all earnestness.

"We certainly did." The earl took her hand in his. "No one

worked harder. I chose my team well. Shall we go back inside?"

He offered his other arm to Lizzie Gaynor, who took it and chattered gaily all the way back to the house. But before Christina could come to claim her daughter and whisk her up to the nursery to remove her outdoor garments and comb her hair, he managed a private word with the child.

"I will have an announcement to make in the drawing room while we are all warming up with chocolate and something to eat," he said. "I shall see to it that you young people are all there to hear it. And then I have a suggestion to make to you. Just to you. It will be our secret."

"Even from Mama?" she asked him.

"Especially from Mama," he said and winked at her again.

"It is not wrong?" she asked anxiously. "It is not evil?"

He felt the old flash of annoyance for a moment against a mother—and a father—who could so have burdened a young child with a morbid conscience.

"It is not wrong," he said. "It is not evil. It is going to make Christmas happier for everyone. Are you interested?"

She nodded slowly. "Yes, my lord," she said.

Christina came for her then while everyone else dripped melting snow onto the hall floor and stamped feet and rubbed hands and exclaimed loudly to one another that they had only just realized how cold they were.

"Come," she said, reaching out a hand for Rachel's. "Let us go and tidy up quickly."

For just a moment she held the child's one hand while he still held the other. And their eyes met. He relinquished his hold and she turned away, taking her daughter with her.

Tall, slender, elegant even after vigorous outdoor exercise. And graceful and beautiful despite the gray of her garments. And perhaps, just perhaps, sheltering his child in her womb.

"The widow grows lovelier and more animated with every passing day," a voice said at his shoulder. It was languid, self-satisfied—Luttrell's voice. "She is ripe for the picking, would you say, Gerard?"

The earl's immediate impulse was to swing around and plant his friend a facer. He raised his eyebrows instead.

"You are the self-proclaimed expert on such matters, Harry," he said. "Do you need to ask my opinion?"

"It was a rhetorical question," the viscount said with a chuckle. "Are we to be doomed to chocolate, Gerard, as the only beverage with which to warm ourselves?"

"By no means," his lordship said, striding off in the direction of the stairway arch. "Come with me."

Chapter 13

There was to be a Christmas service in the village church during the evening. Most of the guests were planning to attend, Christina had learned, despite the snow and the absence of any sleighs in the carriage house. It would be a walk of more than a mile through the snow, but several of the gardeners and stable hands had made an attempt to clear the worst of the drifts from the driveway—though apparently the prospect of walking to church on Christmas Eve through snow had its attraction for most of them.

Between an early dinner and the service, they were expecting the village carolers to call, as they did every year. But this year fires would be lit in the large fireplaces in the hall. They would not give a great deal of heat, but they would take away the worst of the chill and they would at least make the hall look more cheerful than usual. Also this year there would be hot spiced wassail for everyone after the caroling, and mince pies and Christmas cake. Usually only lemonade was served. The carolers had not come at all the year before because the countess had been in mourning.

The evening would be busy enough. And most of the guests had tired themselves considerably with the morning's frolics. The afternoon, then, had been intended by most of them as a time for relaxation, perhaps even sleep. Until, that was, the Earl of Wanstead made his announcement in the drawing room after they had all come inside and assembled there.

"Tomorrow is Christmas Day," he said. "I have a notion that several of you will wish to be left to your own resources during the morning. I will be spending some time entertaining the servants in here. In the afternoon, if everyone is agreeable and if the weather cooperates, there will be skating on the lake—and doubtless a bonfire again." He paused for the flurry of enthusiasm to die down. "But the evening might be a problem—the ball is not scheduled until the day after tomorrow."

"We can dance in here again tomorrow evening, Cousin Gerard," Margaret suggested eagerly.

"I have another idea." He smiled about at them. "It will involve all of us in hard work."

There was a general groan.

"We are going to have a Christmas concert in the ballroom," he said. "I am putting Lady Hannah in charge of drawing up a program. She has already agreed to do it. She will see to it that there is some variety of items—one would hate to have twenty or so people stand up one after the other before the gathering in order to give a rendition of the same Christmas carol."

"Why not form a choir, sing the one carol—preferably one that does not have twelve verses—and get on with the dancing, Gerard?" Ralph Milchip suggested.

"No, no." The earl held up his hands to quell the laughter. "We are going to do this thing properly. We are going to entertain one another. We are going to enjoy ourselves."

"I think it a splendid idea, my lord," Susan Gaynor said. "We will play our pianoforte duet, Lizzie, will we?"

"There is only one rule," his lordship added. "Everyone is to take part—with no exceptions. And anyone needing the ballroom or this room for rehearsals is to consult Lady Hannah, who will draw up a schedule. Now, if you will excuse me, Lady Rachel and I have a matter of importance to discuss."

"But we have only a little longer than twenty-four hours, Gerard," Jeannette complained.

"Ample time," he said unsympathetically, taking Rachel by the hand.

Christina was looking at him in surprise and some alarm. She got to her feet. But he held up a staying hand.

"This does not concern you, my lady," he said. "It concerns Rachel, Margaret, Aunt Hannah, and me. No one else."

She opened her mouth to protest.

"It is a secret, Mama," Rachel said solemnly.

She had a sweet singing voice. Meg and Aunt Hannah knew that. They were probably going to have her sing at the concert. The children were to take part too, then? Christina would not object to the secret, she decided, though she knew very well she would have done so just a few days before. There could be nothing wrong in it if Aunt Hannah approved.

But any chance that the afternoon would be a time of relaxation was gone. Everyone looked inward, many with severe misgivings, to discover what talent, if any, they might display for the general entertainment the following evening. And then almost everyone looked outward to protest to one another that they *had* no talent. Lady Hannah went quietly about among them, making lists of items for the program and of rehearsal times and places—and even a few suggestions. If Mr. Campbell had a good singing voice but was too bashful to sing a solo, why did he not sing a duet with some lady who was too shy to sing alone? Might she suggest Miss Milchip? The ballroom and the drawing room were declared out of bounds to everyone except the person or persons whose rehearsal time it was.

The children, Christina decided, would put on a Nativity play. But there were only six of them, and they would need a Mary and Joseph, an innkeeper and his wife, shepherds, kings, and angels. There were a few adults without any individual talent at all—or so they claimed—who would be only too glad to appear in the play, Laura Cannadine suggested. And she was right, of course. Lord and Lady Langan leaped at the chance to be the innkeeper and his wife. They would quarrel quite convincingly, they promised; she would box his ears; he would bluster and threaten all sorts of retaliation; they would offer the stable to the Holy Family with the most grudging reluctance.

And Viscount Luttrell with the Milchip brothers, after

looking somewhat taken aback when Christina suggested it to them, agreed to be the shepherds, and disappeared in the direction of the conservatory to whip into shape a scene on the hillside in which they would feed one another comic lines appropriate for the ears of ladies and children.

Laura agreed to form a heavenly host with Alice, singing offstage while her daughter stood in the stable and on the hillside looking angelic. Rachel and Paul Langan would be Mary and Joseph, and Tess, Matthew, and young Jonathan— if he could be persuaded not to exit stage right or stage left in the middle of his scene with his thumb in his mouth—would be the Wise Men. After all, Laura said briskly, the play would not be ruined if he *did* wander off. Nowhere did the Bible specifically state that there had been *three* Wise Men— though it would be a shame if the casket of myrrh did not find its way to the foot of the manger.

Rehearsals proceeded all over the house during the very time when everyone had hoped to relax. Christina was forced to admit, though, that despite the fact that many of them had done their share of grumbling, they had all thrown themselves into the preparations with a cheerful will.

She went down to the conservatory while the younger children were having their afternoon nap to see how the shepherds' part was progressing. It was funny, she was forced to admit. Jeremy Milchip was a shepherd who could not remain awake for longer than a minute at a stretch but nodded off and snored convincingly and believed nothing he was told when he *was* roused. His brother was a loud, superstitious complainer, who was quite convinced that the heavenly host was an army of extraterrestrials come to carry him off to the moon, and Viscount Luttrell was a gentle idiot who gazed vacantly about him and giggled whenever directly addressed.

The children would love it, Christina concluded. And Gilbert would surely turn over in his grave at this attempt to inject humor into the Christmas story.

"But you must, of course," she reminded the shepherds, "realize the truth when you finally go down to Bethlehem, and be transformed by it."

"We plan to work on that after tea, ma'am," Jeremy told her. He yawned hugely and noisily. "*If* I can stay awake long enough to go to Bethlehem, that is."

"Bethlehem, ha!" Ralph roared. He wagged one finger close to the side of his head and half closed one eye. "I were not born yesterday, I weren't, fellers. I don't trust no coves wot sings instead of talking like sensible folks and wot has wings sprouting from their shoulders and rings of light about their noggins. Stealing sheep they will be while we toddles off to see a babe wot ain't there."

The viscount giggled.

Christina laughed. "It is time for tea," she said. "I am sure you must be ready to rest from your hard labors."

They did not need any further persuasion. The brothers went on ahead while Viscount Luttrell laid a staying hand on Christina's arm. "I wonder if you could identify this plant for me, Lady Wanstead," he said while there was still a chance that he might be overheard. But he grinned when they were alone together and drew a pathetically droopy sprig of mistletoe from his pocket. "This one. I was despairing of ever finding a private moment in which to ask you."

"It is mistletoe, I believe, my lord," she said. "Shall we go up for tea?"

"Let me see." He reached up and rested it on the branch of an orange tree above their heads. "Yes, that will do nicely." And he reached for her, drew her close with circling arms, and kissed her.

She was a little more ready for his expertise today. She did not allow him to part her lips though he licked invitingly at them and murmured softly to her.

"Christmas aside," he said after he had lifted his head until his mouth was perhaps an inch from hers, "I suppose you must know you are the most beautiful, most alluring woman it has ever been my privilege to know." His voice was low, seductive, not at all teasing.

"And the most stupid or naive if I believe you," she said, smiling at him.

"I scarce know if I believe it myself," he assured her. "It is, I confess, a line I have used before. But never have I used it with so little forethought. I want you, my dear. I do believe I have fallen in love with you. What a nasty ailment that may prove to be! I have not suffered from it before. Is it deadly, do you suppose? Is it a terminal illness?"

She liked him, she realized. He was a rogue and a rake, but there was such a mingling of practiced gallantry and blatant teasing in his approach that it was impossible to be deceived and therefore hurt by him. He was not in love with her—he did not expect her to believe that he was. He wanted an affair with her, one in which he would make it clearly understood that there was to be no deep sentiment and no commitment. Only a shared enjoyment. And she would enjoy it, she thought. Or she would have if . . .

She wondered, and was not at all sure of the answer, if she would have been tempted had the situation been different.

"I like your silences," he said. "I like that enigmatic smile. It would look even lovelier framed by a pillow behind your head. You would not remain silent for long, though. I do not permit my women to love in silence." He grinned wickedly at her and kissed her again.

After which, she decided, she must firmly declare that they had paid enough homage to one small sprig of mistletoe for this occasion.

Someone cleared his throat from the open doorway of the conservatory.

"One hates to interrupt," the Earl of Wanstead said.

"But—" Viscount Luttrell had lifted his head and was looking down into Christina's eyes. "I hear a *but* about to be uttered. You cannot be persuaded to go away, Gerard?"

If the floor had opened up beneath Christina's feet, she would gladly have dropped through it. She resisted the urge to push violently away from the viscount and start trying to explain.

"I need to talk to her ladyship," the earl said. "About tomorrow's concert. Ralph told me she was here a few minutes ago."

"I must have a friendly word with Milchip," the viscount said with mock menace, stepping back. He bowed to Christina. "Until later, ma'am."

She turned away as he left the conservatory, and fingered the leaves of the orange tree.

"Should I have allowed myself to be persuaded to go away?" the earl asked softly.

"There was mistletoe," she said, despising her own eagerness to justify herself. "It would have been ill-natured to refuse to be kissed beneath it."

"Your head *does* look lovely framed by a pillow," he said.

She whirled around to face him, her eyes flashing. "I would have you know," she said, "that I am not your possession, my lord. Neither am I Viscount Luttrell's. I am not answerable to either of you or to anyone else." Which was a foolish thing to say, she knew even as she said it. She was this man's dependent.

"You are right," he said curtly. His face had that hard-jawed, cold-eyed look she remembered from his arrival at Thornwood. "And this scene ought not to have been surprising to me even without the existence of the invisible mistletoe. I know from bitter experience how well you are to be trusted, after all, do I not?"

Her eyes widened. "Trusted?" she said. "To do what, pray? To stay away from all other men for the rest of my life merely because of what happened yesterday? If you will remember, my lord, you yourself said that yesterday was an ending." And perhaps a beginning, he had said—if there was a child.

"If there should happen to be a child," he said coldly, echoing her thoughts, "I would like to know whose exactly it is, my lady."

She swayed on her feet and only half heard him swear profanely.

"I do beg your pardon," he said, running the fingers of one hand through his hair. "Devil take it, Christina, why am I always at my very worst with you? Do forgive me, I beg you. That was a—a filthy thing to say."

"If there should happen to be a child," she said, "the whole world will know exactly whose it is. It will be *mine*, mine alone. And I will love it with all the love in my heart, just as I love my daughters. Fortunately children need not bear the stigma of their paternity, whether legitimate or illegitimate. They are precious in themselves. If I am with child, you need not ask who the father is or whether I even know. It will not matter who the father is, and none of you will ever know—you, Viscount Luttrell, any other man I may allow into my bed during the next month or so."

His face was very pale. She was glad of it.

"I am sorry," he said. "The words are inadequate, but I mean them. I am sorry."

"For making it possible that *you* might be the father?" she asked. "For lying with me yesterday?"

"Yes, for that too," he said quietly. "It should never have happened. I am sorry."

She had felt only angry until this moment—blindly, furiously angry. But now she felt unaccountably hurt too, and empty, and bereft. She turned her back on him again and took a few steps farther away from him.

"Why did you come?" she asked him. "Just to ensure that Lord Luttrell did not enjoy today what you enjoyed yesterday?"

She heard him draw a deep breath and hold it for a few moments. "It sounds trivial now," he said. "I need your assistance—in a magic act I intend to put on at tomorrow's concert."

"Magic?" she said.

"A few things I have learned over the years," he said. "Mostly objects vanishing and reappearing elsewhere. It will amuse the children and perhaps some of the adults too. I need a female assistant."

"And you think I may be willing." She half turned to him.

"I *thought* you might," he said. "Now I think you probably will not. Will you?"

"Yes," she said.

Why? Just to prove him wrong? Because she was intrigued? Because it would solve the problem of what *she* was to do for the concert? Because such an act must be rehearsed and they would have to spend some time alone together? They always quarreled bitterly when they were alone together—or they made love.

"Thank you," he said. He had taken the few steps to the branch of the orange tree, beneath which she and Viscount Luttrell had been kissing when he had arrived. He reached up one hand and smiled rather ruefully. "There really was mistletoe. I suppose he has been carrying it about with him in the hope of getting you alone."

"Yes," she said.

Their eyes locked. She almost walked toward him—and toward the mistletoe. She almost acted as much without conscious thought or decision as she had at Mr. Pinkerton's hut the day before. But she caught herself in time.

"Come for tea," he said, breaking a moment of unbearable tension.

"Yes."

He had never really had much of a feel for Christmas. During his childhood it had been an occasion for adults only, a time when his uncle had invited guests, almost exclusively male, for hour upon hour of drinking and carousing. He had always been very careful to avoid his uncle as much as possible during the week or so following Christmas, when the man's temper had been more volatile even than usual.

In Canada he had always been invited out for Christmas while in Montreal and had celebrated with other winterers during his three stints in the Northwest. But really the day had always seemed much like many other days of the year.

This year was very different from any other. It was not just being in the vast comfort of Thornwood and knowing that it was his. It was not just being surrounded by congenial friends and even a few family members. It was not even just the snow and the greenery and the carolers and the rich smells escaping from the kitchen. It was not entirely the anticipation of the following two days in which the celebrations would reach their climax.

It was everything all combined and something over and above the sum of all the parts. He admitted that to himself as he sat in the earl's pew in the village church late on Christmas Eve, Margaret on one side of him, his aunt on the other. The church was full. The carolers were not perhaps the most musical choir he had ever heard, but the angel choir outside Bethlehem could not have warmed the hearts of the shepherds more thoroughly than they had warmed his heart earlier in the evening in the gloomy, chilly great hall at Thornwood—which had seemed neither gloomy nor cold with the carolers and all his guests and servants in it and Christina serving the mince pies while he ladled out the wassail.

Christina. She was seated on the same pew as he. If he leaned forward a little or back a little he could see her in her gray cloak and bonnet, seated next to Rachel, who was next to his aunt. Tess, who had been at her other side, was on her lap now and would doubtless be asleep soon. When he had been her age, he thought suddenly and for no apparent reason, his own mother had still been alive. He had only vague, flashing memories of both her and his father—they had died when he was five. Had he been able to climb upon his mother's lap when he was tired and curl against her, his head on her bosom, knowing the world to be a safe, nurturing place?

He would see to it, he thought, that the world was always like that for both Tess and Rachel—until they were old enough to cope with its uncertainties alone. Even if he was at the other end of the earth he would see to it. They would remain here. She would not have to marry again and risk another bad marriage. The marriage to Gilbert must have been bad. He had not missed what she had probably not meant to reveal in her anger during the afternoon—her assertion that children, even *legitimate* children, did not have to bear the stigma of their paternity.

He listened to the service, gloried in that warm and wonderful but entirely intangible atmosphere of Christmas that was really so new to him, felt his heart expand with love for the Child who was being born into the world again tonight as He had been at Bethlehem almost two thousand years ago—and rested that love on the small family sitting just beyond his aunt.

He would never marry now. He would give no other

woman a claim to Thornwood. It would be *her* home in which to bring up her children in safety and peace. And after the children were grown up and married and moved to the homes of their husbands? Well, then, it would be her home to grow old in. She would never have to face the humiliation of being compelled to live with younger relatives, who might not want her. Immediately after Christmas, certainly before he returned to Montreal, he would rewrite his will. Unlike his predecessor, he would see to it that the countess had some private settlement, some modest fortune on which to live in the event that he predeceased her.

Tess was fast asleep by the time the final hymn came to an end and the church bells peeled joyfully. Rachel was big-eyed with fatigue, the side of her head against her mother's arm.

"They will wake up in the fresh air," Lady Hannah said cheerfully, "poor little lambs. But they will sleep as soon as their heads touch their pillows at home. Would you like to hold my hand, Rachel?"

Rachel was a polite little girl and would have accepted the offer without a murmur. But it was very clear to the man who had remembered losing his own parents at the age of five that she wanted only Christina tonight.

"Perhaps," he said, "Rachel could hold her mama's hand, Aunt, if I carried Tess." He looked at Christina. "It would be a shame to wake her, but she is too heavy for you to carry all that way."

"Thank you," she said after a moment's hesitation.

She had had the forethought to bring a warm blanket. They wrapped it carefully about the sleeping child, and he took her into his own arms, pillowing her head on his shoulder. She was all warm, limp, trusting babyhood. He felt curiously like crying.

And so they walked home together, he and the countess and her family. He met Lizzie Gaynor's eyes briefly as he stood up from the pew—they had walked to church together. But she was far too well-bred to show any disappointment she might have felt at seeing him encumbered with a child. She turned and smiled beguilingly at Sam Radway.

It was not a lonely walk home. All about them were family and guests, some of them conversing quietly and walking as fast as they could in order to get in out of the cold, others laughing and dawdling and resuming some of the games that had occupied them during the morning. And yet it felt curiously like a lonely walk—or at least a lone walk.

It felt like family—the family he had not known as a child beyond the age of five, the family he had never had as a man because . . .

Because the woman at his side had chosen to make this family with another man. With his childhood tormentor. She was not his wife. These were not his children. He heard a gurgling in his throat and swallowed.

"There is not too much farther to go, sweetheart," she said to Rachel, whose footsteps were lagging. And she opened her cloak, wrapped it about the child, and drew her close against her side. Her eyes met the earl's. They had not spoken a word to each other since leaving church.

"If you think you can carry Tess the rest of the way," he said, "I'll carry Rachel—if she will permit me."

"She is heavy," Christina warned him.

He smiled at her. Rachel's large, overtired eyes were gazing longingly up at him from the folds of her mother's cloak.

And so Tess once again changed hands—she did not awake though she grumbled sleepily. And he opened his greatcoat, stooped down, enveloped Rachel in its folds, and stood up with her. She was cold. She snuggled against him and yawned.

"I suppose," Christina said as they walked on, "I should have left them at home. But they both wanted to come, and Gilbert always insisted upon it. Besides, tonight seemed—special. I wanted them there with me."

She felt it too, then—the specialness of this Christmas?

"Christmas was always celebrated as a strictly religious occasion," she said. "There was never any fun, never any real joy."

The best thing Gilbert had ever done for her, he thought without even a twinge of guilt, was to die young.

"This year," she said, "there is such joy." And yet she

spoke the words with a wistfulness that made her sound
more unhappy than joyful.

"We have been blessed with the perfect setting," he said.
"I am accustomed to winter snow, but I remember how rare
it is here, especially at Christmas. Have you noticed the sky
tonight, Christina? The moon and the stars seem so close
that one might expect to be able to reach up and pluck one."

"It is as well we cannot do so," she said. "Happiness cannot be plucked or held and hoarded. It has to be recognized
in fleeting moments and accepted wholeheartedly and remembered with gratitude."

Had she remembered with gratitude?

He had suppressed memory with bitterness.

"I will remember this Christmas," he said.

"Yes."

It had been a short conversation. It had also been the kind-
est they had shared in longer than ten years.

Rachel did not fall asleep. She was still half awake when
they arrived back at the house. But the hall was full of chattering, laughing people removing outdoor garments before
going up to the drawing room for promised hot drinks. It
would seem cruel simply to set her down.

"I'll carry her up," he told Christina, and followed her up
the stairs to the nursery.

He set Rachel down in the bedchamber she shared with
Tess. Christina bent over one of the beds, intent on undressing the younger child without waking her.

"Good night," he said.

But before he could straighten up and take his leave,
Rachel wrapped her arms about his neck.

"I wish," she said, her voice fiercely passionate, "I *wish*
you could stay forever and ever. Mama says your home is
far away. I wish it was here. I wish you were my papa."

"Rachel!"

Christina clearly shared the embarrassment he felt.
Though there was something stronger than embarrassment
in him. He hugged the child and then released her firmly.

"Any man would be honored to be your papa, Rachel," he
told her, "and Tess's. I am your papa's cousin and therefore

your relative too. I always will be. When I have gone back home, perhaps your mama will let you write to me occasionally, and I will write to you with her permission. I will always think of you and always love you. But we still have some days together here—all of Christmas. Go to sleep now, and when you awake there will be one of the happiest days of your life awaiting you. Good night."

"Good night," she said—and yawned loudly.

Christina, he noticed, had not turned. She was still bent over Tess's bed. He left the room, passing the children's nurse in the doorway.

Chapter 14

Christmas morning had always been busy. In Gilbert's time there had been extended prayers for family and servants early in the morning, followed by visits made to the cottages of the farm laborers and other poor people of the village. The visits had been grand, formal affairs. The family had remained in the carriage for the whole tedious ceremony, while the recipients of the Hall's munificence had been called from their houses to pay homage in shivering discomfort in exchange for their basket of food.

This Christmas morning was to be just as busy, if not more so. But whereas Christina had never particularly enjoyed it in former years, this year there was the anticipation of joy beyond the morning and even during it.

This year there were to be gifts for the children, and Christina hoarded to herself the novelty of the occasion by taking them into her private sitting room and enjoying the luxury of almost an hour alone with them. She had bought them porcelain dolls, which she had dressed herself with meticulous and loving care, as well as books and a few other small items. But there were gifts too from Meg and Aunt Hannah and their nurse—and little fur muffs from the earl.

Their excitement brought tears to Christina's eyes. And the tears brimmed over when they presented *her* with gifts—a bright painting from Tess, who explained that the fat yellow blob with four pink projections, the whole surmounted with a curly black fringe, was her mama, and a linen handkerchief from Rachel, who had embroidered with rather ragged stitches a blue flower in one corner.

"I could not have done it alone, Mama," she admitted gravely. "Nurse helped me."

Christina hugged them both tightly. "They are the most precious gifts I have ever had," she said. "I would not exchange them for all the gold, frankincense, and myrrh in the world." Her children were well versed in the Christmas story.

But the hour could not be prolonged. There were other duties to be performed. Besides, the children were eager to return to the nursery to show their gifts to the other children and see what they had had.

There were the guests to greet at breakfast and then the servants to entertain in the drawing room while the earl spoke with each of them and gave each a Christmas bonus—a new experience for them. It was a vast improvement, Christina thought, on the old tradition of prayers, at which the servants had stood at silent attention while the family sat in solemn state. Gilbert's version of piety had been so very lacking in warmth and compassion. This morning there was not a single prayer or reading from the Bible or reflection on the religious significance of the day. But if what had begun in the stable at Bethlehem had been all about love and hope and joy, then it was being continued this morning, as never before, in the drawing room at Thornwood.

When the housekeeper finally signaled to the servants that it was time to return to their posts, Christina would have left the room with them. She did not wish to be alone with the earl. She had been considerably embarrassed the night before by Rachel's words. The worst of it was that she had been weaving fantasies of her own, even if only half consciously. Walking home from church, they had seemed so much like a family—a close and loving family. The sight of him walking beside her, first with Tess in his arms and then with Rachel right inside his greatcoat, had turned her quite weak at the knees. And then his presence with her in the girls' bedchamber . . .

And then Rachel's words!

"Please stay a moment," he said now, and she was forced

after all to be alone with him in the drawing room. She turned to look at him as calmly as she could.

"Thank you for the children's gifts," she said. "They will thank you themselves, of course, but it was very kind of you."

He inclined his head to her. Had he too been embarrassed last night? she wondered. Or horrified?

"Do you have a spare moment in which to practice magic?" He grinned suddenly and her heart somersaulted—he looked so very like that exuberant boy of her memories.

"Not this morning," she said. "There are all the baskets to deliver." She might have given directions that some of the servants take them, but it was a duty she did not choose to delegate.

"The baskets?" He raised his eyebrows.

She explained.

"I really do not know much about life on a great estate, do I?" he said ruefully afterward. "It is a lovely idea. May I help?"

"That will not be necessary, my lord," she said. "Aunt Hannah and Meg have promised to accompany me."

But three is an awkward number," he said. "If you all go together, the task will take just as long as if one went alone. If you form two groups, one person is doomed to be alone. Two groups of two would be better."

"Yes," she admitted.

"And the deliveries could be made in half the time."

"Yes."

"We will send Margaret and Aunt Hannah out together, then," he said. "And you and I will go together. We will need two carriages, will we not? I had better go and see if it is possible to take them out this morning. Will you speak with the other two ladies, Christina, and organize who is to go where?"

He opened the door for her, followed her out of the room, and then strode off about his own business.

Less than half an hour later they were on their way, the earl and the countess in one carriage, Margaret and Lady Hannah in the other. But although they had only half the cottages to visit, this particular duty did not take any less time than usual. For one thing the coachman drove at cautious speed through the snow. For another they descended from the carriage at each cottage, stepped inside, and stayed to talk. Wherever there were children, his lordship gave them sixpence each—he seemed to have an inexhaustible supply in the deep pocket of his greatcoat. They left laughter and genuine smiles behind them as they moved on.

"It has been a pleasant morning," he said after they had made their last call and were seated inside the carriage again. "One misses a great deal of the warmth of family life in a large home like this when one is—alone."

"Yes." She turned her head away to look out of the window.

"I often wonder what my life would have been like if my parents had not died when I was so young." His voice sounded nostalgic, as if he were thinking aloud rather than addressing her. "I was younger than Rachel is now, you know. And then brought up by an uncle of uncertain temper and with two male cousins who resented me for companions—my aunt did not die until I was eleven, when Margaret was born, but she was a shadowy figure. I was almost unaware of her presence. I believe my mother must have been constantly present in my life before she died. There is a feeling of warmth and safety associated with her memory. I believe I spent the rest of my childhood missing her."

She could not look away from the window, could not say anything. The urge to reach for him, to try somehow to soothe him for the loss of a mother years and years ago was almost irresistible. He would think she had windmills in her head. She did not want to think of him as a man who was perhaps essentially lonely.

"You had the love and stability of family life that I missed," he said. She could tell that he had turned his head toward her now. His voice showed that he was aware of her. "You were older when your mother died. Sixteen, was it not?"

"Yes." She nodded.

"I remember," he said, "that you still grieved for her when—when we met."

"It had been only two years," she said.

There was a short silence. "Is your father still living?" he asked her then. "Pardon me for not knowing the answer. And for not asking you about him before now."

"He is still living," she said and tried to think of some other topic with which to change the subject. Nothing presented itself to her mind.

"I am most dreadfully sorry for not asking until now," he said. "It was very remiss of me. Perhaps you would have liked to invite him to join the house party. Would you have had him here for Christmas if I had not suddenly announced my intention of coming to Thornwood? Or would you have gone to spend the holiday with him? He must enjoy seeing his granddaughters."

"No," she said, "there were no plans. I believe he had made other arrangements."

"I see," he said. "He was an amiable gentleman, Christina. I liked him. Everyone did."

Yes, everyone had liked Sir Charlton Spense.

"That letter was from him," she said abruptly. "The one you handed me a few days ago." She remembered too late how he had witnessed her reaction to that letter, how she had asked for an advance on her allowance soon after reading it.

His silence told her that he remembered too.

"He is living at home," she said. "He is in good health."

She could tell that his eyes were watching her closely. "When did you last see him?" he asked.

She considered not answering at all. Or lying. She laughed instead. "Ten and a half years ago," she said, "on my wedding day. After that I was forbidden to communicate with him or even to speak his name—just as I was forbidden to speak yours."

"Ah," he said softly as the carriage was drawing to a careful halt before the horseshoe steps outside the house. "There was more to it than I ever knew, then, was there?"

It was not phrased as a question that required an answer. He did not wait for one. He opened the door even before the coachman could descend from the box, and vaulted out onto the snowy terrace. He set down the steps and reached up a hand to help her down.

"We will speak of it before I return to London," he said. "It is time the truth was spoken, Christina. But not today. Or tomorrow. It is Christmas."

"Yes," she said.

"Let us enjoy it," he said, his eyes looking directly into hers. "We are both in need of some good memories, I believe."

"Yes."

She half ran up the steps ahead of him and proceeded directly through the great hall to the staircase arch without looking back. She might have disgraced herself and burst into tears if she had done so. It was not a day for tears. It was a day for joy.

And part of her, strangely enough, was bursting with it.

It was Christmas. And she was spending it with her children, her aunt, her sister-in-law, congenial house guests, and—and him.

It was a time for gathering good memories.

Not everyone went skating during the afternoon. Some protested their need for quiet rest in preparation for the evening's concert. Others chose to stay to rehearse. But a sizable group of young people and children trekked off to the lake in the wake of three grooms, each of whom carried a large box of skates.

The Earl of Wanstead walked with Margaret. He had watched with interest and approval her transformation from the restless, almost petulant girl who had greeted him on his arrival at Thornwood to the smiling, exuberant young lady of the past few days.

"You are enjoying Christmas, Margaret?" he asked her.

"Oh, yes," she assured him, her eyes aglow. "I have always hated it until this year. You must remember what it was like when Papa was living."

There had never been gifts. Never anything to make the day much different from any other except that there would be goose for dinner and rowdy, drunken adults to be avoided at all costs.

"It did not change when Gilbert was master here?" he asked. He partly knew the answer, but he was curious to know more. If he had thought of Christina at all during the lost years—and despite himself he *had* thought of her, of course—it had been to imagine her living in the proverbial lap of luxury, all her whims indulged. Though Gilbert had never been the most amiable of boys, it was true.

"Oh yes, it changed," Margaret said with a grimace. "Totally. Gilbert discovered God soon after he married Christina—that was how he described it to us, anyway. I did not say so while he was alive, but I really had no wish to discover or worship his God. All was sin and penance and sobriety and morality and—oh, I could go on and on. Rodney was fortunate. He was old enough to leave home. He went traveling. Though that did not turn out to be fortunate for him in the end, of course—he drowned in Italy. But I was a girl and still a child and stuck here. It was dreadful, Cousin Gerard. I even used to long to have Papa back—and you. You were always kinder to me than anyone else after Mama died."

He hated himself for asking the question. It seemed somehow underhanded. "Christina did not try to make Thornwood a happier place?" he asked.

She looked at him and then straight ahead through the trees. "No," she said at last. "Except occasionally when Gilbert went to London. He never took her with him. He would not take me either when I was old enough to make my come-out. He called it the most sinful and the most extravagant city in the world, unfit for either his wife or his sister. Sometimes we used to have picnics when he was gone. Sometimes we used to laugh."

"You have laughed a great deal in the past week," he said. "As you used to do when you were a child."

"It is good to have you home again, Gerard, and to find that you have not changed." She smiled at him. "Is skating as difficult as waltzing?"

"The essential difference," he said, "is that there is no

shame in having to lean on your partner when you are skating. Do you want me to teach you? Or is there someone on whom you would prefer to lean?"

Her eyes danced with merriment. "I believe," she said, "Lizzie Gaynor would be severely disappointed if I monopolized your attention, Cousin Gerard. Before we left the house I overheard her telling at least half a dozen people in a group together that she was *terrified* of ice, that she would *never* in a million years be able to skate, but that you had promised to teach her and to keep her safe. She trusts you to do just that—you are *so* strong, you know." She batted her eyelids at him in a fair imitation of Lizzie.

It was true. He had said that, or been maneuvered into saying it. He had given up all thought of courting Lizzie with a view to marriage. Indeed, he had given up all thought of marriage to anyone—ever. But he was painfully aware that her interest had been piqued by the invitation to Thornwood and that both she and her mother were eager to bring him to the point over Christmas.

"And has anyone promised to keep *you* safe?" he asked Margaret. "Is there any one special gentleman?"

"Not really," she said after tipping her head to one side and thinking for a few moments, "though I like Mr. Frederick Cannadine exceedingly well and I believe he likes me. You cannot know how wonderful it is to meet and mingle with people of roughly my own age, both ladies and gentlemen. And to know that enjoying oneself is not prohibited. I do not want to make the mistake of fixing my interest on one single gentleman too soon, Cousin Gerard. Did you mean it when you said I am to have a Season this coming spring?"

"With all my heart," he said. "It is a crime that you have not already had one."

"But then I would not have it to look forward to," she said, smiling brightly. "Perhaps it is frivolous to long so much for a Season with all its balls and other entertainments, but if it is, then I am frivolous and do not care. I want to be free when I go there, Cousin Gerard. I want my hand and my heart to be unattached. Perhaps I will bestow both eventually on Mr. Cannadine—if he is willing to bestow his on me. But I want to be quite, quite sure first."

It had been his opinion on meeting Margaret a week and a half before that she was immature for her years. But he could see now that he had mistaken innocence and naïveté for immaturity. She had a great deal of common sense, even wisdom.

"As the daughter of an earl," he said, "you could probably snare a duke, Margaret, if there is one available."

They both laughed.

"If he is young, handsome, wealthy, kind, and inclined to love me to distraction," she said, "then I will grab him." She laughed again. "Provided I love him to distraction too, of course."

But they had arrived on the bank of the lake. The gardeners had done a superb job of sweeping the snow from a large expanse of the lake's surface so that the ice was smooth and gleamed in the afternoon sunlight. There was a great bustling as everyone rummaged through the boxes to find skates the right size for each pair of boots.

Some of them could already skate well and took to the ice with effortless confidence. Several had tried it before and were willing to venture out on their own to slide gingerly forward, arms outstretched, legs braced apart. A few had never before had the opportunity or the courage to skate.

Frederick Cannadine, a competent, if not an accomplished skater, offered his assistance to Margaret. Andrew Campbell took both Susan Gaynor and Clara Radway out, one on each arm. Geordie Stewart took Christina's arm firmly through his. Jeannette, laughing, not with derision but with the sheer pleasure of the occasion, took a wobbling Ralph Milchip by the hand. John and Laura Cannadine were instructing the children, he on the ice, she safely on the bank, though Rachel had gone off on her own to one end of the skating area and had quietly set about teaching herself.

The earl looked into the wide, nervous eyes of Lizzie Gaynor and smiled. "I will not let you fall," he promised her.

But not letting her fall, he discovered over the next hour,

involved holding her left hand with his left while his right arm circled her waist, held her close against his side, and supported almost the whole of her weight. She was small and shapely, his body told him, as his eyes had done before. Very feminine. She was timid and trusting and bright and laughing. Very alluring, he thought dispassionately.

"I do not know how you can possibly be so steady on your skates, my lord," she said admiringly as they glided together across the expanse of the ice, half turning her head toward him so that her pretty profile showed to advantage framed by her fur-trimmed hood. "I know that I could trust my life to you."

"With practice," he said, "you would be just as steady, Miss Gaynor. There are certain techniques to successful skating, but mainly it involves a combination of balance and confidence."

"I could never have either, I do declare," she said. She laughed lightly. "And why should I when I have such a steady partner to lean upon?"

Milchip, he noticed, had just taken a tumble to the ice, pulling Jeannette, a surefooted skater, down with him. They were both finding the situation vastly amusing and were being teased mercilessly by Luttrell and John Cannadine, who was also offering to haul them both back to their feet. Christina still had her arm through Stewart's and was moving slowly, but she was using the supporting arm merely for confidence. She was doing the skating herself. She was frowning slightly in concentration.

Life with Gilbert had been undiluted gloom, he thought—but of course he had suspected that even before Margaret had confirmed it. Christina had never tried to lighten the gloom. She had never laughed except when Gilbert went away, leaving her behind. He should be gloating, the earl thought. It should give him a fierce sense of satisfaction to know that she must have been unhappy. But he could only wonder that he had not realized before this morning that there must have been more behind her sudden rejection of him and acceptance of his cousin than had appeared at the

time. Gilbert had never allowed her to mention his name—
or her father's. Why her father?

Rachel fell, picked herself up without a murmur, and kept
on trying to skate. One day he would teach her, he thought.

Jeannette had skated ahead of Milchip, goaded by the
teasing though she was still laughing. She performed a few
graceful spins and then a twirling jump. She was moving at
some speed too. She stopped and executed a deep curtsy in
response to the applause and whistles that greeted her performance.

"Oh," Lizzie said, "how I wish I could do that. I suppose
I could if only I had the courage."

"It is usually advisable," he said, chuckling, "to learn to
walk before one tries running. Miss Campbell grew up in
Canada and is accustomed to long winters and frozen rivers
and lakes. She has been skating since she was a child."

"You are telling me that I am incapable of skating well,
then, my lord?" Lizzie said, pouting prettily up at him. "I
must certainly prove you wrong."

At first it seemed that she was merely going to try to do
what Christina was doing. She shifted her weight over her
feet and slid her arm through his. She performed a few sensible glides, using his arm for a prop. But then she laughed
gaily and released her hold altogether.

"Watch me!" she commanded him and pushed off alone,
extending her arms gracefully.

Fortunately for her he had the presence of mind to in-
crease his own pace so that he was close enough when she
lost her balance to catch her before she fell all the way to the
ice. But she bit her lower lip and lifted her right foot from
the ice as he held her up.

"Oh!" she said.

"You have hurt yourself?" he asked in some concern.
Deuce take it, he had promised not to let her fall.

He held her tightly to his side while she gingerly moved
her foot and winced.

"It will be better in a moment," she assured him.

But there was no point in taking any further risks even

though she set the foot back to the ice and smiled bravely at him.

"I do not want to spoil anyone's fun," she said, her large eyes suddenly bright with unshed tears.

"Nonsense!" he told her. "You will spoil everyone's fun only if you insist upon making a martyr of yourself. Look— the bonfire has been lit and the chocolate brought down from the house." And on his instructions broad logs had been drawn up as close as possible on three sides of the fire, so that they might sit in some comfort to remove their skates and consume their hot drinks. "We will go and warm our-selves and you can rest your foot."

"I can sit there alone, my lord," she assured him as he guided her slowly toward the bank. "You must come back and skate longer. There are other ladies who would welcome your escort, I am sure. You cannot possibly wish to skate only with me—or to sit beside me and watch everyone else. It has been selfish of me to take all your time."

"Nonsense!" he said again briskly, stepping up onto the bank and bending down to scoop her up into his arms and carry her across to the fire.

But they were not the only ones leaving the ice. The fire and the arrival of the chocolate pots were enticing some. Others had realized there had been an accident and came to inquire.

"I was attempting to skate alone," Lizzie explained gaily. "I had already taken too much of Lord Wanstead's time. I would have fallen and perhaps broken a leg but for him— silly me. But he came skating after me and saved me." She bit her lip as he unstrapped the skate from her right boot though he did so carefully without moving the foot. "Oh dear, I fear I must have sprained my ankle. How fortunate for me that his lordship was unwilling to let me leave him." She winced—and smiled bravely with watery eyes.

She would not hear of spoiling everyone's enjoyment by allowing the earl to take her back to the house immediately. Her ankle would surely be better if she but rested it and warmed it at the fire, she insisted. But after they had all drunk their chocolate and were warm again inside and out and had sung some Christmas carols at Laura Cannadine's suggestion, it was clear that the ankle really had sustained some damage.

"If you will but give me your arm to lean upon, my lord," Lizzie said, "I shall contrive quite well."

But he could not allow her to walk the distance to the house. She was no featherweight, but he had grown accustomed to heavy manual labor over the years. He instructed her to set her arm about his neck and carried her home. She talked cheerfully the whole way to the rest of the party, raising her voice and protesting that the accident had been entirely her own fault and not at all his lordship's. Indeed, but for his devotion in following her when she skated away from him, her injuries might have been considerably worse.

"How romantic it is," she said gaily, "to have such a sturdy champion."

He was very glad—for more than one reason—to reach the house at last. But of course he would carry Miss Gaynor all the way up to her room, he insisted when she told him in the great hall that he must set her down. She laughed merrily and looked back at everyone else as they stripped off scarves and gloves and hats.

"And no one is to be naughty and accuse us of doing anything improper," she said, raising her voice again to carry over the hubbub of noise. "Billings will send for my maid and my mama to come to my room immediately, will you not, Billings?"

The earl's eyes met Christina's across the hall and he raised his eyebrows in mute appeal.

"Of course no one would say or even think any such thing, Miss Gaynor," she said with all her usual cool dignity. "We have far too high an opinion of your integrity. Lady Gaynor will come without delay when she hears of your mishap, I am sure. In the meantime I will come up with you and see that you are made comfortable and have everything you need."

The earl half smiled at her as she swept past him and through the stairway arch. He followed her with his heavy burden.

Chapter 15

The guests assembled an hour earlier than usual for Christmas dinner, which was to be taken in the state dining room. It was a very splendid setting indeed, everyone agreed. Christina, gazing about the table, remembered words that had been spoken to her that morning—*It is Christmas. Let us enjoy it. We are both in need of some good memories, I believe.*

All day she had tried consciously to enjoy each passing moment. She had tried to store away memories.

In some ways neither was difficult. This was Christmas as she had never celebrated it before. With the exception of Lizzie Gaynor's accident, which had not after all been serious enough to keep her from the dinner table, the day had been perfect. It had seemed that everyone was happy, that everyone was in harmony with everyone else. If there were such things as peace on earth and goodwill among men, they had been found at Thornwood this year.

There were people who were already looking beyond Christmas, of course. There was the earl himself planning to return to Canada during the spring; there was Lizzie, for whom the courtship she had expected was not progressing fast enough, making a determined push to bring it to a successful conclusion; and there was Mr. Geordie Stewart, for whom the New Year was to have more happy significance than Christmas.

Christina smiled as her eyes met his briefly along half the length of the table. Then she gave her attention to Lord Langan beside her, who was telling his table companions about his race horses.

Mr. Stewart was to attend another house party—at his sister's home in Scotland—for the celebration of the New Year. There was to be a lady guest there, a widow, who had chosen to spend Christmas with her late husband's family in order to inform them of her intention of marrying again during the spring. She and Mr. Stewart were to announce their betrothal next week. He had confided the news to Christina while they had skated together during the afternoon.

How glad she was that she had given up the idea of courting Mr. Stewart for herself. Mrs. Derby, he had explained happily, had three children, all below the age of ten. He was eagerly looking forward to being a stepfather. Mrs. Derby was a fortunate lady.

Oh, yes, Christina thought as the final covers were removed, it had been a happy day. If she did not look ahead, there was happiness to feel and to hold inside, and numerous memories to carry forward with her. And the day was not yet over. The gentlemen were not to linger over their port this evening. There was the concert in the ballroom to be enjoyed—and enjoy it they would even though it had taken some hard work to prepare and many of them professed to feel nervous or inadequate or both. It was nothing so very out of the ordinary, after all. Most of them were adept at providing drawing room performances for small gatherings.

But dinner was not quite at an end after all. Christina looked along the table, expecting the earl to signal her to rise. But he merely smiled at her and got to his feet, holding out his hands to indicate that his guests were to keep their places. Private conversations ended, and everyone turned his way.

"We have made merry today," he said. "It has been a happy day, at least for me and I hope for everyone else. I wish to thank you, my friends and my family, for coming here at my invitation and making it a Christmas to remember. And I wish to thank her ladyship, the Countess of

Wanstead, for acting so tirelessly and so graciously as my hostess."

"Yes, indeed," Lord Milchip said, and led enthusiastic applause.

In a few more days, Christina thought, inclining her head in acknowledgment of the compliment, this would all be over. She would come into this room from time to time and gaze at its empty magnificence and try to remember where everyone had sat for Christmas dinner. She would try to remember the Christmas decorations and the smells of the food. She would try to recall how he had looked, how he had sounded, what he had said.

He would be gone.

But there was the rest of Christmas to enjoy.

"It has struck me," the earl continued, "that this is what Christmas was always meant to be like—family and friends together, simply enjoying one another's company. But even so I have been aware all day that the peculiar wonder of the church service last night has formed the very basis of today's happiness. It seems to me that it would be a good idea to recapture some of that wonder now before we proceed to the ballroom for the concert. The candles, if you please, Billings."

Soon the only candles still burning were those in the candelabra that stood on the table. Their light cast shifting patterns of brightness and shadow over their faces. There was an immediate feeling of intimacy and coziness.

"We are going to listen to the Christmas story again," his lordship said. "Mr. Colin Stewart has agreed to read it from the Bible. He was the only one of us, you see, who protested that he has no talent to share with us at our concert. But I can recall meetings chaired by him, and I can remember my attention being held by the deep, rich tones of his voice as much as by what he said. Colin?"

The story of the Birth had a beauty and a simplicity that could never be spoiled—even when it had been read in Gilbert's toneless voice while his family had sat in stiff-backed silence and his servants had stood like stone statues. Its power could never be dimmed—even when it had been read from the lectern of the Norman church with all its rich evocation of history. Repetition and familiarity could never trivialize it.

But this evening there was something about the story that held them all more than usually spellbound. There was the focus on the gathering of friends that the dimming of the candles around them had created. There was the memory of a happy day and the culinary satisfaction of a superb meal just consumed. There was Colin Stewart's melodious speaking voice with its attractive Scottish burr. There was . . .

No, there was no real explanation, Christina thought when the reading came to an end and no one moved or said anything. Christmas was just this—peace, joy, love. But none of those words was quite adequate. Nor were all of them combined. No words could quite describe what it was. She only knew that whatever it was, she would never forget it.

"Thank you, Mr. Stewart," Winifred Milchip said, the first to break the silence, and doubtless taking herself as much by surprise as everyone else.

Christina met the earl's eyes along the length of the table, and they both smiled. She got to her feet.

"Yes," she said. "Thank you, Mr. Stewart. Shall we all gather in the ballroom within the next half hour?"

In one way, she thought as she led the way from the dining room with Lady Gaynor, living in a cocoon was preferable to stepping out into a larger, brighter, freer world. There were light and joy in this world—she seemed to have lived more intensely in the past week than she had done in all her life before. But there was the anticipation of pain too. The house was going to feel quite unbearably empty. . . .

Her life was going to be unbearably empty.

But then cocoons were not necessarily warm, comforting places either.

"How kind of his lordship," Lady Gaynor was saying, "to insist upon carrying my poor Lizzie down from her room to the dining room and now into the ballroom when he might as easily have summoned a servant for the purpose. Of course, I do believe he is quite devoted to her. Not that I ought to say so aloud, ought I?" She tittered. "Not yet at least."

"Excuse me." Christina smiled at her. "I must go up and prepare the children for their play. I do not doubt they are all almost sick with excitement."

Lady Hannah had scheduled the Nativity Play early in the program. It would have made an excellent finale, she had explained to the earl, but she was afraid that the children would grow tired and restless if they had to wait too long.

It was a great success. The Langans, usually very quiet and refined, were quite convincing as a vulgar, quarrelsome, bad-tempered couple; the three shepherds drew almost constant laughter. Laura Cannadine sang like an angel. But none of the adult performances could outshine those of the children, who had been well coached but whose individuality shone through nonetheless. The angel, decoratively placed behind Mary and Joseph at the manger, moved to one corner of the stable until she had a clear view of her papa in the audience. One of the kings grew tired of her beard and lifted it to her forehead. Another king walked off the stage with his thumb in his mouth before he had deposited his gift at the manger. The Virgin Mary ran after him and took it gently from him. Joseph picked up the baby to show to the shepherds and was seen to be holding it feet uppermost. The third king tripped over his robe and made a grand entrance.

But they played their parts with an earnestness that was endearing and as touching in its way as the reading of the Christmas story in the dining room earlier had been.

The Earl of Wanstead watched attentively. But he was equally aware of two other things—or rather, of two other persons. Lizzie Gaynor sat beside him, her injured foot propped on a stool. She leaned slightly toward him and turned to him every few moments to share some observation on the play. He wondered uneasily if he had said or done anything to compromise his honor with regard to her. Did he owe her a marriage offer? But then she was not the only single lady he had invited to the house party. Yet none of the others appeared to believe that he had invited them with the sole intention of proposing to them.

And he was aware too of Christina, who was frequently visible off at one side of the stage, directing her players and prompting them. He wondered if she realized how dazzlingly beautiful she looked tonight in her bright red gown. It had the elegant simplicity of design that he was beginning to recognize as characteristic of her. What an idiot he had been, he thought, imagining just two days ago that it would be possible once and for all to work her out of his system if he but completed what they had started at Vauxhall.

He knew that he would be bonded to her forever, more so now than ever before. There was a physical connection now. He wondered if she was with child and how soon she would know. He tried to remember why he hated her, why he would never again be able to trust her. And he wondered again what it was about the events of ten and a half years ago that he had not understood at the time.

But the concert moved onward, and it was certainly his duty to give it his whole attention. There were numerous musical items though none quite the same as the ones that had gone before. The magic act had been placed halfway through the program, not too late to be appreciated by the children. The earl and Christina had not had a great deal of opportunity to rehearse together, but they contrived well enough. She succeeded in looking lovely and charming and suitably startled as he drew colored silk scarves from her ears and—a little risqué, perhaps—a gold sovereign from the bosom of her gown. She held his hat while he dropped into it the silk scarves and drew out a silver-topped cane. He bowed over her hand and kissed it at the end of the act while she curtsied to the audience.

She looked, he thought, as if she was enjoying herself. She looked as if she might have put on weight, though that was doubtless an illusion. But somehow the tight-lipped, stiff-spined, too thin look had vanished, and her body appeared more supple, more curvaceous, more alluring. Her complexion appeared to glow with the flush of returned youth.

But he was nervous. Jeannette was to sing a few Scottish folk songs next to her own accompaniment. After that it was Rachel's turn. He hoped she would acquit herself well. It was hard to know with that child how easily she would hold up under the onset of nerves. She was almost always quietly grave except in flashing moments when one became aware of her as a child with deeply passionate feelings. And he hoped Christina would not disapprove. He did not know why she should. Aunt Hannah and Margaret both had approved. But one never knew with Christina. He well remembered that first afternoon in the ballroom.

Lady Hannah got to her feet after Jeannette's performance had been properly applauded. But the earl had already moved out of sight beyond the screen that hid future performers from the eyes of the audience. Rachel was there with Margaret, dressed in the flowing white-and-gold gauze dress her nurse, Margeret, and Aunt Hannah had made between them in secret haste, her loose hair entwined from crown to tips with finely cut gold ribbons. She looked terrified. He went down on his haunches and took both her hands in his.

"Remember," he said, "that you are the most graceful lady of my acquaintance." She and her mother.

Lady Hannah was speaking beyond the screen. "The Star of Bethlehem plays such an important role in the Christmas story," she said, "that sometimes it seems almost like an animate character in the drama. It is beautiful and serene and embodies brightness and hope and peace. Tonight we bring the star alive in the person of Lady Rachel Percy."

She had taken her place at the pianoforte, the earl saw when he looked beyond the screen. He squeezed Rachel's shoulder and released it. He set himself to watch both her and Christina, who was seated in the second row of chairs, a rather sleepy-looking Tess on her lap. She was looking, he thought, somewhat apprehensive.

But he could not keep a great deal of his attention on her during the next few minutes. He had seen the performance a number of times. Indeed, he had helped choreograph it with his cousin and his aunt. He had thought it sweet and musical and graceful. But tonight Rachel made it her own.

She danced as if she had all the stars at her feet, as if she were supreme among them, as if they must surely pay her homage. She danced on air. It seemed as if her silk slippers scarcely touched the floor. And she danced to some inner vision that set her face glowing though she did not once smile.

She was a child with so much beauty, so much imagination, as much passion locked within that one could only guess at the full extent of them and marvel at the occasional glimpse into the treasure that was Rachel.

She looked a little bewildered for a moment when she was finished. But when everyone clapped, she dipped rather stiffly into the curtsy she had practiced. And suddenly she looked again simply the rather plain, grave little girl she usually was.

The earl turned his gaze on Christina. She was not clapping. She was holding Tess and looking as if she had been sculpted of marble. Her face was pale in the candlelight. But when Rachel went to her, she hugged her close with her free arm in such a way that he could no longer see her face.

He did not know if he had made a mistake, if he had taken an unpardonable liberty with her daughter. He tried to feel the old irritation. If she was such a killjoy that she could not bear to see Rachel dance when the child was so very gifted, then perhaps she deserved to be shaken up.

But he could not feel irritation. Only anxiety, Rachel was her daughter, and she was a good mother. They were essentially strangers to him. He knew almost nothing of their lives as they had been lived before his appearance a week and a half ago. How could he presume to know what was best for her child?

Suddenly he felt depressed. Suddenly he wished he had not leaped so impetuously into this plan of coming to Thornwood for Christmas. He should have stayed away. The memories were going to be very sweet, it was true.

They were also going to be unbearable.

*   *   *

The concert was over. Christina had hugged and kissed her children and sent them off to bed with their nurse. Her presence was needed in the drawing room, where everyone was to gather for tea and conversation. After a long and busy day, no one seemed eager to see it end.

But she could not bear to be with everyone else just yet. She felt pained, desolate, guilty, bewildered—she did not know quite what word to put to her feelings except that they were hard to bear and harder to hide.

She let herself quietly into the state dining room, which was in darkness now though she could see quite clearly— the night sky beyond the windows was bright with moonlight and starlight just as it had been the night before. She moved to the table and set her hand on the back of the chair at its head. Where he had sat tonight. Already it seemed like a dream. Already she felt the painful loneliness of the coming weeks and months—perhaps years.

When the door opened and someone stepped inside and closed the door behind him, she felt her heart leap for one moment. But it was not so very dark. She could see clearly enough that it was not he.

"The room is rarely used," she said. "I enjoyed sitting in here tonight."

"So did I," Viscount Luttrell said, strolling toward her. "The candlelight was full on your face and your gown. It was difficult to keep my attention on my food. I understand, though, that it was appetizing fare."

She smiled at him.

She could have moved away. She could have turned the moment. But she was feeling bruised and lonely and upset, and for a moment too long she thought that she might find comfort in human contact. She made no resistance when he took her in his arms, though there was no mistletoe as excuse this time, or when his mouth came down open on hers. She even relaxed almost gratefully against him. But she drew back when she felt his hand on her bosom.

"Yes," he agreed softly against her lips. "That *was* indiscreet. My bedchamber later? There is a lock on the door and even a key, I am delighted to say. I am sure you can contrive to get there and back without being seen."

"No," she said with a sigh she had not intended to be audible. "You have misunderstood, my lord."

"Have I?" He still held her close. He looked deep into her eyes in the near-darkness. "Yes, by Jove, I have. You are no tease, are you? No with you means no. What a regrettable fact. You do not by any chance mean no tonight but perhaps yes tomorrow, do you?"

"No," she said.

"No," he repeated, "I did not think so. I do not often miscalculate." He loosened his hold on her. "I beg your pardon if I have caused you distress."

"You have not," she said. "Perhaps under different circumstances—" But she stopped abruptly, bit her lip, and then laughed.

He chuckled too and released her. "One can only imagine what those circumstances might be and regret that they cannot be contrived," he said. "Shall we adjourn to the drawing room?" He bowed and offered his arm.

But she shook her head. "Later," she said. "There is something I must do first."

There was not, of course. She wandered about the room after he had left, wishing that she had a shawl with her for greater comfort. She wondered how possible it was going to be to start a new life. She had married at the age of eighteen and had been wed for nine years, nine of the formative years of her life. She was now eight-and-twenty, with no idea how to be happy except in brief moments, and no idea how to create happiness about her. She only knew how to retreat inward to avoid pain.

And she feared that Rachel had learned the lesson as effectively as she.

It was for Rachel that she grieved tonight. If it was too late for her to change the direction of her own life, so be it. But something had to be done for Rachel. She owed it to her daughter. . . .

The door opened again and then closed behind the back of another man. Her eyes had grown accustomed to the darkness. There was no mistaking his identity even for a moment.

"I have brought you a shawl," he said, coming toward her. "Luttrell told me you had come in here."

It was a warm woolen shawl. He set it about her shoulders and she held it close.

"Thank you," she said.

"Did I do wrong, Christina?" he asked her. "Should I not have encouraged her to dance?"

She did what she had no idea she was about to do until she did it. She burst into tears and realized even as her hands shot up to cover her face that there was going to be no way of controlling them for a while. She felt his hands close about her shoulders, but she had leaned into one man already this evening for comfort and found none. She turned away from him and went to stand before the embers of the fire, her back to the room.

He handed her a large handkerchief without a word when her sobbing finally ended. She wiped her eyes and blew her nose firmly. She was not even sure herself why she had wept. It just seemed to her in a moment of painful clarity that she had never learned how to cope with life and that she had dragged her children into her own helpless darkness. And so the cycle would be perpetuated. . . .

He was kneeling before the hearth, she realized, in all his evening splendor, building a fire and then lighting it. He drew a chair close to it and motioned her to sit down.

"Tell me," he said, standing before her, one elbow propped against the mantel. "Did I do wrong? I did not mean to hurt you."

"You did not," she said, watching the flames catch hold, feeling the first thread of warmth. "I am the one who has done wrong. Always. All my life, it seems. Bringing misery to everyone I have ever loved. To Rachel." Only as she heard her own words did she realize how melodramatic, how self-pitying they sounded. And how true.

"Tell me about it," he said.

And so she told him about Rachel as a very young child, quiet and affectionate and trusting. Choosing Gilbert as a hero. Worshiping her father. Following him about whenever she had been allowed out of the nursery. Always wanting to do things for him to win his approval, his praise, his smiles. Persevering even when it had been obvious to her mother that even for his own child there would never be any warmth.

"She found her way into his study one day," she said. "She had watched him trim his pens once and thought she could do it herself to please him. When I came into the room with him, she was busy ruining his favorite pen, and she was humming a tune and dancing about the room at the same time." She swallowed awkwardly. "She smiled at him with all the sunshine behind her eyes and held out his pen." She bit hard on her upper lip.

"He was angry?" he prompted.

"He hit her so hard across the head," she said, "that she fell over. Then he spanked her more methodically. Then he made her stand on a chair in the hall for two full hours—at a time when the vicar and his wife were expected for tea. It was not just the broken pen. It was the singing and dancing that really infuriated him. He told her she was a child of the devil. She was four years old."

"The bastard!" the Earl of Wanstead said, barely suppressed fury in his voice.

"And I did nothing to defend her," she said, staring unseeing now into the fire. "Nothing—except to keep her away from him as much as possible afterward and to make sure that she did nothing to attract his attention. No singing, no dancing, no smiles, no laughter. I did nothing to defend my own child, and now I fear she will never recover."

"She will," he said. "All the beauty is there inside her and she is capable of letting it out. You saw that tonight."

"But she has me for a mother." She spread her hands over her face again, but wearily this time. There were no tears left.

"She is fortunate," he said. "You must not blame yourself, Christina, because she had a brutal father."

The silence extended between them. A silence that was gradually filled with unspoken words, almost as if their minds connected though they did not speak. She knew what he was going to ask next and was powerless to stop him. The words were quietly spoken.

"Christina," he asked her, "did he ever beat you?"

Sometimes out of anger, vicious cracks across the face or arms, once even with a whip. But he considered uncontrolled anger sinful and usually apologized very formally for such outbreaks—though he always went on to explain what shortcoming in herself had tempted him. At other times the chastisement had been more formal and methodical, punishment for sins, usually involving the way he claimed she looked at other men—correction he had called it. Painful and deeply humiliating.

"I cannot forget," the earl said, "that on two separate occasions you have cowered away from me as if you expected me to strike you. He was a wife-beater?"

"Yes," she admitted.

"It is as well for him," he said, "that he is already dead. He would suffer this night if he were still alive, Christina. He ruled you with terror? No, do not answer that. He is dead. Gone. I am the Earl of Wanstead now. I am master here now, though never yours. You and your children are free to be and to do whatever *you* wish. You are free. Look at me, please?"

She raised her eyes to his. To the golden boy who had lit her world for a couple of months one springtime long ago— so little happiness to occupy the space of twenty-eight years.

"You are free, Christina," he said. "Perhaps I did not like your choice of husband, but you could not have known what your decision would involve you in. I did not suspect it myself though I grew up with him. You must not blame yourself—for anything. You did protect your children as best you could and I can assure you that your love for them is quite apparent to them. You must not bear the burden of guilt any longer. You must understand that you are free. He died over a year ago. He is gone. You mourned him very correctly for longer than a year. You have paid your dues to both him and society. You owe nothing more to his memory."

She was still gazing at him. "Do I understand," she asked him, "that you are forgiving me?"

He stared back, the side of his hand against his mouth, his eyes unusually bright. "Yes," he said at last. "I am forgiving you, Christina."

She had not even known until that moment how much she had always craved his forgiveness—and his understanding. He still did not understand, but he had forgiven her anyway. The bitterness that had been between them for over a week was gone, she realized. It seemed like a precious Christmas gift.

"Go to bed," he told her. "I must return to the drawing room. I will make your excuses for you."

"Thank you," she said.

"And, Christina?" he said as she got to her feet and crossed the room to the door. "Rachel is very precious and not in any way crushed in spirit. She learned to go inward for strength—it is not a bad lesson to learn. But she is still capable of an outpouring of beauty for those around her. She will be a rare gem. I will not betray the trust she showed in me last night. I will write to her—all my life. And you will love her all yours—it will be sufficient."

"Thank you," she said again.

Chapter 16

The snow was beginning to melt—not off the lawns and fields and hills to any significant degree, but off paths and roadways from which it had already been partly shoveled. It was sad, some of the guests declared as they came down in gradually swelling numbers to a late breakfast. Their lovely white Christmas was almost at an end.

But it *had been* lovely, they reminded one another, and all good things had to end.

In fact the warmer weather and the melting snow were a blessing, Lady Hannah declared. Clear roads and driveways would enable all the invited guests to come to Thornwood for the ball. Her words served to remind everyone that in fact Christmas was not yet over after all. Perhaps the best part was yet to come.

And the snow was by no means gone. There was still at least one full day in which it might be enjoyed. The earl had purchased two sleds at the same time as he had bought the skates. Two ancient ones had been dug out of the loft of the coach house and put into smart working order again. One of the gardeners had made another new one.

A number of guests went sledding late in the morning—on the once forbidden hill. The earl went with them though he was aware that there was a great deal of work to be done in preparation for the ball. The countess was busy directing operations. He would only get in her way, he persuaded himself, if he stayed and tried to help. There was some truth to the old adage about too many cooks. Besides, it would not do to neglect his house guests.

He was rationalizing, of course. The truth was that he accompanied the sledders because he wished to escape from two problems, both female.

He had carried Lizzie Gaynor down to breakfast, though she had protested—through the person of Lady Gaynor— that she did not wish to be a nuisance and would gladly eat in her own room. And then he had carried her into the morning room, where he had left her with other company. She had insisted that she did not wish to keep him from his duties—and for once he had taken her at her word. But he could sense entrapment with every passing hour. His friends were even teasing him about it.

"I suppose," Ralph Milchip said when they were on their way out to the hill, "you will be carrying the fair Lizzie to the altar within the next month or so, Gerard?"

"You know, Ger," Luttrell added, "when you allow a young lady in your care to stumble on the ice and, ah, sprain her ankle, it is clearly understood by all her relatives and friends that you are obliged to make amends by marrying her."

"Sounds reasonable to me," Ralph agreed, shaking his head sadly.

And then there was Christina. He found it hard to look her in the eye this morning. He had spent a sleepless night remembering how he had always hoped vindictively that she would live to regret her choice of husband, that her marriage would prove to be a less than happy one. He had hoped she would grow sorry for putting money before love. He had never for a moment suspected how thoroughly his wish had come true.

He felt guilty.

He had wished her harm and Gilbert had done her harm. Was there any essential difference between what he had wished and what his cousin had done? He felt savagely regretful that he could not get his hands on Gilbert in order to punish him—but was it himself he found impossible to punish?

Christina—his beautiful, sunny-natured, warm, passionate Christina—had been the terrorized victim of a wife-beater, who had hidden his viciousness behind a mask of religion and morality. And now she blamed herself.

How could he look her in the eye?

But he had no choice when he came back from the hill with everyone else, all of them noisy and laughing and chilly. She appeared in the great hall while they were all disentangling themselves from scarves and muffs and other outdoor garments, and touched him on the arm.

"May I speak with you, my lord?" she asked him.

She looked her usual calm, dignified self—but he had learned last night, if he had not suspected it before, that she had had long practice at donning this particular mask, The hint of violet shadows beneath her eyes suggested that perhaps she had slept as little as he.

"I will come to the library in a moment," he told her. It was inevitable, of course, that she would need to consult him several times in the course of the day on the preparations for the ball.

She was standing in front of the large oak desk when he entered the room a couple of minutes later, her hands spread flat on its surface, her head bowed. She looked elegant and fragile and—and he did not know how he could speak to her except briskly, impersonally, as if he were speaking with a business associate.

"Is there any problem?" he asked. "I should have stayed instead of leaving the whole burden with you."

"No," she said. "Even my presence in the ballroom is unnecessary. The servants have everything well under control."

He stood where he was just inside the door. He licked his lips and rubbed his hands together. "What may I do for you?" he asked her.

"You said I was free," she told him. "I have never been free—very few women ever are. How free am I? Am I free to—to leave here without sacrificing my allowance?"

Ah. So he was not going to have even the dubious comfort in the coming years of picturing her living here in comfort, was he?

"I know you are my daughters' trustee," she said. "The

law, so ably administered by men, cannot trust a woman to look after her own children, you see. Are my children free to leave?"

"Where are you planning to go?" he asked her.

He heard her draw an audible breath as she examined the desktop with lowered head. "Home," she said. "I need to go back there."

To her father? In a way it was surprising she had not fled there soon after Gilbert's death. Surely being with her father would have seemed a more pleasant fate to her than remaining here when he was the new earl. Why had she been forbidden to communicate with her father? Why had she almost fainted when she had received his letter? Had it been the first in over ten years?

"The answer is yes," he told her. "Yes, you may leave. Yes, you may take your children with you—and the quarterly payments that are rightfully yours. Was that your first letter from him, Christina?" But she had been bound to remain here over Christmas because she had agreed to be his hostess?

"The first in his own hand," she said. "I have had two other letters in the past year, both written by someone called Horrocks."

"Your father is ill?" he asked gently. He remembered his impression from the handwriting on the outside of the letter that it had been written by an elderly or infirm person.

She shook her head slightly but did not immediately answer.

"It must be a shock," he said, "after ten years to find that his health has broken down. Would you have gone to him immediately if you had been under no obligation to me? I am sorry, Christina. Shall I arrange to have my carriage take you tomorrow. I will even escort you if you will allow me."

He was, he realized without any real surprise, quite irrevocably in love with her. Her joy was his; her pain was his. There was no point in further denial—not to himself at least.

But she was shaking her head more firmly.

"I think I should go alone at least at first," she said. "I shall leave Rachel and Tess with Aunt Hannah and Meg.

They will not mind, I think. I do not know quite what I will find."

He acted from instinct. He had not realized he had moved up behind her until his hands were clasping her shoulders. She turned and looked at him with a pale, wan face—the shadows beneath her eyes were quite pronounced now.

"What happened?" he asked her. "May I know? Was it me, Christina? Did I do something? Did I *not* do something? It was not just Gilbert's fortune in comparison with my mere competence, was it?"

She was shaking her head slowly and biting her lower lip. "You did nothing wrong, Gerard," she said. "Nothing was your fault. You were young and high-spirited. You did some foolish things, like risking your neck by racing a curricle to Brighton. You used to tell me some of your escapades. I daresay you drank and gambled and—and had women—"

"No!" he said sharply. "Not after I met you, Christina. I *loved* you. I wanted to marry you. I could not crave any other women when there was you. I can remember only three occasions in my life—not one of them during the months I knew you—when I drank to excess. Each time I vowed never again. The most I ever won at the gaming tables was fifty guineas. The most I ever lost was sixty. Both times I decided afterward that I had been rash. Money is not easily earned. It should be spent wisely and well. Did you believe at the time that I was irretrievably wild?"

"He told me what I already knew and then made me realize I did not know the half of it," she said. "He made me—see you as you really were. Or so it seemed at the time. I believe now that I was mistaken. I *know* I was." She closed her eyes and rested her forehead with every sign of weariness against his cravat.

"Gilbert?" he said. That bastard Gilbert! He might have guessed it. That had always been one of his favorite methods of getting his cousin in trouble at Thornwood—establishing the truth, twisting it and turning it without ever lying a great deal.

"Yes," she said.

"And he convinced Pickering too, I suppose," he said.

"And your father forbade you to see me again. You believed that you had been deceived in me and married Gilbert instead." It was simple really—and quite worthy of Gilbert. "You might have trusted me more, Christina. You might have confronted me, given me a chance to defend myself."

She lifted her head and looked into his face. She raised one hand and cupped it lightly about one of his cheeks for a few moments. "I had to believe it all," she said. "I had to go on believing it all these years. Only so could I remain sane."

She drew away from him and walked over to one of the long windows. Melted snow was dripping from the eaves across her line of vision, he could see. He did not attempt to follow her. He stood where he was.

"The whole world loved my father," she said. "Everyone thought him amiable and charming. Even I was not immune to his charm."

Why should she have been?

"And I knew him." She rested her forehead against the glass of the window. "I do not suppose there were many people who suspected that he was two persons—the gay and charming and very likable public gentleman and the dark, moody, often violent private man. He had enough control over himself or enough pride—call it what you will—to do most of his drinking alone. He drank only enough in company to be the life of every party. In his defense I believe it was like a disease with him—if drinking can be called a disease. He could not stop even though he always said he could if he wanted. He did his heavy gambling in private hells. The public gentleman appeared comfortably wealthy—he was generous and spent lavishly. The private man was often plunged dangerously deep in debt. The two conditions—uncontrolled drinking and reckless gaming—made his moods very unpredictable. My mother was the one who suffered from them."

He gripped the edge of the desk with one hand as if he needed it to prop himself up.

"She used to shield me from his wrath," she said. "So much so that until recent years I have not really admitted to myself that she was the innocent party, the victim of his violence. He was almost always loving and indulgent with me and I would not face what I did not want to see. I came to despise her almost as much as I loved her. Why did she always have to provoke him and bring on those dark days when everyone had to tiptoe about the house? Why did she hide away for days at a time until the bruises faded when she might have avoided them in the first place? I was even angry with her when it became clear that she was consumptive and Papa used to shut himself up and weep and drink more. Everyone pitied him for his grief in the loss of a wife he had loved so tenderly in public."

Even at the age of eighteen, he thought suddenly, she had been an expert in the wearing of masks. One would never have known that the sunny-natured girl had grown up in such a home.

"By the time I was eighteen and my mother had been dead for two years," she said, "I understood the situation better. Not that he was ever violent with me, but I could see the instability of his character, his total inability to control his addictions. I did not stop loving him—he was my father. But I was determined when I went to London to make my come-out and to look for a husband that I would not make my mother's mistake. I swore to myself that I would not be beguiled by a charming man whose life and character had no substance. I was determined to choose with my head and to marry a man of steady character. But I fell in love with you."

But? She had fallen in love against her will? He felt suddenly cold.

"You were so like him in many ways," she said. "You had all his best qualities. I persuaded myself that you were unlike him in all the ways that mattered. But I was vulnerable, you see, to anyone who told me otherwise—especially when he was a man of sense and good character."

Gilbert!

She laughed softly without humor. "Oh, the ironies of life, Gerard. They would be funny if they were not so very tragic. It was head over heart, you see. That is always the wise way, is it not? And so I walked with wide open eyes into a marriage that was even worse than my mother's—at least there were moments of light for Mama."

"Christina," he said.

She laughed softly again and drew her head back from the pane. "My father charmed everyone as usual in London," she said. "I can even remember someone saying in my hearing that he seemed more like my brother than my father and that he was as likely to make a dazzling marriage as I if he wished. But he lived his usual private life. He lost a fortune one night—or what was a fortune to him, at least. I knew nothing about it until the—the Vauxhall night after I had returned home though it had happened a week before that. He was ruined—*we* were ruined."

And so they had tricked Gilbert into marrying her? Gilbert with all his wealth? But Gilbert had had his revenge. He had poisoned her mind, cut her off from her father, and then terrorized and beaten her.

"Gilbert had redeemed the debts," she was saying—he almost missed hearing it. "To this day I have no idea how he discovered them. He told Papa—during that evening while you and I were at Vauxhall—that he had done so out of concern and respect for me. He did not ask for repayment."

"Except in the form of your hand in marriage." He closed his eyes and clenched his teeth. Yes, this sounded like Gilbert in action—like a wily serpent.

"He did not make it a condition." She paused and drew a slow and audible breath. "And Papa did not try to insist either. He merely pointed out to me what a humiliation it would be to have to accept charity from a man who had no connection to us. He wept. When Gilbert came the following morning to make his offer to me, he insisted that I must not be swayed by Papa's indebtedness to him. I was free to accept or reject his suit. But he did talk about you—with great restraint and sympathy as your cousin. He pointed out with seeming reluctance how unstable you were—how you had spent your boyhood years turning his father against him and his brother through lies and trickery, how you had then broken his father's heart by leaving Thornwood and sowing your wild oats, how you had grandiose hopes of making your fortune in one toss of the dice when you might have settled to a respectable gentleman's life with your modest competence or else have allowed him to buy you a pair of colors—and how you would doubtless lose what little you had before the summer was over. He pointed out how you loved to make merry with your friends—often at brothels. He did not say that word, but he made his meaning clear. He told me how you often had to be carried home drunk. He made me see the similarities between you and my father that I had been trying not to see."

"No," he said. "No, Christina. How could you have thought that? How could you have believed him?" But he knew how, of course. Gilbert had always been capable of projecting an image of quiet dependability—and he had been working on the weaknesses and fears of a very vulnerable girl.

"He seemed to be everything Papa was not," she said. "Sober, steady as a rock, trustworthy. And everything he said seemed believable. I told myself I had been blinded by love. And then after I had asked for a few hours in which to consider my answer and Gilbert had left, I found Papa in tears again. He seemed so genuinely remorseful for everything. Yet he pleaded with me not to sacrifice myself. I—" She could not seem to continue.

"You were eighteen years old," he said, "and easily manipulated by selfish and unscrupulous men. You had no one to whom to turn for solid, sensible advice. And I, God help me, was one-and-twenty and tasting the pleasures life had to offer. I was, moreover, restless and unsettled in life. But I was never reckless or depraved or vicious, Christina. Why did Gilbert twist the truth? Why did he go to such lengths to win you? Did he love you so much?"

She turned to look at him at last. "I believe," she said, her voice trembling almost beyond her control, "he hated *you*, Gerard. He never talked about you after our marriage and forbade me to do so, but I have pieced together enough knowledge over the years to understand that you were his father's favorite and that he hated you for it. He took me from you—it was as simple as that. He did not love me. I do not believe he even liked me. Sometimes I thought I actually repelled him. Whenever he punished me, I believe in his mind he was punishing you."

They gazed at each other across the space that divided them. It was a space vaster than a mere few yards. It was a space of years and the experiences that had matured them over those years in different ways. Had they married ten years before, their minds and hearts and aspirations might have twined together; they might have grown together as couples in particularly good marriages sometimes did. But they had been robbed of those years. And now perhaps there was no way of closing the distance between them.

He could only shift the focus of the conversation somehow. It had become too unbearably painful.

"And after all this, Christina," he said, "you are willing to go back to your father? To live? Your children with you?"

"Not to become his victim," she said. "Not of his violence, not of his tears. Not even of his pleas for money, though my first instinct on reading his letter was to ask for an advance on my allowance so that I could send what he says he needs to avert ruin. But to see him again. To somehow free myself of the past completely. And perhaps to nurse him if he is as ill as I suspect he is. To love him. He is my father. He is my children's grandfather."

If he had a father, the earl thought, or a mother, he would perhaps be willing to forgive almost anything for the mere sake of the bond. Yes, he would give anything in the world to be able to see his father again.

"You will go to him, then," he said. "And you will do what is best, Christina—best for him, for yourself, for your daughters. I know you will do what is best. I will not try to interfere from any male conviction that you cannot manage without a man's help. But if there is anything I can do, I am at your service."

"Thank you." She visibly straightened her spine and raised her chin. "Thank you, my lord. But I will not impose upon you further. You have a home and a business in Canada that I know you are eager to return to. I will be happy when you are gone, knowing that I did not ruin your life, knowing you are back where you belong. And I will be happy with my freedom. You have given me that gift and I am going to use it. You cannot understand, perhaps, how it feels to be a woman of eight-and-twenty, knowing suddenly that for the first time in your life you are free to shape your own destiny. A man could never understand. But I am grateful to you because you have made it possible for me to be independent, and you have helped release me from the feelings of guilt and fear that have kept me bound even since Gilbert's death. Thank you." She smiled at him.

Ah.

There was nothing left to say. He had helped her find freedom and now he was the last person in the world to try to persuade her to give it up again.

"Gerard," she said, walking closer until she stood a few feet from him, "I married for a number of reasons. One was that it seemed the sensible, the wise thing to do. I was proud of myself for giving you up. I thought I was proving my own good sense and maturity. I heard nothing of you until after Gilbert's death, but I hoped that your dreams had failed you. I hoped that all my fears had been well founded. I hoped I had not given you up in vain. I—I was wrong. Forgive me. Please forgive me." Her dark eyes gazed directly into his.

"And I hoped," he said, "that you were unhappy, that you regretted your decision. I have been suitably punished. I have to live with the knowledge that all the time I was wishing for your unhappiness he was beating you instead of me and making your life a hell. Forgive me."

"I am glad you succeeded so magnificently," she said. "I am glad you have been happy." She held out her right hand to him.

He took it in his, held it in a firm clasp for a moment, and then raised it to his lips. If he tried to say anything more, he thought, smiling at her, he would surely disgrace himself by weeping, heaping an emotional burden on her as her father was clearly adept at doing. He released her hand.

"Shall we go and enjoy the rest of Christmas?" he suggested.

"Yes." Her smile was suddenly brightly amused, reminding him of the girl he had once known and loved. "I understand there has been some friction between the kitchen servants and the extra hands hired for the occasion. Cook's feathers have been ruffled, never a comfortable omen for all around her. I had better go belowstairs to find out if anyone has come to fisticuffs with anyone else yet."

"Kitchen disputes," he said firmly while grinning at her, "are entirely your domain, my lady."

"Perhaps," she agreed, sweeping past him on her way to the door. "But the leader of the orchestra, *my lord,* was behaving on his arrival earlier suspiciously as if he thought he outranked Billings—and Billings was anything but pleased. I left the ballroom in a hurry, before anyone could conceive the notion of appealing to me as adjudicator."

"Sometimes," he said, following her, "I wish I had never allowed myself to be lured even one mile east of Montreal."

She laughed.

Chapter 17

Christina was dressed early for the ball. Mainly it was because she had promised that Rachel should see her in her
ball gown, yet she knew that a simple appearance in the
nursery would not suffice. Tess would want to prattle to her
and would want the usual bedtime story, and Rachel would
need to be made much of though she would not make any
demands for attention.

Partly it was because she was too excited to wait. There
was to be a Christmas ball at Thornwood—it was a dizzying
wonderful prospect. She felt rather as she had on that long-
ago evening of her come-out ball in London when she had
been eighteen and full of eager hope.

It was difficult to realize that she could be the same
woman who had reacted with such shocked disapproval less
than two weeks before to the suggestion of a ball. It was difficult to realize that she was the same woman who had lived
for nine years under Gilbert's strict, oppressive regime, so
terrorized and so demoralized that it had taken her a year
and a half to break free.

She was free! She tried to think only of that and of the
coming ball as she hurried down from the nursery to the
ballroom, afraid that after all she might be late. It was important to her to be there before any of the guests arrived so
that she might be standing in the receiving line. It was important, not because she would be abused verbally and chas-
tised physically if she were a minute late, but because she
chose to aim for perfection in her duties as hostess.

And because—oh, and because she could not wait to

stand beside him in the line. She could not bear the thought of missing a single minute this evening in which she might be either looking at him or at least feeling his presence.

She almost collided with Margaret in the doorway of the ballroom. She smiled brightly. "Oh, Meg," she said, reaching for her sister-in-law's hands and squeezing them, "how very pretty you look."

Margaret had wanted a brightly colored ballgown, but Miss Penny had tactfully persuaded her to wear white. She had not yet made her come-out and the ball was to be attended by several members of the *ton*. White would be the proper color to wear. And the best color for her too, Christina thought. She looked young and pretty and eager and innocent.

"Oh." Margaret sighed. "And you too, Christina. Not pretty, but *beautiful.*"

They both laughed.

Christina's gown was pale gold and as simple and elegant in design as all her other new clothes. But this one was cut a little lower at the bosom and had short sleeves and a small train. And it shimmered in the candlelight as she had guessed it would. Sophie had threaded pearls through her dark hair. She felt as far removed from the days of black dresses and caps as it was possible to be.

"I feel that I have been neglecting you," she said. "We have scarce talked alone since the guests arrived. Have you had a happy Christmas, Meg? Have you enjoyed yourself? *Are* you enjoying yourself?"

But the answer was self-evident. There was a glow about the girl's face that had not been there before. She had come alive to her own youth in the past week.

"I could not possibly have imagined anything more wonderful if I had tried," Margaret said. "I can hardly wait to go to town in the spring. But then I do not want to wish away the next few days either—tonight especially."

Christina squeezed her hands more tightly. "You should have been enjoying this sort of life long before now," she said. "I blame myself, Meg. I—"

"No!" Margaret said firmly, and she leaned forward and

kissed her sister-in-law on the cheek. "No, Christina. It was you who made my growing years bearable—you in my girlhood, Gerard in my childhood. You gave me everything you were able to give—you gave me love. It has been enough. It is the only thing that really matters, you know."

There was no chance to say anything more. Lady Hannah was approaching the ballroom in company with Lord and Lady Milchip and Lord and Lady Langan, and the earl, who had been talking to the leader of the orchestra at the other side of the ballroom, was striding across the empty floor toward them.

Christina could not—would not—draw her eyes away from him. He was wearing a chocolate brown satin evening coat over cream-colored knee breeches. His brown waistcoat was heavily embroidered with gold thread. His linen and stockings sparkled white. There was a quantity of white lace at his throat and wrists. Tonight he looked nothing short of magnificent, she thought. She realized even as she gazed that he was looking at her just as intently. She smiled.

"Beautiful!" he said, reaching out a hand for hers and carrying it to his lips. He turned to look at Margaret. "Both of you."

She loved him, Christina thought quite consciously. She always had and always would. She was *in love.* But she would not think for the moment—for tonight at least—of the implications of that fact when he was to return to Canada within a few months and they would never see each other again. Tonight she would not believe in tragedies or impossibilities. Just two weeks ago all this—*all this*—would have seemed impossible.

"If you will excuse me," he said, "I must go up and carry Miss Gaynor down. But I will be back in time to stand in the receiving line."

"I do believe," Margaret said to Christina after he had left, keeping her voice low, "that the sprained ankle is not sprained at all. It was a clever ruse to have Gerard carrying her everywhere and being her slave. I wonder if at the time she realized, though, that she would be unable to dance tonight."

"Meg," Christina said sharply, "you are being unkind."

But they looked at each other and both laughed. Lizzie probably really had twisted her foot and hurt it, Christina thought. But she had had the same suspicion about the sprain. There had been no swelling or bruising about the ankle when she had helped ease Lizzie's boot off her foot after their return from the lake.

"We will not be laughing," Margaret said, "if we suddenly find that she is to be our cousin-in-law. Frankly, Christina, I do not like her for all her smiling sweetness. Neither does Gerard. But she is determined to have him if he can be had."

More of the house guests had come down. Christina turned her attention to the ballroom itself, giving it one final visual check to see that all was in order. The room was decked with pine boughs and holly and lavishly draped with red ribbons and bows and hung with gold bells. The last act of a warm and wonderful Christmas was about to begin.

A Christmas to remember. For the rest of her life. But how would she remember it? With the ache of sadness and loneliness and loss? With sweet nostalgia?

She was *free*—she found she could not repeat the idea often enough. She could make the rest of her life whatever she wished. There were limits, of course. For any number of reasons one was not always able to do what one wanted in life. And when other people were involved in one's wants, their wishes had to be considered too. But—

But she was free at least to try to shape her own destiny. She had been a victim for long enough. There were no more excuses for holding back, for retreating inside herself, and for allowing life to happen to her, merely intent on not getting hurt.

There was life to be lived. She was alive and still young and healthy. And she was in love. She turned back to the door, about which were clustered most of the house guests, all gorgeously clad, laughing and conversing and looking admiringly about them, smiling at her as she approached.

She felt aglow with happiness. What a ridiculous thought! She smiled at it and joined the group.

*   *   *

He was not sorry after all that he had come to England, and that in the end he had come all the way home to Thornwood. A great deal of good had happened. The past had been explained and forgiven. The bitterness of years had been purged. There could be some peace now for two people because he had come home.

And yet a part of him longed for Montreal and the home he had made there. Part of him wished—as he had said to her as a joke earlier in the day—that he had not ventured even one mile east of Montreal. Better the dull pain of bitter memories, he was half inclined to think, than the raw pain of this new parting that was upon him. And there seemed to be nothing he could do to avert it. He could not try to take the freedom she had so newly found. If he asked her to marry him, she might feel an obligation because of the pain she had caused him in the past. He could not do that to her.

Of course, there was still the possibility that she was with child. But he hoped not, much as his heart yearned toward the idea.

But there was tonight left, he told himself and a few more days after that. For tonight at least he refused to have his spirits dragged down by gloomy thoughts.

He was almost late in joining the receiving line of his own ball. Lady Gaynor had informed him that her elder daughter was ready to come down, but she had not accompanied him back upstairs as he had expected. He was admitted to Lizzie's dressing room, where she sat on a stool in front of the dressing table, looking very handsome indeed in white satin and lace. But the arrangement of a few of the ringlets at the back of her head did not quite suit her, and her maid had to work on them for a few minutes longer. And then she did not like the particular strand of pearls she was wearing—it was too long. Her maid had to rummage for the other strand—the one her grandmama had given her for her eighteenth birthday. And then she decided that the silver gloves she was wearing were quite wrong with her gown. The maid was set to finding the white gloves.

His lordship had been all of ten minutes in her room before he was finally able to carry her down to the ballroom. He had had a chair and stool prepared for her close to the doors, where she would not feel neglected or lost to view.

It became quickly apparent that there was no danger of either. With her slippered foot resting on a stool, Lizzie Gaynor quickly became the center of attention as she smiled bravely and even laughed gaily and informed everyone who asked that she was in very little pain, certainly nothing she wished to burden anyone else with, and that she had every intention of enjoying the evening by watching the dancing. No one was to pay her any mind at all. She wafted a graceful hand in the air. She was not going to pin anyone to her side or spoil anyone's evening.

The earl joined the receiving line with the countess, his aunt, and Margaret. The outside guests were beginning to arrive. He greeted them cordially and set himself to be the attentive host. He was well aware that there had been no balls at Thornwood for many years and that even an invitation to the house had become a rare and coveted event.

And all the time he stood there, smiling, talking, kissing hands, he was aware of Christina beside him, beautiful, elegant, gracious, smelling of lavender—and for this evening and a few more days his to look at, to admire, to yearn for.

"Christina." He detained her with a hand on her arm when the last of the guests had arrived and it was time for him to begin the ball with Margaret. "You will reserve a set for me?"

"If you wish," she said coolly.

The tone would have annoyed him a few days before. He ignored it now.

"The last waltz?" he said.

Not the first. It would come too soon in the evening, and as the host he could not dance with the same partner more than once. His dance with her was something to be deferred as long as possible, then, so that he could anticipate it as the crowning moment of the evening—of the whole of Christmas. He had not waltzed with her since that one afternoon here in the ballroom. It seemed like forever ago.

"Yes," she said. "Thank you." For a moment the cool, impersonal look went from her eyes to be replaced by—by what? Pleasure? Longing? Nothing at all of any significance? The look was gone too soon to be interpreted.

And so the Christmas ball began. He danced with Margaret, with Mrs. Ferris, one of his closest neighbors, with Winifred Milchip. And he looked about him and observed that everyone seemed to be delighting in the splendid surroundings, in the novelty of a grand ball in the country complete with full orchestra, in the company of so many other people. And all the while he was aware of Christina, who had clearly changed her mind completely since declaring less than two weeks before that she would not dance at all during the ball. She danced with Geordie Stewart, Mr. Evesham, Viscount Luttrell.

It was after the third set that disaster almost happened. He had strolled over to Lizzie Gaynor's chair to make sure she needed for nothing though it was perfectly clear that she did not. There was a small crowd of people surrounding her, both house guests and neighbors. She was holding court with her usual bright gaiety.

"May I fetch you anything, Miss Gaynor?" he asked. "A drink, perhaps?"

She stretched out a hand to him and he took it and bowed over it. But he could not immediately release it—it had closed about his own. She was smiling at him brightly and —fondly?

"Nothing, thank you, my lord," she said. She looked about at her audience. "You see how very well I am cared for? I am really not a *cripple,* and I might easily have remained in my room both yesterday and today. But his lordship has insisted upon carrying me about and on coming in and out of my room very like a husband." She clapped a hand over her mouth, tittered, and blushed prettily. "He came up early to bring me down here. I was *almost* in a state of deshabille. He was alone in my room with me for fully ten minutes, I declare. Some might call it improper. But how could it be called that when—"

He had no idea how she might have ended her sentence. He knew only that with every playful word she was tightening the noose about his neck, making it appear to her avid listeners that he had taken enough liberties with her reputation that he must surely intend to make her his wife. And he was quite powerless to do anything to stop her. Their hands were still clasped, their arms stretched out toward each other.

"Gerard?" The countess's voice spoke rather more loudly than usual. She set one hand on his outstretched arm and smiled dazzlingly, first at him and then at the whole group. "Is it time, do you think?"

"Time?" He stared at her blankly. He felt rather as if he were drowning.

She bit her lower lip. "For the announcement?" she said.

Had he forgotten something important? He would not be surprised. His mind seemed not to be functioning at all well at the moment.

She laughed and spoke low—though everyone about them heard the words quite clearly, of course. "Of our betrothal," she said. "You *did* say just before supper, and the supper dance is next."

His mind jolted back into motion even as his hand parted company with Lizzie Gaynor's. He understood immediately. He did not even for one moment believe that he must be either mad or living through some bizarre dream. He took the hand that still rested on his arm, drew it through his, and smiled warmly at her.

"Then it will be made now," he said, looking deep into her eyes before leading her off in the direction of the orchestra platform, "without further delay—the moment for which I have waited all Christmas, my love."

"Oh, dear," she murmured, her voice not quite steady, as they crossed the floor and a semihush fell on the occupants of the ballroom as if they sensed that something extraordinary was about to happen.

"Indeed," he agreed fervently.

And then they were together on the platform, and he was announcing to his friends and relatives and neighbors that the Countess of Wanstead had done him the great honor of consenting to be his wife and the new—Countess of Wanstead.

There was laughter, applause, exclamations of surprise, whistles, a lone cheer. And his betrothed, her teeth biting into her lower lip, her dark eyes large in her face, her cheeks glowing with color, gazed back into his eyes as he raised her hand to his lips and bowed to her.

"I would suggest," he said, "that the gentlemen take their partners for the next set. It is the supper dance. Her ladyship and I will go and see that all is ready in the dining room."

But if all was not ready there, then his guests would have to go hungry for all the checking either of them did. They proceeded in silence until they reached the library, which was in darkness, there being no fire and no candles lit. It did not matter. He closed the door firmly behind them and backed her against it. He did not need eyes to feel her or smell her—or to hear her laughing.

He leaned against her and laughed with her—idiotic, helpless laughter that neither of them could control for several minutes.

"Oh, the *minx*!" she said at last. "She had you backed into a corner, Gerard. You should just have seen the frozen smile on your lips and the hunted look in your eyes. In another minute she would have had you proposing in public."

"Instead of which," he said, "you had me announcing my betrothal in public."

The exchange merited another prolonged bout of shared laughter.

"*Are* we betrothed?" he asked her—a light, teasing question that nevertheless had his stomach performing strange contortions. Her answer, he realized, could change the whole course of both their lives.

"No, of course we are not." The laughter had gone out of her voice. "You needed rescuing. You set me free last evening. I have returned the favor this evening. We are even. You need not fear scandal when we break it off or when we just let it lapse. You will be far away where gossip does not matter. I will be with my father or here at Thornwood."

"We will talk tomorrow about how it is to be done," he said, his heart suddenly in his dancing shoes. "There is no time now. We had better be in the dining room when everyone comes there after the set is finished."

"Yes," she said.

"There is going to be a deluge of congratulations and other remarks," he warned her.

"Yes. I shall merely smile graciously," she said.

"Let's go, then."

But instead of pushing away from her and opening the door, he leaned more heavily against her and found her mouth with his own in the darkness. And slid his arms behind her and about her when he felt hers twining about his shoulders. He could feel the fingers of one of her hands pushing up through his hair as she opened her mouth against his and moaned.

He was not sure how many minutes passed while they held each other and kissed each other as if they could never be close enough to satisfy the craving of their hearts. The depth of their very obviously mutual passion left him shaken and disoriented. But he was aware as he finally lifted his head away from hers that the music in the ballroom had not yet ended.

"There is still the chance that you are with child," he said, his lips light against hers again.

"Yes." She whispered the word and pressed her lips softly against his again.

He stepped away from her then and opened the door. Light from the candles in the wall sconces outside beamed in on them and brought a strange assurance of reality to the last few minutes. He smiled at her. She smiled back. They walked to the dining room without exchanging another word.

"I have never been more happy or more surprised in my life," Lady Hannah said hyperbolically, dabbing at her eyes with a lace-edged handkerchief. "You and dear Gerard, Christina."

"But I had the impression you disliked each other," Margaret protested.

"We did," Christina said. "But we don't."

"I am so happy I could scream," Margaret told her.

"Please don't." Christina felt a strong urge to laugh. This whole episode was strangely hilarious to her. She was bubbling over with happiness—which was peculiar under the circumstances. She would not be able to take the children to London in the spring after all. She would have to remain quietly in the country, either at her father's or here. Unless . . .

She did not know if she dared.

But of course she dared. She was free. She could do anything she liked.

She turned to greet other well-wishers.

"A leg shackle, old chap," Viscount Luttrell said, clapping a hand on the earl's shoulder. "My commiserations. Why am I feeling envious?"

"Because you fancied her yourself?" his friend suggested.

"You might have warned me, by Jove," the viscount said, sounding considerably aggrieved. "You might have saved me from making a prize ass of myself."

The Earl of Wanstead grinned at him. "It all happened rather suddenly," he said.

He was not finding it at all difficult to smile, to accept handshakes and back slaps and kisses and congratulations— and even tears from his aunt. He felt rather like laughing out loud—which was not at all appropriate when he considered the reality of the situation.

But what *was* the reality? She had lain with him a few days ago. She had just kissed him with the same passion she had shown then. She had meekly agreed that she might be with child—and then kissed him again. She had laughed with him.

Was the reality quite what he had been telling himself it was? Of one thing he was sure. He was not going to go back to Montreal merely because of assumptions he had not tested. No indeed.

He turned with a smile to see who had just placed a hand on his shoulder.

There had been two other sets of waltzes earlier in the evening. Christina had danced neither of them, protesting to the two gentlemen who had asked that she really was not confident of the steps. Gerard had not waltzed either. She had not failed to notice that. She would have been disappointed if he had. She wanted the last waltz to be also their first waltz.

It was the final set of the evening.

"My dance, I believe," he said, bowing to her and looking at her with bright, intent eyes as she stood with Lady Milchip, Jeannette Campbell, and a group of neighbors.

"Yes."

She set her hand in his, and suddenly there seemed to be no one else in the ballroom but the two of them as he led her out onto the floor. She neither knew nor cared how many other couples stepped onto the floor with them. She did not notice that by some strange, unspoken assent all those couples stood back so that the newly betrothed couple could dance at least the first few measures alone together.

She even forgot to be anxious about the steps. They moved into the music as if they had waltzed together all their lives.

"It is surely the most lovely dance ever invented," she said foolishly.

"Without a doubt," he agreed.

"Gerard—"

"Christina?" He had that dreamy look in his eyes.

"If you really *want* to go back to Canada—"

"I do not."

"If you would really like to stay here, then. Not just in England, I mean, but here at Thornwood—"

"I would."

"If there is any chance at all that you still feel—"

"I do."

"So do I," she said.

They had understood each other perfectly.

"I love you."

"So do I. I love you too."

"Will you marry me?"

"Yes."

"Shall I announce our betrothal, then?"

"You already did."

They grinned at each other and gazed into each other's eyes until their expressions softened to smiles of warmth and love and wonder—and of a tenderness that was unmistakable to the onlookers. He was twirling her about the perimeter of the dance floor, she realized suddenly. They were waltzing together, perfectly in time to the music, perfectly in step with each other. And perfectly in tune—

"Why are we dancing alone?" she asked him.

"I have no idea," he said *"Are* we?"

But even as they noticed that indeed it was so, other couples were taking to the floor with them and those who were not dancing were returning to their conversations.

"You dance as if on gilded clouds," he said. "You always did. You were born to dance."

She was aware then with startling clarity of the whole wonderful scene in which they danced—of the rich greens and reds and golds of the Christmas decorations spinning and mingling and merging about them like a kaleidoscope, of the distinctive smell of pine, of the gorgeously clad relatives and friends and guests dancing or chattering about them. And in the very center of her vision—and of her heart and her life—Gerard, the man she had always loved and always would.

There was perhaps a twinge of bittersweet sadness in the moment—it was the last watlz of the evening.

But there was also an inner welling of joy, reflected in the eyes of the man who gazed back at her—it was the first dance of the rest of their lives.